"Fast-paced and funny—a debut with style."

—*Kirkus Reviews*

"A well-written suspense [novel] that has a captivating conclusion." —*Romantic Times BookClub Magazine*

"As someone who loves mysteries—and, of course, fashion—I couldn't wait to read the book. I was not disappointed. Klensch ably pulled it off, with the kind of plotting that kept me awake and guessing till the end."

—Evelyn Theiss, *The Cleveland Plain Dealer*

"A stylish work of fiction. Suspects abound throughout the mystery like celebrities at a Hollywood premiere."

—"Fashion Flash," *Tulsa World*

Sonya Iverson is an ambitious Midwest̲̅͟ ̲͟ing to succeed as a prod̲ ̲ ̲ ̲ ̲ ̲ ̲ ̲ ̲ ̲ ̲frustrated at being trapp̲ ̲ ̲ ̲ ̲ ̲ ̲ ̲ ̲ ̲ ̲ ̲ ̲ ̲ ̲ wants to cover hard new̲ ̲

Sonya is abo̲ ̲ ̲ ̲ ̲ ̲ ̲ ̲ ̲ ̲ ̲ ̲ ̲ ̲ ̲ ̲re.

Behind the s̲ ̲ ̲ ̲ ̲ ̲ ̲ ̲ ̲ ̲ ̲ ̲ ̲ ̲y awards dinner, Sonya̲ ̲ ̲ ̲ ̲ ̲ ̲ ̲ ̲ ̲ ̲ ̲ ̲upermodel clutching a bloody dagger and standing over the body of the glamorous wife of a fashion industry mogul.

Suspects abound. Was the killer the supermodel, whose comeback Harriett was threatening to derail? The internationally renowned designer recently fired at Harriett's bidding? The fashion magazine editor Harriett first bribed and then blackmailed? Or even Harriett's long-suffering husband, who may have finally had all he could take of his shrewish wife?

Eager to break this career-making story, Sonya doesn't realize that her interviews are bringing her closer and closer to the murderer. Close enough to become the next fashion victim. . . .

BOOKS BY ELSA KLENSCH

Style
Live at 10:00, Dead at 10:15

LIVE AT 10:00
DEAD AT 10:15

Elsa Klensch

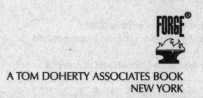

A TOM DOHERTY ASSOCIATES BOOK
NEW YORK

This is a work of fiction. All the characters and events portrayed in this book are either products of the author's imagination or are used fictitiously.

LIVE AT 10:00, DEAD AT 10:15

Copyright © 2004 by Elsa Klensch

A Forge Book
Published by Tom Doherty Associates, LLC
175 Fifth Avenue
New York, NY 10010

www.tor.com

Forge® is a registered trademark of Tom Doherty Associates, LLC.

ISBN 0-765-34680-X
EAN 978-0-765-34680-3

First edition: September 2004
First mass market edition: September 2005

Printed in the United States of America

0 9 8 7 6 5 4 3 2 1

To my husband, Charles, for his love and support

ACKNOWLEDGMENTS

Without the critical encouragement of my longtime advisor and friend, Jerry Krone, my resourceful agent, Kay Mc-Cauley, and my nurturing editor, Melissa Singer, this book would not have been written.

**LIVE AT 10:00
DEAD AT 10:15**

ONE

6:30 PM, Sunday

Isaac Franklin paused at the door of the den and looked down at his two sons, both curled up on the paisley shawl that covered the long sofa. Byron was 11, Henry 10. With their dark, tousled hair and slim bodies, they looked as if they were his biological children.

The TV set was on, but the boys were half watching, half asleep. They'd been swimming, as they always did on Sundays. It was a family tradition; Isaac's father had risen at five every morning and gone to his club to swim.

Isaac had been captain of the swimming team at boarding school, which pleased his father enormously. He still remembered his father's voice saying, "Swimming was my salvation; it kept me sane. It will do the same for you."

His father had said this so often that Isaac tired of hearing it. When he was 12, he had threatened to give up swimming as an act of defiance. His father said nothing at first. And then the same litany: "Do what you want, but swimming will keep you sane."

That was the way his father had been: adamant about what he believed. Isaac had inherited that strength. Without it, he would have divorced Harriett long ago, before they adopted the boys.

In fact, his father had been right. Isaac still loved to swim. It put him in touch with himself. One of the four elements was water, he often thought. One of the pure things of the earth.

In 1920, Isaac's father, Murray Franklin, had immigrated to America to join his uncle's business—a grimy sweatshop on the grim Lower East Side of Manhattan. He was barely 16 and barely able to hide his horror at the exhausted women slaving over their sewing machines 12 hours a day.

He had left behind his home on Hvar, an idyllic, small island off the Dalmatian coast. The beauty of the islands rising steeply from the calm, deep blue of the Adriatic was a memory that haunted Murray Franklin all his life.

He had swum in Hvar's bays every day. With the warm waters flowing past his body, he forgot the stigmas of poverty, of being Jewish, forgot the anxiety of waiting for his uncle's money to arrive from New York.

"When the time to leave came, swimming gave me courage," he told Isaac many times. "Swimming built my mental and physical strength. How I needed that strength to say good-bye to the family, to friends. They all kept telling me I was lucky, and so I was. But in my heart I longed to stay with them."

And now Murray's grandsons were swimmers too. Murray had arranged for their adoption. He insisted on it when Harriett's first baby was born with Down's syndrome and she refused to have any more. How Murray enjoyed them for the few years before he died at 87.

Isaac smiled at the memory, and he smiled at the boys as he sat down beside them.

"Almost time for supper," he said. "And remember, only two hours of television before bed at 10. It's school tomorrow and you've had a busy day."

Although he knew they'd showered, he caught a whiff of chlorine.

"You'd better give your mother a fast kiss tonight," he told them. "If she catches that chlorine you'll be right back in the tub. Next time use shampoo when you wash your hair."

"I want to watch TV until 10:30," said Henry.

"I said 10 and I mean it."

He put his hand on Byron's knee.

"I've got a feeling that before long you'll be beating me at the pool. You're getting on so fast that maybe I'll have you coached twice a week."

Byron was a natural swimmer; he had grace and was developing stamina. Isaac felt pleasure just watching him from the moment he dived into the pool.

"I'm 10, almost 11—why can't I have extra coaching?" Henry always wanted what his elder brother got.

"Henry, you can join Byron in another year. You're coming along nicely. But you need to develop a little more."

Like his father, Isaac was always honest with his sons. And quietly firm. It was necessary. They were Jewish boys and despite the wealth they would inherit, the boys would have to be strong. Life was never easy for Jews.

They had done very well for a poor Jewish family from a little village, Isaac knew. One of those only-in-America stories. He sank back against the fringed, satin cushions and looked around the room. It was meant to be a family room, but for two young boys about to enter their teens it was as suitable as an antique store.

Like every room in the apartment, it was decorated to reflect Harriett's image.

"Of course I want the den to be a place where the boys can play. But I also want them to grow up with an appreciation of antiques, of fine painting and rich living," she had said. "That will be their heritage. And if they don't learn to appreciate it when they are young, they never will."

But what did the huge 19th-century landscape that hung

over the table on the opposite wall mean to them? It was dark and gloomy; the only bright spots, the grazing sheep. And the small TV set was placed low in the corner so it was half hidden and difficult to see.

What the boys would enjoy was a flat screen, on the wall where the painting now hung. Then they could really watch their sports.

The antique carpet was almost in shreds. Impossible for teenagers to walk across without damaging it further.

Yes, Isaac planned to make a stand. He wanted the boys to develop as individuals, to feel as loved and cared for as he had as a child. They needed their own space—a place to play their music, to smoke their pot. Do what teenagers did these days with their friends.

But making a stand against Harriett's iron rules was not easy to do. He didn't like confrontations. She relished them.

Usually, Isaac knew, he was a decisive man. And once he made a decision, he stuck with it. But with Harriett he was a different person. He would agree to her demands and then passively ignore them under the pressure of work. With her he felt less than himself.

But there was one demand in his life that he never ignored, and it didn't come from Harriett. It came from Jeremy, his oldest son. Isaac called him every evening, and tonight would be no exception, even though he and Harriett were preparing to leave for the annual fashion award ceremony of the International Designers Association.

He rose, picked up the phone, and walked to the window. Speed dialing brought the upstate clinic for retarded children on the line in seconds.

"May I speak to Dr. Hoffman, please? Isaac Franklin speaking."

"Dr. Hoffman is with Jeremy now." The voice was familiar, the same nurse who answered each night. "We were waiting for your call." Franklin didn't like the tone of her voice. She seemed anxious.

"Is there something wrong? Is Jeremy all right?"

"I'm connecting you to the doctor."

There was a moment of silence, then Hoffman spoke.

"Jeremy has had a fall," he said.

Isaac felt the panic rise. "A fall? How? Is he injured?"

"He was running along the pathway, tripped on something, and fell. It happened just a few minutes ago. He wasn't conscious when we found him, but he's coming around now. He should be fine, just shaken."

"Does he need me? Should I drive up tonight?"

Isaac knew Hoffman could hear the guilt in his voice. Like the parents of many Down's children, he was torn apart. Should the child come home? Should he stay in an institution?

After Jeremy was born, 15 years ago, the doctors assured the Franklins that an institution was the best place for him. The child could get the best care and treatment and his parents could get on with their lives as a young society couple.

But times had changed.

At their latest annual conference, Dr. Hoffman had told the Franklins that studies now showed Down's syndrome children were often better off with their families. At home, Jeremy could develop many more social skills.

Jeremy was an unusual boy. His IQ was 55, higher than most Down's children his age. He could be expected to be completely independent, at least at home.

"He should be able to take care of himself, make meals, do housework, and take a bus to the store to buy food," Hoffman had said. "He might even earn money working in a sheltered workshop. He could lead a much more fulfilling life."

Isaac wanted his child to come home, but Harriett opposed it.

For Isaac, this fall was just the kind of emergency that could be avoided if Jeremy were at home.

"Jeremy is in no danger," the doctor told him now. "But these kinds of things shock him. Discuss it with your wife and if you decide to come, call me back in the next few minutes. I will wait for you. If I don't hear from you in half an hour, I'll expect your call first thing in the morning."

Franklin put the phone down slowly. Jeremy needed him.

Or perhaps it was that he felt he needed to be with Jeremy. He wanted to go.

Harriett had been planning the award party for weeks. It was part of the campaign she believed would help launch their first fragrance. Isaac knew that he wouldn't go to his son unless she agreed.

"What is the matter with me?" he asked himself angrily.

He poured a stiff scotch and walked into his dressing room.

Harriett was in the adjoining room, having her hair combed while her favorite manicurist, Maggie, did her nails.

"Isaac," she called, "Maggie says I look wonderful. The diet's worked so well I'm bony. My figure is perfect for the dress I designed. Have you seen it? It has a very thin, stretchy fabric on top. And the bottom is just a whiff of parachute silk—not transparent but almost.

"It's modern, sophisticated, and very glamorous. And I think perfect for the fashion awards."

Isaac had already seen the dress in the design studio. He thought it was too edgy, too punk for the Franklin image, but he had said nothing.

"You know, all the other designers will be there watching what I'm wearing." Harriett hardly stopped for a breath. "I always put my best foot forward and tonight is so important because of the fragrance."

Every word made Isaac angrier, and he tried not to listen.

He walked into her room. He seemed to be living in two worlds. One in which a disadvantaged child was crying for him, and the other in which the desires of his self-absorbed wife threatened to overcome him.

"And Isaac," continued Harriett, "wear what I laid out for you. The tie you wore last week looked so cheap. You have to be extra careful now you're so middle-aged. I hate butterfly bow ties."

He'd been here so many times before. Unable to cope with the hopelessness welling up inside him.

"Harriett," he said, "Jeremy has had an accident. He's in pain, calling for us. Dr. Hoffman would like us to visit him tonight."

"What do you mean? We can't possibly go anywhere tonight except to that dinner. The hospital will take care of Jeremy, whatever's wrong." Her voice was icy.

"Harriett—" Isaac started.

She cut him off. "Tell me, exactly what has he done now?"

"He was running along the pathway and stumbled. He hit his head. He was unconscious when they brought him in. We should be there. You know how frightened he gets."

Isaac was not so sure of the facts, but he didn't care. He wanted to go to Jeremy.

"What can you be thinking of? We've been told repeatedly that we shouldn't respond to every hysterical outburst from him. In this weather it will take three hours to get there and by that time he will be in a calm, sedated sleep. He won't even remember any of it by the time we get there."

"Harriett, Hoffman says he is frightened. I think we should go."

"Hoffman is a doctor whose life is justified by those retarded children. You're running a multimillion-dollar business. We are hosting this table. I have to be there and so do you. It's not just for pleasure. You remember. It's business, big business. And business isn't exactly bright right now. We are launching our first fragrance: We have to be seen. Be part of the 'in' fashion crowd. And you know what I expect to get out of this—an interview in *W* or *Vogue* with photos of my table settings. What I've done tonight is really amazing."

"Harriett," he protested, "the table settings are not important and for that matter they are not even yours. Mari worked them out."

"Isaac, it was my idea."

"I don't care. Our son has had an accident and needs us with him."

"No," Harriett screamed. "No!"

She rose and reached for her dress, almost ripping it off the hanger. She stepped into it defiantly and turned so Maggie could zip it up.

"See what I have created. See how beautiful this is. See what I'm doing for you and your company. I am the future of the company. So get used to it. You may not love me, but you have to support me. Forget Jeremy. I am going to this party, and so are you."

Isaac stepped back. Her fury exhausted him. He had no response. He would never win.

"Can't you say something!" she shrieked. "This will be the most brilliant dress at that party. And *I* designed it."

Isaac looked at her. The stretchy gauze hugged her body. Every rib showed. She was too thin, anorexic, a skeleton.

"You look wonderful," he lied.

How easy it would be to slip a knife in between those ribs to end her life, and with it, his torture.

TWO

7:00 PM, Sunday

Sonya Iverson raced up the rain-soaked red carpet as fast as her high heels would allow. She was late and that was something she hated. It was not her idea of what a TV producer should be—especially not a producer for the *Donna Fuller Show*. Never late.

In fact, Sonya never understood why anyone should be late. It wasn't professional.

She ran under the canopy that covered the path up the steps of Manhattan's main public library on Fifth Avenue. The canopy did almost nothing to keep off the rain and shook with every gust of wind. Who could have foreseen the pelting rain that had whipped through New York all afternoon? Rain that had turned the traffic into almost impassable turmoil even though it was 7:00 on a Sunday evening.

It was a terrible night for a party.

The wind burned as it touched her face. It had been barely two weeks since her face-lift.

All around the canopy, bright lights had been put up to give the rainy evening an opening-night feeling. For Sonya, those bright lights were the enemy.

Though she had let Sabrina, the studio makeup artist, come to her apartment to do her face, Sonya was sure that not even Sabrina's skill could hide the puffiness and discoloration. But Sabrina was a friend, and she'd insisted that Sonya look her best for the gala night. So Sonya had agreed.

At the top of the library steps, Perry Dalton, her cameraman, was waiting for her. His sturdy right arm was draped over the camera. He waved to make sure she saw him. Perry was not handsome; his ears were too big and his curly brown hair was thinning. But under his droopy mustache, there was almost always a smile.

Perry was a friend, and a producer in the television business needs good friends. Especially good cameramen. Perry was one of the best at the network.

A bad relationship with a cameraman could break you. The tape could be bad when you sat down to edit it. Or perhaps one of those unexplained and mysterious technical problems had erased everything. But not with Perry. He was kind and thoughtful. He was also tough and reliable.

As usual, he had one of the best positions behind the barriers put up for the press. The tripod and camera were right in the middle of the space, facing down the center of the steps. There was no way he would miss a celebrity.

"Perry, you're wonderful, as usual," Sonya said as she reached him. "I'm sorry I'm late. Damned rain. Damned traffic!"

"Cool it," he said, sensing her anxiety as she positioned herself beside him. "You haven't missed a thing. No one worth taping has arrived yet. It's the weather. And anyway, you know the really rich and the famous wannabes always wait to the last moment to arrive.

"This isn't the Oscars, remember?" he added, laughing.

"I know it isn't the Oscars, but it is my job to see that you get a good position and that I identify the people I want you to shoot."

Sonya could be very serious. She could sometimes sound like a grade school teacher, and behind her back some of the studio staff imitated her tone. Still, she was respected for her work.

Sonya loved her job as producer, collecting material for the *Donna Fuller Show* and helping the on-air reporters shape and write the segments. And she was certainly well paid for it even if her own mother never quite understood what she did. She asked Sonya over and over if she was ever going to be on-screen—"like Donna."

"You're as pretty as Donna Fuller. Why don't you try?"

But the behind-the-scenes job suited Sonya. Perhaps it was her conservative Minnesota background. Perhaps it was because she loved to observe people, to judge them even. Guessing whether they were truthful had almost become a habit.

"Come off it," Perry came back at her, teasing. "I've covered the fashion crowd as many times as you have. I can spot the designers and even ask the questions if need be."

Sonya nodded; he was right.

Fashion was getting monotonous. With global marketing, it was the brands—the Guccis, the Pradas, the Christian Diors—that made the news. There weren't' all that many new, creative, young talents around. And what talents there were got their real breaks by joining one of the megahouses.

That was one reason Sonya was trying to get out of covering fashion stories. From what she could see of the fashion world, there was commerce, but not much room for creativity. She wanted to do more serious stories, yet here she was again at a fashion party.

Sonya unbuttoned her raincoat, folded it carefully, and handed it to Perry.

"Put this under the tripod for me. I mustn't look too bedraggled. You know what Donna is like; she wants her producers to look as glamorous as she does."

And Sonya did look glamorous. For the season, she had bought herself a black Gucci suit. It shaped her body as neatly as a swimsuit. But despite its simplicity, the details spelled quality. Every fashionista there would note the set of the shoulders, the hand-stitched lapels, the impeccable tailoring of the pants that made her legs seem longer than they were.

"Is my hair okay?"

Perry grinned. "As okay as red curly hair ever is."

Unbelieving, Sonya bent forward and looked at her reflection in the lens of the camera.

She grinned back at Perry. "You're right."

"He is right," the low voice of Mari St. Clair echoed behind her. "Ask my advice and I'd put you in front of the camera, not behind it."

Sonya turned, and there stood Mari. Another friend. Her best friend.

Mari looked perfect as always.

"Save those kinds of comments for your clients," Sonya said. "You may be the best PR in town, but you don't have to flatter me. I know where I want to be and I'm happy there."

"You don't have to be so serious. And I mean it, Sonya."

Sonya smiled.

"Here, let me look at your face," said Mari, putting her hand on Sonya's shoulder and turning her so she faced the light.

"Fresher, younger, and yes, there is very little swelling. If Sabrina did your makeup, she did an excellent job. How do you feel?"

Looking at Mari's pale face, Sonya thought that her friend probably was truly concerned about her. But she also knew the power of the *Donna Fuller Show* and that being one of its top producers meant she had to be handled with care. Getting on that show was important to Mari's clients.

"A bit shaky," Sonya answered. "This is my first time at work. You think I should be on camera, but I thank God I never have to do that. I don't want to be a star, or look like one. I just want to produce great shows for the rest of my career."

They all turned as strobes flashed at the bottom of the stairs.

"Can you see who it is?" asked Sonya.

"I can't tell. Someone so wrapped up, they're unrecognizable."

"Well, zoom in," Sonya urged.

"Yes. Okay, but even when I zoom in," replied Perry, "we won't get many glamour shots tonight. No one looks good battling a gale. I'll bet the only usable stuff you get is during the award ceremony. At least they'll have their coats and scarves off. Oh, I see now—it's nobody."

Mari turned to Sonya. "Do you want me to bring my two designers over to you for interviews, or can you manage to grab them?"

"Better bring them over as soon as you can," replied Sonya. "You never know when people will turn up and what Perry will have to shoot. I would hate to miss your people in a crush."

"Thanks. Novelli will probably be the first to arrive. He's usually early, and he told me he wanted to make sure it was all okay backstage. He likes to check the position of the podium, so he'll be comfortable when he walks on to give his speech.

"I hope in the story you'll be able to give some real play to the humanitarian award he's getting for his work for breast cancer. Kim Kelly is giving it to him."

"Yes, I know. I'm anxious to see what she looks like. And it's a good sidebar for the story. You know. Famous model returns after rehab. But I'm more interested in getting a good go at Jason Sarnoff," Sonya said.

"He's new, up-and-coming, and just arrived in New York. French *Vogue* calls him star material . . . and on and on. You must have lots of PR requests for him. How's his English?"

"No problem," Mari replied. "In fact, you'll see, his accent is charming. He can be difficult, but right now he loves the press.

"Sonya, please be a pal and see if you can get a good shot of the Franklins when they arrive. I know you won't use it, but it will make Harriett ecstatic and my life easier."

"Sure. I'll do my best, and if I get a good one I'll try and work it in with something like 'and many Seventh Avenue garmentos also turned up.'"

Mari laughed. "Thanks. You'll come to our table when the lights dim to signal the cocktail party is over. It's number 24, at the front."

"Right," said Sonya. "As usual you've got us all under control."

Mari laughed again as she headed down the steps to find her clients.

Leonard Novelli was the first of the two Franklin design-ers to climb the soggy stairs. As soon as he saw Sonya, he came over to greet her.

"Congratulations," she said as he bent over to give her an air kiss, first on one cheek and then on the other.

Sonya could never quite get used to all this artificial friendliness. After all, she hardly knew the man. Maybe she had too much Minnesota in her. She smiled as she remem-bered her aunt saying to her, "You are going into such a kissy business." It was.

"Thank you," Novelli said. "My dear, it's a real honor. It will be a great evening for the House of Franklin. I am mov-ing on to a new life. And with their new design philosophy, the Franklins are too. We have a lot to celebrate."

Pompous ass, thought Sonya. He must have rehearsed that lie with a coach. But she said only, "Let me get some of this on tape."

She turned to signal to Perry to start rolling the tape, but her ever-ready cameraman had the red light on. Sonya spoke into the mike. "Leonard Novelli, N-O-V-E-L-L-I," she spelled for the editor who would later have to put the man's name at the bottom of the screen.

Then she added, as an oral note to remind her when she wrote the story, "The retired Franklin designer will receive the Humanitarian Award of Honor tonight for his fund-raising efforts for breast cancer research."

She turned to Novelli and put the microphone close to his face as Perry focused the camera for a tight shot. "Leonard, when and why did you decide to work for breast cancer research?"

"My sister got breast cancer in her late 30s—that was some 20 years ago. She suffered greatly and so did her husband and three children. She died before she turned 40. Our family decided the best way to remember her was to help prevent other women and other families from suffering the same tragedy. As my brother-in-law had children to raise, I took over."

Another well-practiced answer, Sonya recognized. But too long for a sound bite.

"Have you any idea how much money you've raised?"

"It's now in the millions," replied Novelli. "But to me, it isn't only the money. It's the work I've been able to do as a designer, making clothes for women who've had surgery. I cannot tell you how grateful they have been and how much that gratitude has meant to me. I was able to do so little for my sister, but I can say that I have helped many women in their fight against cancer."

Sonya, surprised at herself, swallowed tears. Maybe all this was not so artificial after all. Novelli seemed genuinely moved and proud.

"What will you do now you have left the House of Franklin?"

Novelli smiled, seemingly content. "Two things: paint and work to help find a cure for breast cancer."

"Where will you work? Do you have a studio in the city?"

He didn't answer directly. "I have a studio at my country house in Connecticut. That's where I've done much of my painting."

"Well, thank you, and good luck in your new life," said Sonya. She was already going over the interview in her mind. Which section would be in the finished story? Most likely it would be where he talked about how little he could do for the sister and how he wanted to help others. The part that touched her would also move the audience.

"I'll see you later," Novelli said. "We're sitting at the same table. The Franklin table."

He glanced over his shoulder, then turned back to Sonya.

"If you want to talk to my successor, Jason Sarnoff, he's behind me, talking to *Entertainment Tonight*. You can't miss him. He's wearing a weird outfit, one that—believe me—will never sell in the Midwest, or anywhere else."

Sonya recognized the nasty turn Novelli had made. Where was the feeling, caring man she had on tape? Sonya also knew Novelli was wrong.

Jason Sarnoff had replaced Novelli as the Franklin designer only three months ago. He was the French bad boy of fashion. He had done a series of extraordinary, beautiful collections for the long-established house of Jacques Forcade.

They had caught the favor of the world press, and his name had become quickly famous in the international fashion world. Buyers loved the pared-down versions of his runway collections too. They were chic, wearable, and casual enough for the American way of life.

"That's the way it is in fashion now," Mari had said to Sonya. "Usually young, kooky designers are hired to do sensational runway collections, mainly for the publicity."

Sonya had been around the fashion world long enough to know that the runway clothes are unwearable for most women; back in the showroom, it was a different story. She had interviewed enough buyers who told her they only took pieces that were simple and clean and worked in the reality of today's fast-paced lifestyle.

Sonya never liked being part of the game. She knew companies used her work to get the public to buy fragrances and accessories. Every time she put one of those fashion stories on the air, she somehow felt a little wrong about it.

She had asked to do a piece that would tell the real fashion story. But Matt Richards was her boss and he thought that truth was something most viewers didn't want to see.

Sonya believed the game would not finish well for the industry. "Those crazy clothes are turning women away from fashion," she was convinced.

Jason Sarnoff certainly fit Mari's description of the "young, kooky" designer. No tux for him. He wore a cardigan, knitted from what to Sonya's eye looked like black string. His black jeans tapered over his workman's boots. A black pearl hung from one ear, and when he smiled, Sonya caught the glint of a silver stud in his pierced tongue.

He moved toward her with absolute confidence, a preening animal prancing through a mating dance.

She nervously pulled the mike cable to get more reach. When the camera rolled she extended the mike, standing as far away from him as she could.

"Who is the woman you want to dress with your clothes?" she asked.

"My clothes stand out. They have a certain attitude. They are meant for a woman who wants to express her individuality. There are many different women, both young and not so young, who are attracted to them. I offer what I call 'comfortable couture'—fine clothes made with the best fabrics, the best craftsmanship. But always clothes that are real. Not a fantasy. Women are losing the ability to fantasize. Fantasy is out in fashion."

Not only was his English good, but his accent had a carefully developed charm about it.

"Will fantasy come back?" asked Sonya.

Jason sighed. "Everything that goes around comes around in fashion. We all know that. Fashion is change."

"What tempted you to leave Paris for New York?"

"Money. What else? Isaac Franklin needed a new name to boost sales. He was willing to pay enough for mine, and I accepted."

He paused. Sonya could see that he had come to the end of what he had to say.

"They want me over there. Have you got what you want?"

Sonya looked down at the crowd mounting the steps, shrugged her shoulders, and smiled. "You've given me some great sound bites. Go on your way."

Sonya didn't like him. As he moved away, she felt there was something dangerous about him. But she knew he would make great TV.

THREE

7:15 PM, Sunday

Kim Kelly clutched the huge black umbrella with both hands as she fought against the gusting wind and rain. With her heavy black bag slung over her shoulder, she had to struggle to stay on her feet.

But Mari St. Clair had insisted she avoid the photographers who would line the steps to the library entrance. To do that, she had to come in through the loading dock off Fifth Avenue on 40th Street.

Long experience had taught her that it was best to do what Mari said. Not that she liked Mari. She was efficient, but she was also cold and dominating.

"The guards will be on duty and they'll let me in," Kim told herself. "I must stay on the ground floor and find my way to the dining room. That's where the presentation will be.

"If I go up to the second floor, I'll walk into the cocktail party and without makeup I can't face anyone."

She had agreed to do her own hair and makeup, and now

she wondered why. It wasn't such a big deal. What if the makeup artist did see the new lines around her eyes, the droop of her mouth? She'd lost a lot of weight. At 5 feet 10 inches, she was down to 103 pounds, too thin even for a model. The designer samples, which were size two, would have to be taken in. But surely she could force herself to eat. To put on 10 pounds. Everyone else did, why not her?

On the other hand, no one could do her makeup as well as she did it. She'd packed it so carefully in her model's bag . . . the concealers, the foundations, the eye shadow, the lip colors, the powders. Her hair was already in pin curls under her scarf. Give her 10 minutes and she'd be ready to go onstage. Why the wave of anxiety?

And why was she being so tough on herself? It was only three weeks since she'd checked out of the clinic after a month-long dry out.

The staff there had been so encouraging, and she had followed the routine religiously. She was going to be okay. She'd had a few glasses of white wine, but had definitely said no to coke.

More important, each week she'd struggled to the meetings. It was tough. She was used to being stared at, but as a beautiful woman, not as a curiosity. The model who had everything—beauty, fame, money, boyfriends. But she hadn't been able to make it through the day without snorting coke.

When she got up at a meeting to tell her story, she felt that no one there believed her. She was famous and because of it she was resented rather than understood.

Photographers were waiting to snap her coming out of the meeting. The second she spotted them, she had run, filled with anger at the invasion of her privacy. When she reached the car, they had crowded around her, their strobe lights flashing as she burst into tears and covered her face with her hands. She had struggled through the most difficult period of her life, she looked like hell, and now they wanted to blow up her frantic face on the front cover of some tabloid.

Once the photographers had been her friends. She had loved playing up to them as she strutted down the runway.

They had whistled their approval, calling, "Over here, Kim! Give me one of those looks." And she had obliged, vamping it up, loving every moment.

Those were the good times. She shuddered at the thought they were over and might never come back.

But she had to be strong. The doctor at the clinic told her she'd be a star again, and so she would. The cameras would be flashing for her tonight. All she had to do was present Leonard Novelli with his silver award.

Leonard Novelli, her mentor and friend. This night she mustn't think of herself. She was there for Leonard Novelli.

There was the guard at the loading dock door. He turned his head and saw her outlined against the street light.

"I'm a model. A presenter. I'm part of the show," Kim called to him over the noise of the wind. Her voice was clear, even strong—her accent a crisp, charming mix of the English she'd spoken at home with her British mother and her father's Dutch, which she spoke at school in Amsterdam.

"I came this way to avoid the crush at the front steps. Mari St. Clair arranged for me to be let in."

It was a new, unhappy experience to have to identify herself. But she was so unsure, and she knew that, for a model, recognition slips away fast.

She flashed him her most brilliant smile. The smile that had brought her so much fame.

"Of course. Kim Kelly, the model," the man said, and grinned. "I know you. I've seen you come into the shows a hundred times."

Kim felt stronger.

Ushering her through the door, the guard took her umbrella, shook it, then closed it and handed it back to her.

"Thank you," she beamed. How good to be back in a familiar place with friendly people.

"I'm presenting Leonard Novelli with his award tonight. I'm so very proud."

It was true. She was proud that Leonard was receiving the award and that she was giving it to him. They had been so close, in work and in personal life. Her first job had been as the Franklin model. That was only eight years ago. Her agency had sent her, a frightened 17-year-old on her first go-see.

Wendy Sharp, her booker at the modeling agency, had assured her, "Novelli is a good person. He'll be nice to you, and if he likes you at all, he'll give you a chance to work in one of his shows."

Kim and Novelli clicked immediately. He liked her so much he started fitting on her the very same day. During those first few years, he taught her about modeling, about fashion, about glamour, about being seductive.

He had pushed Franklin to let her do the Franklin ads. First for the newspapers, then for the glossy fashion magazines. He had supervised her every time she changed her hairstyle or her look. He advised her about jobs, about the right parties to go to. He had even found her an apartment in his building.

How easy it had all been then. She had been so eager to learn. He had been so secure, so willing to teach.

Of course he tried to control her. That was the way he was—a control freak right down to the way the colored pens were placed on his desk, the way the sketches were filed, the way shoes were lined up in the closet, toes out so he could immediately see the style.

Sometimes she teased him. Like the time when she picked up the pins he dropped at a fitting.

"Do I have to have all the pinheads facing the same way?"

Leonard didn't answer and he didn't speak to her again for an hour. He hated being teased, as he hated any kind of criticism.

Of course he had decided on the dress she would wear to the awards. It was one of his early designs. He had made it on her five years ago, a shimmering sheath of bias-cut gold lamé. It slid gracefully over her body, its cowl neckline softening the shape of her small breasts and its low back emphasizing her long waist.

"It's perfect for you; I designed every detail to flatter your body," he had said with pride. "You are my golden girl and the dress sparkles as you do."

A year later, he had insisted she wear it when she went with him to a party at the White House. The First Lady held it to thank celebrities who helped raise money for cancer research. The photographs of them arriving together had flashed around the world. She looked ravishingly beautiful, and Novelli proud, if slightly pompous.

But he had refused to give the dress to her.

"You can't be photographed in it too often," he insisted. "It's yours, but I'll decide when you'll wear it. Anyway, the fabric is delicate and has to be carefully treated. You could damage it if you travel with it."

He was wrong about that, for if there was one thing Novelli had taught Kim, it was to value designer clothes. Other models might throw a dress carelessly on the floor when they changed, but Kim reached for a hanger.

Clothes meant so much to her. She could spend hours trying them on, putting different separates together, playing with accessories to change the look. It was clothes, not family, not friends, not lovers, that gave her the most pleasure.

She reached the end of the long corridor and pulled open the tall oak door. Before her lay the vast book-lined space that had been converted into a dining room for the party.

It took her breath away.

In the front was a velvet-draped stage with ten rows of tables sweeping back from it. The centerpieces were masses of fragrant roses in different shades of red. The tablecloths and napkins were soft beige trimmed with gold, and the party chairs had antiqued gold covers. Kim climbed the steps at the edge of the stage and turned to look at the splendor of the room.

"Only in New York, only in New York," she said aloud, as if she were addressing a crowd.

"It's so rich, so extravagant, and yet on a night like this it's also warm and comforting. The designers try to outdo themselves every year, and this time they've succeeded."

In 45 minutes the room would fill. Movie stars, models, magazine editors, TV hosts, store executives, and, of course, designers would take their seats.

Every important name in the world of fashion would be there.

How good it was that she was making her comeback tonight. What a friend Novelli was. She would never have had the courage to do it for anyone else.

"If you're looking for your dress, you won't find it up front. I've got it here with me backstage."

The voice over the loudspeaker was familiar. It was Andy, the director of the awards show.

"Don't bother to look for me; I'm watching you on the TV monitor," the voice echoed in the empty room.

Kim smiled. She parted the curtain and saw Andy standing near the TV and sound equipment. She walked over to him and gave him a kiss.

"Thanks," she said. "I was just looking over the room. It's magnificent, don't you think?"

"Well it's Harriett Franklin's taste and that can be a little. over the top for me, but I've got to admit it looks pretty when you come in after battling the storm."

Backstage was crowded. Makeup artists were already working at the three small stations. The toilets were the only changing rooms, and they were full. It didn't matter, Kim told herself. She could start putting on her makeup using her hand mirror and as soon as the large toilet for the disabled was free, she'd change.

She pulled her scarf off her head and tucked it into her bag. Next came the pins that let her hair fall freely. She gave it a quick brush and then loosely clipped it back from her face.

Leonard wanted it straight.

"Your face is perfect," he had told her when they first met. "Never let a hairstyle distract from its purity."

Her dress was hanging in a garment bag on the rack among the overcoats. She unzipped it quickly and examined it. Yes, the waistline, the whole body was narrower.

Novelli had insisted that he fit it on her before she wore it that night.

"If it swims on you, you'll look anorexic and I'll look like a bad designer," he'd said.

She lifted it out of the bag. It was exquisite, beautifully made of glowing, sensuous fabric. The memories flooded back. How good the good times had been.

Would they ever come back?

Novelli was retired. But she must keep working. After all, she was only 25. Her whole life lay ahead.

It was different for him.

"I'll do what I want, at last," he had told her. "Work for cancer research, and find out if I can be a serious painter. Painting is what I dreamed about when I was a boy."

He said he didn't miss the power, glamour, or excitement of the fashion world. He was tired of the emptiness of it.

Perhaps he was right. But she knew if she lost it all, she would be devastated. She had to be a star tonight.

But could she? Doubts flooded in. She had modeled before audiences of thousands and never let her nerves show. She had spoken in countless TV commercials and never quavered.

But tonight was different. She had to make a speech in front of a thousand people. The toughest, most critical audience she'd ever faced.

She found a chair and slumped into it, her black bag at her feet. She started to shiver violently. She wrapped her arms around her body to try to control the shakes. Her nightmares were back.

There was no mirror for her to work at, no place to change, and if she didn't make a success of the speech tonight, no future.

FOUR

8:30 PM, Sunday

Sonya walked as gracefully as she could into the almost empty dining room. Her feet hurt and her body ached from standing. Worst of all, her face was so stiff she couldn't smile.

She needed to sit down and she needed a drink. She walked toward the stage, looking for the Franklin table. As Mari had told her, it was right up front. Sonya found her place card and sank gratefully into her chair. At last she had a moment to pull herself together.

Perry, her cameraman, had realized how frail she was feeling. He had taken the mike from her and ordered her inside.

"It's not worth making yourself sick, Sonya. The local station won't use a second of this tonight. The big news is the storm, the damage it caused, and how tough it will be to get to work tomorrow.

"Do me a favor and forget the *Donna Fuller Show* for a few minutes."

It was never easy for Sonya to leave her crew, but this time she agreed with him. They had more interviews and shots of celebrities than they could possibly use.

"Okay. Just keep shooting arrivals. I'll catch interviews inside if I need them." She gave him a quick, one-arm hug, "Thanks, Perry."

Sonya eased her shoes off under the table and sighed. It was true she always pushed herself too hard. Not only Perry but her friends at the studio kept telling her she gave too much of herself to the job.

She had probably even pushed herself into having the face-lift too early.

Sabrina, her friend the makeup artist, had joked about it earlier that evening. Sabrina worked full-time at the studio, but she had taken the night off to help Sonya get ready. "Only a crazy person would go out on a night like this. Believe me, it's so cold that you won't need to ice pack your swollen face when you get home tonight."

"How will I get through the evening, Sabrina?" she had moaned, realizing what she had let herself in for. "Every woman there will know I've had a face-lift."

Sabrina had shrugged. "Every woman there will see it immediately because every woman there has had one. Probably two or three." She had laughed as she closed the three contouring powders she used to disguise Sonya's swollen cheeks.

"Relax. This is the toughest it'll ever be. By the time you want your second lift, the techniques will be so improved it'll take just a week to heal."

"Second lift? What do you mean 'second lift'? Not after this!" Sonya had moaned. "Anyway, that's 10 years away. I'm talking about getting through tonight."

Now at least she was out of the cold and sitting down.

Sonya looked around quickly to see if anyone was watching her. Then she pulled a large magnifying mirror from her bag and closely examined her face.

Why had she done it? Why the face-lift? She was only 39. But 40 was six months away. Only six.

In the television business, looking young was an essential part of the game—even for a producer who was never on camera.

It made the executives think you were in touch with the audience that counted most these days, young people. She smiled as she remembered the story of the brilliant, ambitious 21-year-old assistant who got fired when the network found out she was really 32.

Well, she'd get through the evening somehow. Sabrina had told her, "Keep your hands off the makeup, forget about the face-lift, and get on with the job."

As a finishing touch, Sabrina had given her a light dusting of iridescent powder, "to reflect the light away from the swelling."

"It's that mane of red hair that people notice about you, not your face," had been her parting words. "Go often to the bathroom, wet your hands and crunch up your curls. You look great. And if you do add more powder, do it lightly."

Sabrina was an artist, and as devoted to her job as Sonya was to hers. She was also a great judge of people. She seemed to know instinctively who was genuine and who was lying. How often had she made observations about celebrities that had proven right?

Sabrina claimed she could tell if someone was lying by the way their eye muscles moved when they smiled.

"Watch them," she had told Sonya. "They give you a smile and you think everything is okay. But if their eye muscles don't move, they're hiding something. And that usually means trouble."

Since then, when she was interviewing a person, Sonya watched their eyes carefully. She had learned to tell whether they were speaking the truth.

Right now she needed energy. Something to eat. She leaned over and examined the centerpiece. Nothing. Just masses of exquisite roses in every imaginable shade of red. The colors were extraordinary.

Sonya guessed that each vase of flowers probably cost as much as a week's pay for a farmhand back in Newton, Minnesota. She would never have the ability to put together anything so luxurious. Her sense of reality would stop her.

In front of each place setting was a letter opener, the handle in red, the brass blade curved slightly at the top. Sonya picked one up. It was beautiful, the handle glowing in the dim light. It fit nicely into her hand. It had almost a lethal feel to it. She tested the point with her thumb.

"Pretty sharp, isn't it?" Mari St. Clair said as she came up quietly behind her.

Sonya jumped. "Oh! I didn't see you coming."

"Look at this table, Sonya. Isn't it great?" Mari was showing her first enthusiasm of the evening. "The theme for the night is cutting-edge fashion—Harriett Franklin's inspiration. You know, she heads the awards dinner committee this year. She found the letter opener. And it works, as well as being quite elegant. The handle is leather, not vinyl. Harriett says that party giveaways should be attractive *and* useful. No one wants to take home another piece of junk. And Harriett always gets what Harriett wants."

"What Harriett wants tonight is to put me down, or get even with me for some imagined slight." The voice had a definite Midwestern twang, and Sonya turned to see Lily Allen, the fashion editor of *Fashion Inc.* magazine.

Quickly, Sonya slid her feet into her shoes and stood to greet Lily, whom she knew and respected. Lily was a fashion icon, and she looked it—high maintenance all the way. She could pass for 45, but Sonya guessed she was closer to 60. Her dark hair was swept back from her perfectly rounded forehead, her eyelids darkened at the corners to give them width. Her lips were painted a deep, glossy red.

In one hand she held a glass of red wine. With the other she gesticulated with a glittering Judith Leiber clutch. She had carefully arranged her fur-lined cape off her shoulder to reveal the subtle sheen of her dress.

It was hard to see in the candlelight, but Sonya guessed the fur was golden sable. It was long-haired and certainly expensive. Probably so expensive she had to take it with her. The cloakroom wouldn't accept responsibility.

How did Lily afford it? Sonya wondered. That magazine was notorious for the low wages it paid. Even if she was in her late 50s, she couldn't have amassed that much money.

Was it from her husband? He was a respected editor on one of the newsmagazines, but Sonya knew those magazines didn't pay well either. And they'd had children to support— a daughter who now lived in Europe and a son, who'd died not long ago. Was Lily from a rich family? Sonya doubted it.

But then, Sonya reminded herself, fashion editors at magazines didn't have to follow the strict rules of TV and newspaper journalists. The fashion industry was notorious for its freebies. How often had Sonya herself received a gift from a grateful designer after a piece had aired? Sometimes it was worth hundreds of dollars.

The network's rules didn't allow her to keep anything, so she'd send the item back with a polite note of explanation. The next day, it often arrived at her home address. The Seventh Avenue fashionistas wouldn't take no for an answer.

Back the gift would go again. Sometimes, Sonya admitted to herself, with real regret.

Freebies or not, Sonya liked Lily. She was a pro. If Sonya needed information, Lily was the one to call. And when she called, she got through immediately.

"What's the problem, Lily?" Sonya asked as she bent forward to receive the obligatory kisses.

"Well it's just that Mari, or more likely Harriett, has broken one of my standing rules," the well-groomed woman snapped. "They've placed Henry at a different table. One far away in the back."

She looked directly at Mari.

"It was Harriet, wasn't it? I know she's playing one of her games with me."

Mari tried to answer, but Lily interrupted, turning to Sonya.

"I insist that Henry and I be seated together whenever I accept an invitation to one of these big dinners. It is the only way I ever manage to leave early. Henry is like all men; he has a few drinks, gets caught up in a conversation, and forgets about time. Especially when he's sitting next to a pretty woman."

Lily's voice began to rise. "I can't tell you how many times I've had to walk around the room and drag him away. It is so stressful. It makes me seem as if I'm jealous. Which I am *not*."

Sonya thought Lily's denial was just a little too strong to be believable. Wasn't Henry a few years younger than she?

"Henry can talk to all the pretty women he wants to, but on his own time. I'm the one who brings home the bacon. I have responsibilities. I have to get up and get going. I'm at the office early—before my staff. Harriett knows my problem. Why has she suddenly done this to me? What's going on?"

Sonya felt embarrassed for her. Why be so upset? The problem was not insurmountable. Couldn't Mari simply go across to Henry and tell him when Lily wanted to leave?

Something powerful was bothering Lily. Something unsaid.

Mari placed her hand on Lily's arm in an effort to placate her.

"Please, Lily. There are only 10 places at the table. It's politics. There are the designers, Jason and Leonard. We invited the Tylers because, as you know, their company is launching the new fragrance. There's Harriett and Isaac Franklin and Sonya, Kim Kelly, you, and me."

Lily pulled away from Mari and looked across the room as if she were trying to find someone. Could it be Harriett? Was she going to have it out with her? Surely not here.

Mari continued, "It's a good group politically and socially. The only person we could have gotten rid of is Kim Kelly. But she's presenting the award, and it would create a lot of gossip if we seemed to be dumping her at another table."

"Kim Kelly." Lily spat out the words. "I don't want to see her, let alone sit at the same table with her." She paused for breath.

"I don't care what you say. I know Harriett's doing this,

deliberately dumping Henry at another table. I've known her for a dozen years and I know she is up to something. And if you were the friend you pretend to be, you would tell me."

Sonya looked at the anger distorting Lily's perfectly made-up face. The woman's almost hysterical reaction seemed ridiculous. What did she mean? Was there some truth in her accusations against Harriett?

Sonya was intrigued. Her instincts as a journalist were racing.

Did Harriett hold some power over Lily? Was Lily frightened of Harriett?

Turning to Mari, Sonya said, "I don't have to sit here, Mari. You're a friend, Lily. Henry can have my seat. I'll go and stand by the crew. I need to work anyway."

Mari didn't blink. "For heavens sake, don't you realize Harriett dreams of getting a story about her new perfume on the *Donna Fuller Show*? If you don't sit at this table, she'll fire me."

Lily pulled her arm from Mari's grasp and, without a word, turned and walked away.

FIVE

8:40 PM, Sunday

"Isolate the panic. Pinpoint the cause and control it before it takes over."

That's what the doctor had said to do about her panic attacks. And that's what she must do now.

Mari St. Clair leaned against the damp stone wall of the public library. Her chest tightened as she tried to force air into her lungs. She had to get away. She mustn't be seen like this. Not tonight.

She forced a deep breath. What had brought on this attack?

It wasn't the rain-soaked carpet or the water dripping through the plastic canopy onto the disgruntled reporters and their cameras.

It wasn't that the first few people to arrive weren't worth shooting, and now when the celebrities were arriving, few wanted to pause in the freezing air before the cameras.

And it wasn't the fashion awards themselves.

She'd done this event so many times before. It was 10

years exactly since she started representing the Franklin company as publicist and marketing consultant and she'd been working at the awards ceremony since then. It had been Franklin policy for decades to help promote American fashion. Isaac Franklin was a big contributor to industry events and causes. Mari respected his attitude and did what she could to help, often not charging a fee.

So what could have gone wrong tonight?

Mari put her hand into her bag and felt in the smooth satin pocket for one of the pills the doctor had given her. She didn't need them often. She'd only had one since this morning.

She kept them loose and easy to find in case an attack began. It was a daily ritual. She checked the pills before she left the house, the way she checked her cell phone.

Mari placed one in her mouth and broke it in half with her teeth. She swallowed hard. It would be half an hour before it worked, but surely that was time enough.

She had gone to the psychiatrist a few months after her mother died. That's when the attacks began. At first, she'd ignored them, attributing them to the long hours she worked and the stress of owning her own business. But they didn't stop, no matter how many times she went to the gym, how many massages she had, or how many weekends she took off to go skiing.

They came without warning and Mari, with all her determination and willpower, was helpless against them.

She had told the doctor how she had hated her mother all her life. "She was a pretentious, social-climbing woman who was totally absorbed in buying the latest designer outfits. I'll never understand why she married my father. She thought him beneath her. She neglected him and she neglected me. When he had a heart attack, Mother didn't go to the hospital to see him. And she wouldn't let me go either."

He died soon after.

"I loved my father. He was everything to me. I survived his death; I can't understand why I am having these attacks now."

"You are a classic case of a woman who lost her father as a child," the doctor had told Mari. "You have coped with your loss and fear of abandonment by going to great lengths to ensure that it will never happen again.

"Your work is the replacement for your father's love. That's where you feel you are in control. You have become a drill sergeant to keep the upper hand. We need to work together and solve these problems."

All she had asked for was some anti-anxiety pills to take when she had a panic attack. But he had gone on and on, insisting that she was refusing to understand the depth of her problem. He had asked Mari to visit him every week, or twice if she felt her anxiety was out of control, but she refused. Once a month was as much as she wanted. Just often enough to renew the prescription.

She had told the doctor some of the details of her affair with a married man. He questioned her endlessly about it, saying that she should not be satisfied with having "only the crumbs of a relationship."

"It's destructive," he said. "You are starved for love. Face your fears, learn to love and be loved, and to feel worthy of both."

Mari wondered why she kept going to him. He told her the same things over and over again. While she told him very little.

"I know I should tell him everything," she thought. "But how can I? It would be too painful. And what if he said he would put me away? No, I will never tell another soul."

She managed a deep breath. The pill would do the trick. She felt stronger, almost able to cope. Mari leaned against the wall, remembering the only time in her life when she had really felt totally in control.

That was in those last days when her mother was dying, and Mari had had to take over. She'd had to make every decision. What an enormous relief it had been to realize her own power.

Now she would exert that power with the Franklins. That was the solution—she would make the decisions. If she didn't, the problems between Isaac and Harriett would become even uglier. That could seriously hurt the company.

Isaac had acted so strangely at the office on Friday. He suddenly called a late meeting about the launch of the new fragrance. They had all come running.

Except Harriett.

"I don't want her here, and I don't want you to discuss the meeting or any decision we make with her," he had said. "Things are going to be done my way."

He knew what he wanted to do with the fragrance. So did Harriett. The problem was their ideas were light-years apart. The only thing they shared was a desire for the profit it could make—profits from at least five million dollars of sales in the first year.

Everything else they had argued about—the name, the shape of the bottle, the packaging, the fragrance itself.

Mari knew Harriett wanted the fragrance to have her name. It would be a "testament of Isaac's love for me," she claimed.

But the name "Harriett" meant nothing to the stores, the press, or the buyers. Isaac wanted to call it Franklin to rest on the name that had been so prominent in the fashion world for 50 years.

"Franklin is a name well known to customers across the country," he said. "It's a clean, modern name, a name that is a symbol of style and of quality. It will also be a tribute to my father, the man who started the business and has done so much for us all."

Mari had been disturbed when she found out Harriett was to be excluded from the meeting. She was a difficult woman, but she was creative and her suggestions had often sparked ideas that built sales for the company.

"Isaac, you are asking for trouble. She will be furious with you. You brought her in on the project; you can't reject her now in front of the staff," she had said to Franklin. "Even if she is your wife, she is still part of the team and entitled to your respect. I don't think you understand how ambitious and clever she is."

Franklin had tried to laugh it off, but Mari continued. "She's very bright. But she's never been given the chance to show it. Not with your father, and not with you. She is burning up with resentment."

Mari surprised herself. As close as she and Franklin had become, she never really shared her feelings about Harriett.

"Isaac, please listen to me," she went on. "Take a good look at her. She is deeply, deeply dissatisfied. And dissatisfied people can do a lot of harm."

"Forget about Harriett, I've had enough," he had said gruffly, almost rudely. Mari was surprised. He was usually a kind, thoughtful man. She had never heard him speak that way about his wife. His problems were overwhelming him.

"This meeting has nothing to do with Harriett," he said. "Jeff Tyler is making all the decisions. He's the expert and we're paying him a lot of money for the launch. Jeff finds her too disruptive in the meetings."

Mari had insisted, "She'll find out about it."

"How? You won't tell her, the staff won't, Jeff won't, and I certainly won't. Anyway, she's busy fussing about the dress she is wearing to the party on Sunday night. Just leave this to me."

Mari knew Isaac felt he was losing the battle with Harriett. This might be his last desperate attempt to foil her.

Month after month, Harriett had been worming her way into the business. She now had her own office, between Isaac and the design room. He said jokingly it was to keep his eye on her; but in reality she said and did what she wanted.

Harriett had even approached Mari for support, behind Franklin's back.

"Women have to stand behind women," she had said. "So I'm asking you to stand behind me. I think you understand why it will prove best for you."

It had been an extremely uncomfortable moment for Mari. The Franklin account was important to her business. She had just smiled and said, "You've always had my support, Harriett, and while I'm here you always will."

Today, she felt she had to be careful with Isaac. She mustn't overstep the line, despite having been associated with the company for so long. Despite her close relationship with him. Mari knew that she had a lot to do with the success of the business. She had spent many days and nights mapping business strategy with Franklin. She had worked with their growing number of licensees: first, raincoats, then shoes and handbags, and now the all-important fragrance.

True, her own reputation had grown along with the success of Franklin. It was her major account, and because of it she received constant offers from other fashion and beauty companies.

But Mari wanted to stay with the best. For in the end, it was the best names that lasted.

Still, times did change. Firing Leonard Novelli and bringing in Jason Sarnoff represented a major design shift for the House of Franklin. But was it the right change for this prestigious company?

Thoughts of the two designers brought Mari back to the present. She was beginning to feel better. The tension had eased.

She could always move to another company. Maybe get twice as much as she did from Franklin.

She smiled at the thought.

But first, tonight.

Tonight must be a success. That meant looking after Kim Kelly. She had nearly forgotten about Kim. Kim would need her.

Mari rushed inside and headed backstage.

There was Kim in the corner, on a plastic chair. How

frightened, how fragile she looked, thought Mari. With her arms wrapped around herself like that, she looked as if she were trying to protect herself from the world.

"She has a *real* case of panic," Mari told herself. "She is much worse than I am."

As Mari approached, Kim whispered, "I am so happy you are here, Mari."

Mari knew it would be fatal to show any sympathy. She said, "Kim, pull yourself together. You've walked down a thousand runways in front of hundreds of cameras and never taken a step out of place. What could go wrong tonight?"

Kim's trembling voice sobbed an answer. "I can't do my face here, Mari. You can see there's not enough light. I went to a place at the makeup table, but that blond 16-year-old told me to get away, it was her turn now. She pushed me off the stool. I had nowhere to sit. I didn't know what to say to her. What to do."

"Do what you always do. Pull yourself together." She reached out and took Kim's hands.

"Get up and face the world. Tonight, as much as any-thing else, we're celebrating your return. We all respect you and are so glad you're okay. It was a tough time, but you went to the clinic, you took the treatment, and now you're starting a new life. Every member of the audience out there will be rooting for you. Believe me, there is no need to be afraid."

Kim raised her face, her eyes filling with tears. "Do you really believe that?"

Mari pulled her to her feet.

"Yes I do," she said. "We all know that while Leonard is the one getting the award, he owes a lot to you. You were his devoted helper. You did as much as anyone to see that the shows for cancer research were a success. The industry is in debt to you. Be proud of yourself. This is a time for joy, not tears."

She picked up Kim's makeup bag, led her to the mirrored table, and found a chair for her.

"Look after Kim, she's one of the stars of the evening," she told the makeup artist.

Then she bent down and touched Kim's cheek.

"I'll come back to check on you later. You'll be fantastic. As fantastic as only you can be."

SIX

8:50 PM, Sunday

The lights in the great arched hall of the New York Public Library dimmed. The cocktail party was ending. The time had arrived for the guests to put down their glasses and move to the dining room.

Grace Tyler reached out and placed her almost empty champagne glass on the waiter's silver tray.

"It's both warm and flat," she said with a smile to the waiter. Then she quickly picked up a full one, turned away from him and the crowd, and took a long sip.

How ridiculous it was, she thought, to excuse herself to a waiter. She hated herself for doing it. As if he'd notice or care that she had already had three glasses.

But she didn't want Jefferson, or anyone else for that matter, to see how much she drank. On nights like this, she needed it more than ever. Tomorrow was another day, she told herself. She'd call a shrink and get into a program. She had to take care of herself for the sake of the children. They came first.

In front of her was a wall of sketches, photographs, and posters extolling past winners of the awards. It was amusing to see them. How young and eager those famous designers were once. There were Donna Karan, Ralph Lauren, Karl Lagerfeld, and Calvin Klein, looking as handsome in that old photo as Grace's husband was today.

The cocktail crowd began to thin as the guests, talking and laughing, slowly moved to the passageway.

Most of the women were in black. Black that they wore to emphasize their narrow, muscular bodies. And they had every right to show them off. Their hard-edged elegance came from training vigorously every day of the week. And also, Grace told herself, from their absolute rejection of the trays of delicious hors d'oeuvres the waiters continually offered to them.

They were a tribe unto themselves, these fashion women. How they looked mattered more to them than anything else. In a way she envied them—their passion. She rarely felt passionate about anything. Growing up, her big interest had been avoiding her father's anger.

She had been passionate about Jeff. And of course the children. If Jeff left her, she would always have the children.

One of the young, skinny beauty editors she'd met at a press party caught her eye and waved. "Magnificent pearls," she mouthed. Grace put her hand to the strand of pearls around her neck and then quickly to her matching earrings. "Thank you," she mouthed back, smiling and waving. The pearls were an unexpected present from Jefferson. They were magnificent. She wondered why he had given them to her. He said it was because he had been neglecting her. Over the last few months, work on the new Franklin fragrance had kept him at their apartment in the city most nights.

"I know you don't wear much jewelry, but you have the kind of beauty that pearls accent," he had told her. "And you can wear them with anything, even a T-shirt. I have been searching for the right strand for months. And now I've found it. They are perfect for you."

Was it true? Or had he rushed into Tiffany's to buy yet another expensive gift to placate his guilt? She would never know. Jefferson Tyler was an extremely accomplished liar.

Perhaps her doubts about his motives were the reason she seemed to be constantly misplacing the earrings. Just this evening she had looked for them in their velvet box and found them gone. After a frantic search, she'd called Jefferson for help. He had found them immediately and told her she should have looked beside the bed. She was sure she had.

Jefferson always seemed capable of finding things she had lost.

But where was he? She looked around. He stood under the chandelier, chatting with yet another blonde.

How attractive he was. His dinner suit was perfect on his lean, well-proportioned body. Conservatively cut, yes, but then there was the blood-red handkerchief he had tucked rakishly into his breast pocket. He had a taste for fashion.

He still looked like the agile sportsman he had been when she first met him, even though he had spent 10 years behind an executive desk.

Jefferson felt her gaze and looked at her. He started to excuse himself and turned to walk across the room to her. She waved at him, motioning that there was no need for him to come.

She was happy where she was, and happy to have time alone. It was better than sitting at a table making idle chatter. She could finish her champagne quietly, pretending to be fascinated by the display.

She watched Jefferson charming the blonde, listening with endless fascination to her, laughing at her jokes. He turned on the charm the moment he entered a room. He seemed to signal all the attractive women that he was available. They flocked to his side.

Grace wasn't jealous, not anymore. Even if she were, she would never let it show. She had not been brought up that way. If she had something to say to him, she would wait until they were alone in the bedroom.

*   *   *

She had fallen in love with Jefferson the first minute she saw him. How well she remembered his easy manner as he stood waiting for her beside the small plane.

Her cousin Robbie had given her a parachute jump as a present for her 21st birthday. He was so certain that she would enjoy it, she hadn't had the courage to refuse. They'd gone to the airport in Westchester County together. Robbie, who had always tried to make her life more exciting, introduced her to the instructor pilot, Jefferson Tyler. Grace was so terrified she could hardly speak. Robbie had just told her there was only room for one passenger, so he wasn't jumping with her.

She had felt shy and unprepossessing in her jeans and T-shirt. She held out her hand to shake Jefferson's, and he, perhaps sensing her nervousness, had held on to it.

"Don't be afraid," he had said. "Parachuting can give you a new perspective on life. It opens the world. After you jump, you'll look down and you'll see the world stretched out before you, more beautiful than you ever imagined. You'll never forget it. It'll be one of the most thrilling moments of your life."

It had indeed been thrilling. But more thrilling was the phone call a week later. Jefferson asked Grace to fly with him to Martha's Vineyard for lunch the next Sunday. Her heart raced. She immediately said yes. Since their first meeting, she had spent hours wondering how she could arrange to meet him socially. And now he had called her.

She expected opposition when she told her parents she was going with Jefferson, but she was shocked at the depth of her father's anger. Perhaps he had sensed her strong attraction to the young man. Perhaps he had been jealous.

"He's a fortune hunter," her father said. "He's had a week to research our money. I guarantee he knows all the details of our businesses. He's been busy adding up the worth of the perfume company, the holdings in France, the properties in Manhattan, my trust fund, the trust fund your grandfather set up for you. All of it.

"You may be a lovely girl, but not so lovely that a high flyer like him would fall for you. He wants your money. Stay away from him."

She knew there was no changing his mind. It was useless to point out that Jefferson had no way to discover all that information. Her father was the most secretive man alive.

He was a hard man to understand. He owned and controlled huge plants that manufactured fragrances. Yet, despite having the kind of business that thrived on press coverage, he believed all publicity was bad. He avoided being photographed and refused to have his wife or daughter at any social event that would be covered by the press.

Grace was educated at home with tutors. On her 18th birthday, she had insisted the only present she wanted was to go to college. Her father finally agreed and enrolled her at Radcliffe, the sister school to Harvard, his alma mater. Over the years, he had given substantial donations to both institutions.

Grace was happier than she had ever been. Then trouble struck. A magazine article called her "one of the three most eligible girls at Radcliffe." Worse, the magazine ran a picture of her playing tennis in short shorts and a tank top.

Her father was alerted to it by a friend, who also warned him about the kidnapping of rich children by terrorists. Though Grace denied giving permission to the magazine to take the picture, her father brought her home in disgrace and eventually enrolled her at a women's school close to the estate.

He insisted she come home every weekend, and she had agreed, not knowing what else to do.

But at 21, she was able do what she wanted. She went on the date with Jefferson.

Three weeks later, they were married in the small chapel on the grounds of the family estate. Her grandfather had built it for her grandmother when she'd become too ill to go to the local church. Each week the old man had carefully wheeled her frail body to the altar.

At first, Grace's father told her that marrying in that chapel would dishonor her grandmother's memory and dishonor him. Then, faced with the publicity that a registry wedding would bring, he relented. But he refused to give her away.

"Let Robbie, the cousin you are so fond of, take you into the new life you are so desperate to enter," he had said the night before the wedding.

When Grace walked to join Jefferson at the altar, tears ran down her face. She loved him with a depth of feeling she hardly thought possible. After a lifetime of hidden emotions, she was overwhelmed.

But even then, she had nagging doubt about his love for her. It seemed as if she were two women. One was happy and joyous in her love, marrying a young man with a brilliant future. The other was distrustful, weighing every word he said, doubting his motives, his business talent, and most of all, his love for her.

On her wedding night, still in the simple cream wedding dress her mother had said was appropriate for such a rushed wedding, she had collapsed on the bed, unable to control her sobs. Jefferson stood looking down at her, unable to understand her grief.

"It was all so dreadful," she wept. "My mother did her best to make it the kind of wedding she believes in—a beautiful, solemn exchange of vows in the house of God. But it was terrible.

"My father didn't give me away because his knee was swollen and painful," Grace said, trying to excuse his behavior. "He was frightened he'd fall. That's all. He doesn't hate you. Why did you ignore him when he went to shake your hand? All my family, all our friends were watching."

"*Our* friends?" Jefferson snapped. "Name them for me. I had no friends there. Your mother wouldn't have it. She insisted the wedding be small, like hers had been. That's what she wanted, so that's what she got.

"What about what *I* want?"

Then suddenly calm, he sat down on the bed beside her and began stroking her hair.

"Oh, Jeff," she said as she turned to him. "You'll want for nothing. My grandfather set up a trust fund for me when I was a child. I started getting the interest when I turned 21. When I turn 25, I can take control of the capital. I'll give it all to you."

Jefferson smiled. "I've got what I want. You. My generous, unspoiled Grace. I love you. I love everything about you. The smile you give me when I walk into the room. The way you listen to all my dreams. The belief you have that those dreams will come true.

"You're my refuge. I want you beside me for the rest of my life. I want us to have children . . . a lot of them. Three or four. At last I'll have a family. My own family." He paused.

"Your father judges everything by the amount of money a man has. But I'm young and I have a great future. You know I don't fly just for the fun of it. It's a business. It's already profitable and will be even more so. It will take care of us. We don't need your family wealth. I will support you."

She sat up, and looking into his eyes, believed him. Then she wound her arms around his neck. At last she escaped into the pent-up passion she felt for him. He kissed her long and deeply. Money didn't matter.

And now, as she watched him walk toward her, she felt a wave of love. Money had never mattered.

Since taking over, Jefferson had proved to be a brilliant businessman. He adored their three children. And here he was, still smiling at her as if she were the only woman in his life. She smiled back at him as he took the glass from her hand and put it on table.

"There's plenty of wine inside and good wine, from what Harriett keeps telling me," he said. "She's gone over the menu with me every time we've met."

Grace looked at him, surprised. "How often do you see her?"

"She's always dropping in to see Isaac when I'm in his office discussing the new fragrance. She's become a nuisance—more than a nuisance. She tells me that you were great buddies at college. She's full of stories of your days together.

But I don't know how you, of all people, could have put up with her."

Grace answered coldly, "College was a long time ago." She turned away from him.

Harriett was no friend. Not for years. Not since Grace's mother had told Harriett she was unwelcome in their house. What was Harriett telling her husband?

Her old insecurities swept back. She reached for the champagne glass. It was empty.

"Let's go to the table, Jeff," she said. "I'm cold. I need a drink."

SEVEN

8:55 PM, Sunday

Sonya watched the last of the crowd push its way into the dining room, glad that the award ceremony was about to start.

From what she had seen of most of her table partners, she wasn't looking forward to being with them. She wanted the evening to be over, but she was hungry.

She smiled to herself, knowing that her mind always got down to basics.

The lights were low, and what little brightness there was seemed to be absorbed by the deep color of the wood-lined room. The men were all in black; most of the women wore black and the waiters too.

It was all very chic, very funereal.

She wondered what her mother would think about it. In Minnesota, they prayed for the light of summer. Black was for the dead.

Sonya ran her hand down her leg and massaged her foot.

Thank God she had worn pumps. Her other choice, the
Manolo Blahnik sandals, had four-inch heels. She resisted
the temptation to take her shoes off again.

In this crowd, it wouldn't pay to be seen wiggling her bare
toes. All right in Minnesota, but not at the fashion party of
the year in Manhattan.

She watched Harriett Franklin coming toward her, thread-
ing her way through the chairs and tables, stopping to wave
at people and urging them to sit down. It was clear that Harriett thought of herself as the hostess of the event.

And it was obvious that underneath the smiles, she was
annoyed. And, what's more, she didn't mind if it showed.

Probably the cocktail party had gone on too long.

She is a good organizer, Sonya thought admiringly. She
guessed that if they started too late, the audience would
leave after the award ceremony and skip Harriett's carefully
planned dinner.

Harriett approached the table and smiled stiffly when she
first saw Sonya. Then she apparently changed her mind and
her tactics and came toward her with an outstretched hand.

The smile became even broader as Sonya rose.

A fake smile, thought Sonya as they shook hands. She had
seen those smiles before, when someone wanted something.

"I can't believe Mari let you sit here by yourself. I can't
imagine where she could be. You must accept my apolo-
gies." Before Sonya could answer, Harriett went on. "But it
does give me a chance to chat with you alone. Your crew
filmed my husband and me when we arrived. Will you be interviewing us? I would love that. You know, Isaac and I are
the celebrities of the industry. We have more interesting
things to say about fashion than any actress or model."

Harriett was living up to her reputation.

Sonya took a quick breath and decided to ignore what
Harriett was asking. Instead, she said, "Mari told me about
your dress, that it was designed at Franklin. I have to com-
pliment you. You were brave enough to walk in without a
wrap, so we all could see it."

Sonya had avoided the question, and she saw that Harriett caught that. But the woman persisted.

"I'd love it if you could interview me. I designed the dress myself especially for this evening. I believe that dresses are prettier for parties. And pretty women make a party a party."

Harriett paused, trying to read Sonya's reaction, and then gushed, "Of course you look wonderful in that pantsuit. Do you always wear them?"

Sonya felt irritated. Yes, she did always wear pantsuits. She looked slimmer in them and the pockets were so useful for keeping assignment slips, addresses, and cards—all the essential bits and pieces for her job.

Sonya never even thought about looking pretty. Attractive, feminine, sexy. Those were the words she liked. They were good enough for her. And she was good enough to be an ace producer on an ace program, and that's what she wanted.

She smiled as some of her self-confidence returned. "I wear them mostly when I'm working on bitterly cold nights. They are so much more practical. But Harriett, you do look beautiful in that dress."

She called the woman Harriett—using a first name for someone she didn't know. That was what was done in this New York world, but Sonya had never really gotten used to it.

"Thank you for inviting me to your table. I'll certainly have a good view of the show. I'm looking forward to it."

"Then sit down, so we can convince the idiots running it that we are ready to start. I'm going to speak to the caterer." With that, Harriett headed backstage, walking away quickly. Too quickly, thought Sonya, almost as though she couldn't contain herself. Harriett had a nervous energy that seemed ready to explode.

Sonya slid back into her chair, happy to be off her feet. She looked around and saw Mari pushing through the crowd toward her.

"I'm just checking to see that you're all right," she said when she reached the table. "Perry is okay. I took care of him, got him in a good position to shoot the show."

She paused for moment and then went on hesitantly, "Don't be upset by Harriett. I promise you that she's not always this bad. Something has happened to upset her. When that happens, she strikes out in every direction.

"I'll be right back. I want to check with Kim and track down Isaac Franklin."

As Mari left, the Tylers arrived at the table. Jefferson looked in the best of spirits as he helped seat his wife, then walked around and sat down on Sonya's right. He introduced himself to her, gave her a firm handshake, then picked up her napkin and unfolded it for her.

"I hear we're getting hot soup instead of cold salmon. Better be ready to eat before it freezes over," he said.

He's a party man who plays around, Sonya thought. She looked across at his wife. Grace seemed Waspy, but attractive—the sort of woman who'd be a good mother and a good friend, but hardly a good playmate.

Grace caught Sonya's eye and said, "Well, we got here; let's hope the soup does too."

"And the other guests," Sonya shot back, glancing at the empty chairs. Grace smiled at her. She's determined to play her role well . . . whatever that role is, thought Sonya.

Harriett returned to the table with a slightly tipsy Leonard Novelli in tow. He was waving his acceptance speech at Harriett.

"You can read it now, or hear it later," he offered. "I keep it in my hand because I'm afraid if I put it down, I'll forget where it is." He giggled. "Harriett, I think you should read it."

Harriett ignored his offer, and turned to the table as Leonard took his place beside Grace. "Enduring it once will be enough for me," she said.

Lily came back with Henry beside her. She sat down huffily after giving her husband a prolonged farewell kiss. He waved to them all and walked away laughing.

Jason Sarnoff also took a seat, after air-kissing the two models who had helped him find the table.

Sonya's years in television had made her a keen observer. She watched each arrival, fascinated. She didn't like these people. Except for Mari, not one of them was real. They were bigger than life. But not life.

"Merci, merci, merci," Jason laughed as he waved his napkin playfully at the models. "Be good girls and go home to bed early. It's too cold to go dancing tonight.

"What bores models are," he remarked as they left. "I spend my time propping up the egos of the most beautiful women in the world. Women who have everything but carry on as if they have nothing. They don't realize what they've got until they've lost it."

Sonya took a particular dislike to Jason.

Leonard Novelli turned to Harriett, "And speaking of fools and beauty, where is Kim Kelly?"

Harriett looked the other way, pretending she didn't hear him, but he went on. "Is she setting a new record for being late? Has she run away because she is afraid of making a forty-second speech?"

"Kim is backstage, waiting for the presentation," snapped Harriett. "Wearing the dress we altered for her. But more to the point, where are Franklin and Mari? He's the host; she's the PR. They should be here."

Harriett sat down, and Sonya looked at her face closely as she bent toward the light of the candles. Even with the professionally applied makeup, there was nothing beautiful about Harriett. She was hard and cold. And so thin.

"That's their job," Harriett continued, "as I have told them both a million times. This business has to be run like a business. They've both had time to chat up their friends at the cocktail party. They should be at this table, looking after our guests."

"Mari will come, dear," said Lily, placating her. "I'm sure she's backstage, fussing over Kim."

"Yes," added Harriett with a deliberate hiss, "I'm sure that's it. The way Mari ran after her a few minutes ago amazes me. The woman calls herself a supermodel, but you'd think she'd never walked onto a stage before. She always has to be the center of attention."

Lily agreed, "Kim will do anything to be noticed, and I

mean anything. She started as a sweet young thing, so eager to please. Then success made her a monster. Everyone—the photographers, the stylists, the makeup artists, even the designers—are fed up with her."

"Kim changed, but I'm sure it was the drugs," said Leonard. "Still, at times it was more than I could bear. One moment she was a diva who incessantly demanded her own way. The next, she was a weeping, hysterical wreck who said her life had no meaning. She insisted that we would all be better off if she were dead."

"She probably would be better off," said Lily. "But here's Mari at last. And more important, I see a waiter."

Sonya was glad the soup had arrived. The evening ahead looked almost unbearable. She envied Lily's husband, who had escaped to another table and what had to be more pleasant company. At least Mari was back.

The thick cream soup was amazingly tasty and amazingly hot. Harriett pushed her bowl away, untasted, and looked up as Mari slid into her chair. "Mari, where is Isaac? Where the hell is he?"

"He's backstage, trying to get a clear signal on the cell phone. He was having difficulty getting through, so I gave him mine," explained Mari.

"It's 8:55 on a Sunday night, so who on earth could he be calling?" demanded Harriett. "Everyone important in the business is right here."

"He wanted to check and see if Jeremy was okay after his fall today."

"That's nonsense. Of course Jeremy is all right. He was given a sedative and he'll sleep through the night."

"Oh, Harriett," interrupted Leonard, "you know how upset Jeremy gets when something unexpected happens." Sonya heard real concern in his voice.

Harriett turned to Sonya. "Our eldest son has Down's syndrome. He's being cared for in a beautiful home upstate. This afternoon he had a slight fall and was treated for it. He was perfectly okay an hour ago. It's a small problem, but my husband insists on making a drama out of it. He does it to get to me. I never wanted to have children. In fact, when I was pregnant with him, I begged Franklin to agree to an abortion. Now he blames me for anything that goes wrong with Jeremy."

No one at the table seemed surprised to hear Harriett raging. Only Grace looked at Sonya to see her reaction.

Sonya went stiff, barely breathing. Embarrassed and angry, she felt the heat growing in her sore face. She was hearing more than she wanted to know. She had no idea how to behave. She wanted to leave, to get away from this woman, from all these people.

Mari touched her arm reassuringly. Seeing the motion, Harriett leaned toward Sonya. Her voice rose. "Every little thing turns into a drama. He cares more about that boy than he does about me, his business, and our two adopted sons. Two children who are strong and intelligent. They may not have the Franklin genes, but they have the brains to carry on our firm."

Mari interrupted quickly, "Oh, Harriett, don't let it upset you. Isaac just wanted to see if Jeremy had awakened. He wanted to talk to him. It's a natural reaction."

"How would you know what's natural?" snapped Harriett. "You've never even been married, let alone had a child. I can remember the things your mother told me about you. You are not natural."

Mari laughed. "I guess I have to agree."

Sonya felt the tension at the table ease. She admired Mari's skillful handling of the situation.

"You know, Sonya, for years I listened to my mother complaining that I wasn't married and producing children. How she wanted a grandchild. And I guess, now that she's dead, I really wish I'd produced one or maybe two for her. Well, twins would have been easier."

Mari laughed again, as Grace added, "Every mother wants her daughter to produce grandchildren. I know that's what I want. That's natural."

"Yes," said Mari, still laughing lightly.

Isaac Franklin returned to the table just as the soup bowls

were being removed. He sat down, glowing with pleasure. "Well, I may have missed the soup," he said, "but Jeremy's fine. He was awake when I got through, and he told me everything that happened. He asked me a few riddles, said he was going to have some soup, and wanted to know what we were eating."

It was obvious to Sonya that Franklin adored his son.

"He's a good boy. Mari, will you get me a few photos of the party so I can take them to him when I go up there next week?" Harriett leaned forward and was about to interrupt, but Franklin put his hand on her shoulder and physically held her back. "I want him to know I told him the truth when I said I wasn't there because we were at an important business party. And anyway, Harriett, he loves to see photos of you. Jeremy always says you are the most beautiful of all the mothers who come to visit."

Harriett started to reply, "Franklin, I am sick and tired . . ."

Mercifully, the music started and the show began. It drowned the anger in Harriett's voice but not the fury in her eyes.

EIGHT

9:10 PM, Sunday

Perry had been watching Sonya. She could tell from the look in his eyes as she climbed the stairs to the makeshift platform that had been set for camera positions. She smiled. He grinned in return, standing by the tripod, his arm draped over the camera, ready to roll tape when the long introductions were over and the presentations started.

"What's going on?" he asked. "Why is this beautiful redhead paying me a visit?"

Sonya laughed, relaxing. How normal he looked in his jeans and sweatshirt. How normal he sounded. What a relief from the unpleasantness of the table.

"It's because I can't bear to be parted from my beloved crew," she quipped. "I wanted to see if they had given you something to eat."

Perry grinned. "Don't try to fool me. I know you. You can't sit still until you've seen the angle we're shooting from. Miss Control, always checking me out."

"I'm not. Did they give you something to eat?" Sonya repeated.

"There's a table in a side room for the press. The usual turkey sandwiches. But I managed to grab a lot of those hors d'oeuvres they were passing around. I really liked those tiny potato halves with caviar. Pretty good stuff."

"I couldn't eat very much," said Sonya. She took a deep breath. "I just had to get away from my table. They are so vicious, they're frightening.

"Perry," she said, putting her hand on his shoulder, "wait for me after the show ends. I don't want to stay for the rest of the dinner, I just want to get out of here. Just give me a few minutes at the end of the award presentations to say good-bye."

"My pleasure," he said. "The show is due to end at 10:00. I'll have the gear packed by 10:15. With luck, I'll get you home by 11:00."

"You're wonderful, Perry."

Returning to the table, Sonya saw that Mari was anxious. "Are you okay? You slipped away so quietly, I didn't see you go," Mari whispered.

"I'm fine. I just wanted to have a word with Perry."

"The show's running on time," Mari said quietly, her head close to Sonya's. "Whether it ends on time depends on the acceptance speeches. The winners are asked to keep them short, but you know how that goes.

"They start with the lesser categories and end with the stars. Novelli is the third from the last. Humanitarian work rates high in fashion."

"There's something about him, Mari, I can't put my finger on. He's so polite, but underneath . . . I don't know. Dangerous . . ." Sonya deliberately let her voice trail off.

"I know what you mean. The rumor is that he has AIDS, and now that the Franklins have let him go, lots of people have said he's changed and acting strangely. For one thing, he seems to be drinking a lot more. And that's not good if he really is taking that cocktail of AIDS pills."

Sonya glanced up and saw that Harriett was intently

watching them as they whispered together. Her eyes were narrow.

"Why is he getting this award?"

"Well, they had to give it to someone," said Mari. "And it was the right moment. Everyone in the industry felt he'd been badly treated. Everyone believes the rumor that Harriett had him booted out of Franklin's. It may even be true. I know his clothes were selling, and selling well to his regular customers.

"But Harriett wants to attract new, younger customers. Novelli's name is associated with their mothers, and it would be difficult to change that. At first I couldn't get any of the younger celebrities to wear his designs. But Leonard certainly knows how to cut a sexy dress, and bit by bit I was getting the young stars to borrow things for big parties.

"Then, suddenly, it was all over. Isaac announced Leonard was out and Jason Sarnoff was in. He's supposed to do younger clothes. And as you know, we'll be marketing a new fragrance for those clothes. I'm wearing it tonight. Isaac gave me the only sample of the one he likes, and asked me to test it for him. What do you think?"

Sonya sniffed. The scent was appealing.

"I like it."

Novelli certainly doesn't have much camera appeal, thought Sonya, looking across the table at him. He reminded her of a puffed-up peacock. His speech was still in his hand, and he was clearly eager to be onstage. She saw he was drinking wine and wondered how well he would do with his speech, and if he really had AIDS.

Mari continued, "I think the award was as much against Jason as it was for Novelli. In this world, everyone hates a winner, especially when they are French."

Sonya was silent, slowly going around the table in her mind. Thinking about what each one had said, she only half listened to the acceptance speeches. They wouldn't be worth using in the story anyway. The usual boring recitation of thank-yous.

Exactly 15 minutes later, the humanitarian award was announced.

Kim Kelly walked slowly onto the stage with the elegant silver award, a tall statuette of a winged woman on a black marble base, pressed against her breasts. Her hands trembled as she put the statue on the lectern. She seemed childlike, a lost waif.

Then she lifted her head and smiled a warm, winning, breathtakingly beautiful smile.

A murmur went through the room.

"I'm here full of joy," she said in her charming accent. "I am to give this award to a great friend. A great man, who gave a frightened 18-year-old model from Holland the break of a lifetime. Then he filled her life with love. He helped her through the difficult times and rejoiced through the good.

"I speak of what Leonard Novelli has done for me. But he has extended his love to all women. And he has done it not only as a designer, but also in his work to find a cure for cancer.

"I am so happy to give you, Leonard Novelli, this humanitarian award on behalf of the fashion designers of America. You, who have helped raise millions of dollars for breast cancer research."

The audience applauded vigorously as Novelli rose and headed for the stage.

"That was great. She's a winner," said Sonya. "You certainly built her confidence, Mari." She was surprised to see tears in her friend's eyes.

"I didn't think she'd do it," said Mari. "The drug experience devastated her. But tonight she proved she can put it all behind her."

As Novelli climbed the steps to the stage, the audience rose for a standing ovation. Kim stepped aside. Novelli crossed the stage, kissed Kim, then raised the statuette triumphantly over his head.

Setting down the statuette, he stood still, relishing the moment. At last he took his speech out of his pocket, spread it in front of him, and put on his reading glasses.

He waited for the audience to sit, looked at the crowd, smiled, and began to speak.

"Thank you, Kim, and thank you all for this award. If I have helped in the fight against breast cancer, it is because I had the generous support of all of you in the fashion industry.

"When I say generous, I mean generous. You have helped me every step of the way, and I love you for it. But we must not rest in our fight. We have many more lives to save. That means more research and more research means more money. So please keep giving."

Leonard beamed as the applause broke out again. Like a champion boxer, he held the gleaming statuette above his head and showed it to all sides of the room. Whistles and cheers rose with the applause, but instead of leaving the stage, Leonard returned to the lectern and waited for the room to be quiet.

He certainly understands how to work a crowd, Sonya thought.

He paused for a moment, glanced down at his notes, and began to read slowly.

"As you all know, I have left the House of Franklin and plan to live a more private life. My partner died and I have tested HIV positive."

The audience was absolutely still.

"So this is surely my last chance to speak to you, the leaders of our industry, as a group. Tonight, I want to praise, to thank, to wish well, and also to warn.

"First, to praise and thank. I want to thank Isaac Franklin for his years of friendship and solid support in both the business and my private life.

"I want to wish my successor, Jason Sarnoff, the very best of luck, but remind him that these are torturous times in fashion. Too much emphasis is put on glamorous, bare, unrealistic clothes on the runway.

"The publicity these ridiculous clothes generate has turned women away from fashion. We have made fashion a joke. It is up to you to remedy this. It is a problem that must be faced immediately." He paused, then stared directly at the Franklins' table.

"And now, to my friend, Harriett Franklin.

"Harriett, I hear many rumors of your plans. You want to work alongside Jason. You want to launch the Franklin fragrance. You want your own accessory collection. Whether these rumors are true or not, I say beware. Leave fashion in the hands of professionals like your husband."

His eyes seemed to blaze as he looked directly at Harriett.

"Leave well enough alone," he said firmly.

"You, my longtime friend, are a brilliant party giver, a gifted organizer, and an inspired fund-raiser. The charities of this city need you. Count the blessings you have."

He looked around the room and smiled. "And so should the rest of us."

Novelli took off his glasses. As he did, chairs scraped back as the audience rose again and roared their approval.

Holding his hands high for silence, Novelli finished with, "Thank you, and God bless you all."

He kissed Kim again, put his arm around her waist, and led her off the stage. When they reached the table, their table companions rose to shake Novelli's hand and murmur congratulations.

Harriett alone was silent.

The show resumed with the top awards for the women's wear designer of the year. Soon the last model left the stage, and relieved applause rang out.

Pale but composed, Harriett rose slowly and walked around the table to Mari.

She is majestic, thought Sonya. White-lipped and tense, but not a tremor showing. Here was a woman who'd been frustrated time and time again and knew how to handle herself. But to get the career she so desperately wanted, she was prepared to climb over as many dead bodies as was necessary, thought Sonya, eager to see what would happen next.

"Mari," Harriett said softly, "I want to know if you had anything to do with Novelli's speech."

Mari shook her head. "He surprised me as much as he did you."

"What he said will be in every column tomorrow," Harriett said. "He would never have attacked me without someone goading him on. So, find out immediately who is behind it, so I can stop the damage before it spreads."

She had been ignoring Novelli, but now she turned toward him.

"That was a cruel, mean, vicious attack. I'll sue if necessary. Someone is going to pay."

Sonya had had enough. She just wanted to leave.

"Harriett," she said, rising, "you have no grounds to do anything. Novelli offered to let you read his speech. You turned him down. We all witnessed that." Sonya surprised herself with the vigor of her response. As a producer, she thought she had learned not to get involved. But there was something different this time.

She turned to Mari. "I have to go. I need to check with my cameraman."

She had to escape from them. Any excuse would do.

Harriett stepped aside and let her pass.

NINE

10:12 PM, Sunday

Sonya's hand automatically slid over her cheekbones as she walked along the corridor in search of a ladies' room. Yes, the puffiness was there and she felt that it was growing. It was stupid of her to have let Harriett Franklin upset her. She had to see her face in a good light.

The plastic surgeon had warned her to rest, but if she had to work, to stay calm. Being anxious, he said, would only make her feel and look worse. And she had ignored his advice.

First, she'd gone back to work early. Then she got so mad she felt like slapping her hostess across the face. But Harriett had been rude to Mari, and Mari was a friend. She'd given Sonya good advice and stood by her.

Sonya knew it was not easy for her to control herself when she felt someone had been wronged. She had always been that way. Sometimes that got her into trouble. She was afraid that tonight was one of those times.

As a news producer, she was required to stay neutral. Harriett might complain to her boss, and to placate her, he might agree to feature her in the story. No, she didn't care. There was right and wrong. Mari didn't deserve the treatment she got.

Not only had Mari suggested Sonya have the face-lift, she had gone with her when she consulted several surgeons. Mari had escorted Sonya to the surgery and come back in a limousine to pick her up when it was over. She'd even found a night nurse for Sonya.

It had been Mari who bought the packets of tiny frozen peas the nurse demanded, Mari who had insisted on dividing them into smaller bags so they would not be too heavy on her sore and swollen stitches. It was Mari who listened to Sonya's anguished complaints when the swelling didn't go down fast enough.

Yes, she should return to Harriett's table to support Mari instead of going home to rest and ice her face. Mari would understand her leaving early, but Harriett, never. And Harriett would cause even more trouble for Mari.

Let the mirror decide, she told herself. If the swelling is up, go. If not, stay.

She knew Perry was waiting for her. She could call Mari on her cell phone, then skip around to him and leave quickly.

The corridor was lined with photographs of the venerable founders and trustees of the library. She stopped and looked at her reflection in the glass that covered one of them.

"Stop worrying about how you look. That black pantsuit fits you so well, it must have been tailor-made for you. You are slim, sexy, sensational."

The voice was Jefferson Tyler's. Although he was obviously teasing, Sonya could have kissed him for his compliments. Yes, he was a man who liked women. Sonya saw that his deep blue eyes glowed in the half light.

"Where did you get that suit? I wouldn't mind one like it. But then I don't have the figure to fill it out the way you do," he said playfully.

Sonya laughed. "Do you like women's clothes?"

Jefferson laughed right back. "Not as much as I like women." He paused, then said in a more serious tone, "I'd like to have lunch with you sometime. To get to know you better, and to talk about business." He smiled.

"Sonya, we have the most beautiful plant at Grasse in the south of France. I believe the making of a fragrance would make an excellent story. The visual of the flowers would be breathtaking and the care that is taken at every step is fascinating. I'd love to show it to you.

"You know, it costs millions to develop and launch a fragrance. There's not a man, woman, or child or in the country who doesn't use them in one way or another. I could overload you with facts and figures that show how fragrance is important in all aspects of our lives."

Here it was again. The power of the *Donna Fuller Show*. Everyone wanted to be on it. She wondered if Mari knew what Jefferson was up to. Probably not.

Sonya toyed with the idea that Jefferson might have been indulging in fantasies about being on TV and then having sex with her as a celebration. She laughed to herself; she'd had worse offers.

"I'd love to have lunch. Call me at the studio," she said sweetly. "But right now, help me find the executive rest room that is supposed to be around here."

Jefferson took her arm and steered her around a corner to the right.

"I think you'll find it is the last door on the left. It doesn't have a sign. It's strictly for the VIP women on the board of the library, the wealthy old widows who give their money to educate the kids of New York City.

"You'll find everything you can possibly need in there. Grace tells me it's better equipped than a beauty parlor. Do you want me to wait for you? I'd like to."

Sonya tossed her red hair, then hesitated. "No, I don't think so. I'm sure I can find my way back. But thanks."

"Well"—he flashed her a disarming smile and held her arm gently—"I wouldn't want you to get lost and miss out on the roast beef."

She returned his smile, then turned, quickly walked along the carpet, and opened the door.

Sure enough, the powder room was luxurious. Very luxurious for a public library. The walls were lined in a metallic paper that reflected the subdued pink lighting that was most flattering to aging skin. The closed cubicle door was covered in leather and the floors were a brilliantly matched pale green marble.

The flowers were the inevitable massed orchids, but orchids that seemed to reflect the same flattering pink.

Sonya turned to the gilt Louis XVI table at the other end of the room. Harriett was sitting on a stool, bent over a gold makeup mirror. But something was wrong.

Harriett was slumped forward, as if she had fainted amid the orchids and the array of silver powder boxes and crystal perfume bottles.

Sonya called out as she stepped toward her, "Harriett? Harriett, are you all right?"

Harriett didn't move. Her lip-liner pencil lay on the table, her eye shadows scattered on the floor.

Her body was twisted. Her head rested on one arm. The other arm lay along the counter, with a brush drooping in her hand.

Sonya stood close to her. Under the tight black dress, she could see no motion of breath. She felt that if she touched her, Harriett would crumple to the floor.

She stepped back in horror. "Harriett," she shrieked, "Harriett! My God. What happened?"

Still Harriett did not move.

For a moment, Sonya was paralyzed. Devastated by panic. Then she rushed across the room, through the door, and down the corridor.

Jefferson was still there. She flung herself at him.

"For God's sake, come. Something awful has happened to Harriett."

"What are you talking about?" he asked. He took her by the arm and moved her calmly down the corridor toward the open door.

She pulled at him. "I don't know, I don't know. I was only there for a second. I think she's fainted. No. No. I think she's dead."

Sonya felt her whole body shaking.

Jefferson flung the door wider.

"My God, Kim," he shouted. "Kim, what are you doing?"

Sonya pushed past him.

Kim was standing next to Harriett. She had pulled Harriett up against the chair and was slowly pulling a dagger out of her. The dagger had been thrust beneath her rib cage, toward her heart. Blood had run down the front of the black tulle dress that had been so important to her. A few drops were slowly dripping on the gleaming marble floor.

Sonya looked at Jefferson. "Kim wasn't here when I came in. I only saw Harriett slumped over the table." She turned to Kim. "What are you doing? Where did you come from?"

Jefferson stepped forward and grabbed Kim's wrist. "Let go of the knife," he commanded. He looked into Harriett's face. Her eyes were rolled back. He put his hand to her neck. He shook his head. There was no pulse.

"She is dead."

Kim gasped. "I didn't do anything. It's a letter opener from the table. I'm taking it out. I want to help Harriett. I didn't do anything." She released the handle of the opener. It fell to the floor.

Sonya looked closely at Kim, whose eyes were glazing over. "Kim, where were you when I came in? Tell me."

Kim's voice was unnaturally high and tight; she was becoming hysterical. Her words came in snatches.

"My speech was a success, wasn't it? I said that I love Leonard and he had helped me and other women. I didn't say anything about Harriett. I didn't do anything to make her so angry."

She fell silent. Her thin arms hung by her side. She looked exhausted.

Sonya repeated her question. "Tell me where you were."

Great, gulping sobs racked the model's thin body.

"In the toilet. I went there to get away from Harriett. She

was screaming at me. She told me Isaac wouldn't take me back. They were finished with me. I couldn't bear it. I had to get away from her."

Jefferson stepped forward. "We have to get Franklin. Then the police."

"You're right," said Sonya. She took Kim by the arm and pushed her toward the cubicle. "Get back in there. Try to be calm. Stay there until we come for you."

Jefferson was eager to take control.

"I'll find Franklin and we can get the police."

Sonya turned to him. "No. Stay here and guard the door. Keep Kim under control. She'll listen to you. I'll find Franklin, and Mari too."

"Sonya, just get Franklin. Bring him here quietly. Then call the police." Slowly and deliberately he added, "We have do what is best for all of us."

Sonya closed the rest room door behind her. She felt in the bag for her phone, then ran along the corridor to the window, where she had a chance of making a good cell-phone connection.

For a moment, she hesitated, wondering why Jefferson had asked for the delay. She knew she had to call the police immediately. She dialed 911. CALL FORWARDED flashed on the screen, then it went blank. She redialed. CALL FORWARDED again. Then a voice, fading in and out. She couldn't get through. Interference, she guessed, from the storm.

I'll try the studio, she thought. They can notify the police for me. Then I'll get the party security staff.

This time, connecting was unexpectedly easy. The news department assignment editor's voice came through loud and clear.

"Oh, George, it's Sonya Iverson." She breathed her relief and began to professionally reel off the most important information. "I'm at the fashion awards party. You'll find all the details in the computer. This is for the 11:00 local news."

"What have you got?" asked George rather routinely.

"There's been a murder here."

"A murder? What do you mean? Who?"

"Harriett Franklin. She's the wife of a prominent Seventh Avenue fashionista named Isaac Franklin. Stabbed to death in the third-floor executive washroom."

George didn't hesitate. Unfazed, he responded, "Okay, I'll send a crew."

"Oh, George," Sonya rushed on, "I just found the body and no one knows about it yet. I tried to get through to the police, but the storm must have wiped out a cell relay station. So would you call?"

"Sure, I'll call. And I'll send my crew," George repeated.

"No. Perry is here," Sonya said adamantly. "I'll get him and we'll get to work. I'll get the tapes to you in time to make the 11 o'clock news."

"No, Sonya, I'm . . ."

Sonya wouldn't let him finish. "George, this is my story for the *Donna Fuller Show*. You can use the tapes for your 11:00, but I have to get them back in time for my show's editorial meeting in the morning."

"Sonya, right now it's *our* story for the 11:00 news local." George was resolute. "I'll use what shots I want, and I'll get your precious tapes back to you for the meeting. Haven't I always in the past? But as soon as my crew gets there, it is our story."

Suddenly, Sonya felt worn out. The corridor began to spin around her. She looked at her watch—10:15. No dinner, and her face was beginning to throb again.

She didn't want to get into an argument, but she was determined. She would do it her way, whatever George said. She knew if she stayed for a while with Perry, she could get more shots and perhaps some interviews. That would make a really strong piece for the Tuesday night *Fuller* program.

"Have you got any shots of this Harriett person coming in?" George went on.

"Yes, they are on the first tape with the rest of the arrivals. She came in just after that tall black model, Slim Tamara. You can't miss her. Harriett was the only woman to come in without a coat or a wrap. She's in a long, bare black dress. She's a brunette and her hair is short cut with ragged edges."

"Sonya," George said, "fashion is not our thing. I really think you ought to come in and give us a hand with it."

"George, I can't leave. I told you—I found the body. Slumped over the dressing table. The police will want to interview me. And I'm staying to cover this for Donna."

"Well, if I can't convince you, I'll send someone to pick up the tape. Put it in the camera and see if you can cue up her arrival. Have it ready and call me back. Fast."

"Right," said Sonya. "First chance I have. But first things first. I have to get security, then find her husband and tell him."

"Are you okay?" he queried, apparently realizing that he was pushing too hard. "I'll get the other crew and a producer on the way. If you don't feel up to covering the story, go home after the police have interviewed you. You know, it would probably be better if you got some rest," he continued. "The network will want you to help on the early morning show."

"Yes. Okay. But I'm fine. Just call the police. And remember, I need those tapes back. And George, I want this to be clear. This is *my* story for Donna's show."

She clicked off the phone and raced down the corridor. She had to find Franklin and she had to get security. And she wanted to find Mari. Sonya was going to need a lot of help from her friend.

She suddenly realized she felt fresh again from the rush of adrenaline. This was a serious and important story and it was all hers.

She thought of Harriett and the table of vipers. Where had they all been at the time of the murder? Where were they now? Any one of them could have done it.

Sonya headed for the Franklin table. Get Isaac first. Then security. And Perry, of course. She looked to the platform where the cameras had been set up. Perry was watching for her. She waved frantically, signaling that he join her.

Then she saw Franklin. He was standing alone.

Sonya took a deep breath. She went up to him and put her arm through his.

"Isaac, something dreadful has happened," she said gently. "You have to come with me."

As they walked away she looked over her shoulder. Perry was following, the camera on his shoulder.

TEN

The driver opened the door of the sleek black *Fashion Inc.* limousine and Lily scrambled into the back seat.

Henry watched her as she huddled in the corner, rocking herself like a distraught child.

Was she shivering because of the cold? Or was it fear?

She had behaved like a madwoman. After 22 years of marriage, he was used to her hysterics—her sudden highs, her inevitable crashes. But tonight was something else. Harriett's murder had triggered some deep fear in her.

After the award ceremony, like most of the guests, Henry had left his own table and wandered around the room to chat. He had stopped at the Franklin table as the waiters brought in the roast beef entrée.

Lily had just pulled him into the empty chair beside her when Jefferson approached. Half jokingly, she was repeating her usual instructions, "Don't flirt with the models. At your age, you only make a fool of yourself. They come on to you only because of me. They want to see themselves in my magazine. That's what it is, believe me." She glanced around the table looking for support.

But there was something about Tyler's face that startled her.

Pale and shaken, with all his charm, his man-of-the-world ease stripped away, Jefferson had walked around the table to Grace. He had stood there, resting his hands on her shoulders, as if he were drawing on her strength.

"Harriett is dead," he said quietly, and then continued with a surprising executive efficiency, "murdered in the executive washroom. Sonya found her a few minutes ago. Isaac is with the body, waiting for the police.

"He asks for you all to sit patiently until they arrive. It will only be a few minutes. They will decide what announcement to make and what is to be done."

The table fell silent. Murder was not easy to understand.

Then, "Harriett can't be dead," Lily screamed. "I saw her a few moments ago. I must go to her. She's been fighting with Franklin about the perfume. He was torturing her. She shouldn't be left alone with him."

She had struggled to rise from the table. Henry held her down while Grace rushed over.

"Lily, Harriett is dead, I felt for the pulse in her neck," Jefferson kept his voice low, aware of the sudden interest from people at the adjoining tables. "She's dead. There's nothing you can do."

Lily took the glass of red wine Grace offered, drank it in one gulp, and buried her face in her hands, her body heaving with suppressed sobs.

As he moved away from the table, Jefferson turned to Henry. "Stay with them, please, Henry. I have to go to Isaac. He needs all the support I can give him."

"Where's Mari? I need to talk to her." Novelli clutched his award as if to protect himself.

"I haven't seen her, but she must be with Franklin," Henry replied. "She is the company PR after all, and that's her place."

"Shouldn't we go home?" asked Jason nervously as he

rose. "Surely at this moment he will not want us with him. I would like to feed my cats. Oh, God, what am I saying? I just have to get out of here."

Henry took over. "Sit down. We must do what our host asked," he said firmly. "Wait for the police. As soon as we have given them our names and addresses, we'll be able to leave. They will want to interview us all tomorrow, I'm sure, but not tonight."

He was right. The police had been extremely efficient, taking everyone's name and contact info and asking them to notify the precinct if they were leaving town.

And so now at 11:30, he and Lily were on their way home.

"Lily," he said as he closed the window that separated them from the driver, "you must calm down. Harriett was no friend of yours. She used you like she used everyone."

"You don't understand," she sobbed.

He was constantly amazed that she could become almost paralyzed with fear. One word of criticism and she crumbled.

How many nights had he watched her drink endless glasses of wine as he tried to explain to her that she wouldn't be fired because she hadn't used a photo of an outfit from some important advertiser? Or even if she screamed at her staff to get out of her office because she couldn't take them a moment longer.

She ran the best and most successful fashion magazine in the country. She was respected, admired, loved by designers and manufacturers, even by her staff. But she was incapable of giving herself a moment's rest. She had to walk on the razor's edge. That was the core of her relationship with Harriett. They played a game in which Lily was a willing, even happy, participant.

Harriett gave the Allens thoughtful, expensive gifts that added luxury to their lives. But she was a calculating woman who expected something in return for every gift.

Not immediately, of course. Harriett knew how to bide her time. But the demand would come. Lily had experienced it time and time again. She knew what to expect. And she had learned how to give back.

Henry looked at her. She was on the verge of hysteria. For all of her finery, a miserable, crumpled wreck. And Henry knew that she would need all the protection he could give her.

From the beginning of her career at the magazine 10 years ago, Harriett had wooed Lily. First the lunches, then the theater tickets, the rides to Paris in the private jet.

To say nothing of the clothes. That was taken for granted.

Harriett had supervised the making of the dress Lily was wearing tonight and arranged for her to borrow diamond earrings from Harry Winston. Her gold evening purse with its pavé diamond clasp was Harriett's most recent Christmas gift. The fur-lined cloak was last year's. Even the pantyhose had come from Harriett, who had ordered two dozen pairs for Lily. "Wear them before they go out of fashion," said her note.

Worst of all was the money—the loan Lily had accepted to buy the farmhouse in Connecticut.

How often had he wanted to get out from under it all?

"Let's sell it, repay the loan, and get away from Harriett," Henry had often said. "We'll both be happier. The children are gone; we don't need that house any longer. You and I can visit friends in the country on weekends, or better still, stay at small hotels by ourselves. It would be blissful."

Lily had insisted she was trapped. Harriett would never take the money back. It was a matter of control. And Henry, in his heart, knew it was as his wife had said. There was never any escape from Harriett.

"She'll use that loan to destroy my credibility as an editor, if I ever step out of line," Lily had said. "Every story that I've done for Harriett could be used as evidence that the loan was a bribe."

Henry sighed. If Lily's reputation was tarnished, it would reflect on him. He was a journalist too, one who took pride in his integrity. They could lose everything.

"Henry, we'd have no apartment on Park Avenue, no

country home in Connecticut, no free tickets to first nights at the ballet and opera, no invitations to movie premieres, no celebrity parties—nothing. Our lives would be so different.

"Oh, Henry, what have I done to us?"

What had she done to them, indeed? He'd married her 22 years ago. She was divorced with two young children, a boy and a girl. He was also divorced, with two older sons.

"It's a perfect match," she had said so happily. "A fashion editor and a journalist. We can help each other with our careers and the children will fit in perfectly."

For them, it had been a perfect fit. He loved Lily and would never leave her. He believed she felt the same way about him.

The children were another story. His sons had done well enough—they had gotten through college and were out on their own. But Lily's children . . .

Her daughter hated fashion and everything Lily stood for. She had fled to Berlin at 18 to study German and Russian. She rarely came home and usually refused to meet Lily in Paris during Lily's regular trips to see the new collections.

Her son had been impossible from the moment Lily and Henry began dating. First pot, then heroin and crack. Finally, a body found in a broken-down hotel in lower Manhattan.

Yes, the fashion world had been hard on Lily's family.

Henry turned to her, put his hand under her chin, and lifted her face until her eyes met his.

"I love you and always will," he said, then bent forward and kissed her lightly on the lips.

"Oh, Henry," she sighed with relief, "I have to tell you. I did something at the magazine and Hilda found out." Hilda, Henry knew, was Hilda Gorin, the publisher of *Fashion Inc*.

"It was so stupid of me. Harriett took me to lunch and told me about the Franklins' new perfume. She said Isaac had agreed to name it 'Harriett,' after her. She was full of ideas about it. She said she wanted to take a new approach to the marketing of fragrance.

"She told me that Isaac loved her ideas and was planning an enormous advertising campaign. It would launch with six full pages in *Fashion Inc*. She asked me to do a story about her and her ideas on perfume."

Henry shrugged. "Yes, yes, get on with it."

"I agreed to do the story. It's so hard to get a fresh take on a new perfume. Henry, Harriett's risen to the top of the heap. She even hinted that she would give some of the profits to charity.

"I thought that women would be interested. I sent over one of our best writers to do the story. We took photos and as far as I knew everything was fine. I slated a double-page spread for the April issue."

"Then what is the problem?" asked Henry.

"Hilda decided to get something more definite on the ads. So she called Isaac. He said that the new fragrance was still on the back burner, and that it certainly would not be called 'Harriett.'

"He also told her that if *Fashion Inc*. wanted to get any more advertising from Franklin, I'd better start checking my facts with Mari St. Clair."

Lily reached for Henry's hand and held it to her cheek.

"Of course, Isaac knew that I had talked to Harriett. He really was furious with her, not with me. It was so embarrassing. I had believed Harriett.

"When I called Harriett, she insisted I run the story. I said I couldn't now that Isaac had denied it. If I did publish it, he could sue the magazine and I would be fired.

"Harriett continued to insist. She said if I didn't, she would invite Hilda to lunch and tell her a few things about me. She would start with the $300,000 loan for our farmhouse."

Henry took his hand from hers and ran it over his head.

"That would be disasterous," he said.

"Henry, she was angrier than she has ever been. She said once the story was published, Isaac would fall into line. He would simply give in and let the perfume be named 'Harriett.' He would never sue. It wasn't his nature, she said."

"When did all this happen?"

"On Friday. I didn't want to bother you with it. I was sure Harriett would give up on the story. But before we left tonight, she called and said she had definitely made up her mind. She had counted on me for support, and if I couldn't give it to her, she was prepared to destroy me.

"I couldn't let that happen, Henry. You know that. But now she's gone and I'm sure we're safe. Isaac is a good man. He would never harm us."

They fell silent as the car drew up close to the canopy of their apartment house. Lily gathered her cloak around her. The doorman leaned in to help her step over the roaring gutter. She was unsteady, and suddenly seemed older than her 60 years.

As Henry watched, he wondered. Could this brilliant, ambitious wife of his be capable of murder?

"No, never," was his immediate gut reaction. Lily would risk many things but never a cold, comfortless life in prison. Then he thought about Lily's temper. In a rage, she was capable of anything.

ELEVEN

7:15 AM, Monday

The sun was barely over the horizon when Isaac Franklin drove down Seventh Avenue to his office in the garment district. The city still lay in the icy grip of the winter storm, and Franklin's thoughts were as grim as the dark, windswept streets.

He muttered thanks to his driver and braced himself against the cold as he left the car and walked across the pavement to his building. He leaned against the wall as he fumbled for his keys to let himself in.

Sleep had been impossible. The dread of facing his children, his staff, his friends, the press, and then the police again kept him pacing all night. If Harriett knew how he felt, she would laugh. She would enjoy a last laugh. She always had.

But even as the thought came to him, he was relieved that he wouldn't have to hear that laughter.

At last the key slipped into the lock. Isaac opened the

door, went directly into an elevator, and pressed the familiar penthouse light.

Fear clutched him as he sensed her presence.

Harriett, he thought, I said good-bye last night, but here you are—still beside me.

He had waited, in the powder room and in the hallway, during the three hours it took for the police photographers and crime scene team to arrive and do their work. Then Harriett's body had been placed in a black body bag and lifted onto a gurney. Isaac looked down at her face as the zipper closed over it. She was calm at last, calm, as if she were having a long and restful sleep. Her anxiety and fury had vanished. She was almost as beautiful as when they'd first met on that sunny day in Mexico.

He followed the gurney out of the library and watched the men lift it into the ambulance. Harriett, who had arrived with such splendor, was leaving for the morgue alone.

"Harriett," he whispered as he watched the gurney roll down the hallway, "Harriett, forgive me. I should never have let it come to this."

But now it was Monday morning. Isaac walked slowly through the corridors until he reached his office. Harriett's was adjacent. He stopped at her door and looked in, as he always had.

He almost expected to see her sitting there, fussing with her face in front of the makeup mirror, leafing through a fashion magazine, or writing notes in her spidery handwriting. Turning toward him to talk, to gossip, to complain.

He was happy to be free of that. Strange that with every moment of dread came another of relief.

He walked to the chair beside her desk and sat down.

"Oh, Harriett," he sighed. "Why did it have to go so wrong?"

The problem, he knew, had always been the children. Or rather the fact that Harriett never wanted them. He had known that before he married her.

"I am not the mothering type. I have a brilliant mind and I'm going to use it. I want a career," she had said.

Isaac had found this impossible to believe. Every young healthy woman wanted children. That was what life was about. She was just going through a phase. Once they were married and settled in their own home she would change.

He had once loved her so deeply. He couldn't get enough of her. When they said good night, he counted the hours until he saw her the next day. He would have given his life for her. Then.

Eventually, she had agreed to two children, providing nannies would care for them.

"It's got to be twins," she had joked, "a boy and a girl. I'm only going through this once."

"I'll take what I get," he had replied, overwhelmed with relief and love.

Nine months later Jeremy was born. When Franklin and the doctor had tried to explain that Jeremy had Down's syndrome, Harriett had refused to listen. When they brought him in for her to see, she fainted. One glimpse of Jeremy's small head with its flattened face and slanting eyes had been too much.

Franklin had taken her in his arms to soothe her. "There is every chance in the world that our next baby will be perfect," he said. "We'll get the best possible treatment. We are both young, and the doctors assure me we can have normal children. You just have to give yourself time."

He smiled to himself as he remembered his joy when the nurse gave him Jeremy to hold. Damaged or not, this warm little bundle was still his son.

"And once you get to know Jeremy, you will love him," he had told Harriett.

Harriett had remained silent.

And that was the beginning of their real trouble. She didn't want Jeremy and she wasn't going to try for another child. Later, he came to understand that what she wanted was to control the Franklin business. She had married him only for his wealth and his position in the world.

His father had realized it long before Isaac did. Murray had come to dislike her, even to distrust her. He'd warned Franklin about her.

"She's an ambitious woman, ruthless, and won't stop until she has the power she craves."

When Isaac told Murray that his wife refused to have more children, Murray had said, "Then adopt." When she refused to adopt, he had said, "Then divorce her."

Faced with divorce, she had agreed to the adoption of the two boys. And she held back while his father was alive, playing the dutiful wife, the society hostess.

But the week he was buried, she changed. After that, nothing was too small for Harriett to meddle in.

For the past months, it had been the fragrance he and Jefferson Tyler planned to launch. But she would never have won that battle. The stakes were too high. He was determined to stop her, whatever he had to do.

Yesterday, he had given Mari a sample of the fragrance they intended to market.

"Wear it at the party and see what people say," he had told her, "what comments you get from that crowd. You know they don't miss a thing. Jefferson believes, and I agree, it's young, fresh, and should prove a winner.

"I'll give Harriett the sample of the other fragrance, that heavy one she wants to market."

Franklin closed his eyes and tried to force his mind away from those memories. He must start to deal with the changes that Harriett's murder would bring.

But closing his eyes just meant he could see Harriett's body lying crumpled on the makeup table. Suddenly he gave way. It had all been too much. He put his head between his hands and sobbed.

"Harriett, if only you had worked with us, not against us. What made you so ambitious, so angry? What made you so greedy for power? What happened to the sweet, beautiful young girl I met in Mexico twenty years ago?"

* * *

As the memory came to him, his crying stopped. He felt a warm wave of love for the young woman he had married. The same feeling he'd had when he had first seen her.

She had been sweet and serious. Taking notes and drawing sketches of the geometric Indian designs at the Mitla ruins south of Oaxaca. Her big hat shaded her from the heat of the afternoon sun as the guide showed them around.

She was touring the ancient Indian sites in the area. She was in her last year at college, and this was her final project. She'd been to the Yucatan, to Palenque, and after Oaxaca, she would head for Mexico City and Aztec sites close by.

"With the research I did before I left, I often find I know more than the guides," she said with only slightly disguised disdain.

He had missed her tone then, but came to know it well as the years passed.

"Why are you traveling alone?" he asked.

Isaac stared at her. She was beautiful and her seriousness made her more so. Her skin was glowing under the hat, framed as if by an Impressionist painter. Isaac could feel himself becoming aroused. From that moment, he wanted her.

"My girlfriend was coming with me, but she got sick and at the last moment her parents said no. But that's okay. I'm here to work, not to party."

She walked away from him to study one of the patterns carved in the ancient stone wall.

He thought she wanted to shake him off. It only increased his desire for her.

"I'm holidaying in Acapulco," he said, "but I've heard so much about the beautiful, Spanish-style architecture of Oaxaca, I came over for a few days to see it."

"Alone?" she asked.

"No, with my father. He is passionate about how architectural styles have spread around the world and how various civilizations have modified them. He should have been an architect, but he grew up in a poor family in Europe. He is a whiz, you simply can't hold him back."

Moving close to her, he added, "Why don't you have dinner with us tonight?"

Isaac had never felt such a strong, restless desire. He reached out to touch her slim, bare arm, but she moved slightly, as if she understood what he would do and wanted to play with him.

"I have to be up so early in the morning. I get the best light on the carvings; I photograph them as well as sketch them. It's fascinating to see how the shadows change the shapes."

He smiled. "I know this is an old line, but you do have to eat. So join us."

"Okay," she had grinned. "The food in my pension is terrible."

She had charmed his father. She knew so much about the area. They even agreed to wake up early and meet her at five in the morning.

That night, sitting across the table from her, was almost more than Isaac could bear. He hardly heard what she said, just watched her lips move as she spoke and imagined himself kissing them. Kissing her body. Holding her. Making love to her.

When dinner ended, Harriett quickly excused herself and insisted that she could make her own way back to the pension.

Isaac slept little that night.

The next morning, promptly at 5:00, Isaac turned up at their meeting place.

"Dad has a business problem in New York and is going to fly back," he explained. "And I'm obviously not sorry he has left you at my mercy."

He looked into those big brown eyes. She was irresistible.

Harriett didn't seem to notice that he was falling more deeply in love every minute he was with her. She seemed happy to have him around. Now, looking back, he realized she was lonely and just wanted to talk to someone. Anyone.

Isaac had driven her to Mexico City, found a hotel near her small, cheap hostel, and went with her to the Aztec sites. They spent two days studying at the archeological museum.

He was impressed with her intelligence and discipline. And Harriett had a perfect figure, a flashing smile that showed perfect teeth, and long, luxurious, curly brown hair. What more did a 32-year-old bachelor from New York need?

Once, she let him put his arm around her waist. But other than that brief moment, she seemed to be avoiding getting close to him.

Having her near and being unable to touch her was making Isaac feel totally out of control. He was unable to think of anything but her. It was not just her beauty that attracted him, but her intelligence and wit. She was stimulating, charming, and fun. He felt complete with her at his side. And overwhelmed with passion.

Isaac insisted she spend a few days in Acapulco with him. He hoped that away from her work, she would be less distant. Their last night in Mexico City, she refused to eat dinner with him.

"I have notes that I must coordinate. It's best to do it now. With the glamorous life you are promising me in Acapulco, I'll forget everything. I'll grab something at the hostel. Pick me up in the morning."

When he called for her at seven the next day, he found her deathly ill. She'd been throwing up all night. She was feverish and thirsty, but unable to keep down even a sip of water.

At nine, the local doctor gave her antibiotics and told her to suck ice, provided it was made with pure water. There was none at the hostel, so Isaac went back to his hotel for it.

At noon he called his father. "Get her on the next plane," Murray said.

"I don't think they'll let her board," Isaac replied. "She's barely conscious. She belongs in a hospital. But I'm not very confident in the hospitals here." He paused. "Dad, I really care for her."

"I'll get a private plane. Don't worry."

And his father came through as always. By evening, Harriett was in New York University Hospital's intensive care ward. Deathly pale, but with a faint smile for Isaac.

"Thank you, and thank your father. You saved my life."

Isaac bent down and gave her a first kiss. On the forehead. She took his hand and held it against her cheek.

"I owe you so much. I will do anything for you."

And she had—in her own way. She had married him and borne him a son whom he loved. A son Isaac could now bring home to live with his brothers.

Harriett was dead and he was free. Isaac stood up and walked toward the window. He had the children.

They are the reality of life, he thought, the joy of life. I am blessed with them.

Then he smiled. Perhaps with luck, with another woman, he could even have more. He smiled again.

TWELVE

9:00 AM, Monday

Sonya sat in the small conference room, waiting impatiently with the rest of the staff of the *Donna Fuller Show*. It was time for the morning meeting. Monday's meeting was the most important one of the week, when decisions would be made on the stories for that week's shows.

Looking around the room at the reporters and producers seated at the table, Sonya was secretly pleased to be the center of their interest. She was the reason there was tension in the room.

For a minute, she'd thought that people were looking at her because her face was still slightly swollen. Then she realized it was the events of the night before that excited her colleagues. Sonya had deliberately answered their questions as briefly as possible. This was a competitive group, and she was determined the story would be hers alone.

The hour-long *Donna Fuller Show* aired at 10:00 on Tuesday and Thursday evenings. It was a magazine program that often covered three or four stories in one night. Sonya had always felt it should have fewer light features and more focus on hard news. But as she had often been told when she argued her view, "Ratings don't lie."

It *was* a highly rated program. The host, Donna Fuller, was a respected journalist who had spent 25 years working her way up in TV.

On Monday mornings, the pieces for the Tuesday show were set and the stories for the Thursday show loosely outlined. Since Matt Richards had become executive producer two years ago, the lineup of stories changed often and fast.

He was a hotshot. Only 31, he often joked he would be CEO of the network by the time he was 40. Sonya begrudgingly had to admit that maybe he would. The *Donna Fuller Show* had a four-point jump in ratings since he took over. Matt was riding high, and he didn't care who knew it.

Sonya believed that he often made last-minute changes to keep them all on edge.

"Don't argue," he would bark at her. "The ratings are what matters. Just do what I say."

He told her that her strengths lay in light news features, stories like the fashion awards. Sonya knew she had to keep pushing to get anything more serious. Part of the problem was simple: she was a woman.

She glanced at her watch. Matt was late and that was unusual.

Four hours sleep, that's all she'd had. To bed at two, then up again at six to ice her face. She was strained to the limit. She had to conserve her energy and ignore the chatter going on around her.

At least 15 minutes, she told herself with determination. We must do at least a 15-minute piece on the murder, and the story is mine to produce. Donna will love reporting it.

Harriett Franklin wasn't an international celebrity, but she was rich, beautiful, and powerful. A supermodel had been found with the murder weapon in her hand. The chances were she had murdered Harriett Franklin.

And if not Kim, then who? Anyone at the table. No. Anyone at the dinner.

Sonya thought back to her interview with the police late last night. She and a good-looking detective had sat on either side of a table in a small office at the library. The detective, Keith Harris had been easy with her, probably because of the power of the press and especially the *Donna Fuller Show*. Still, she liked the way he interviewed her. Simple and direct.

But she had been tired and impatient. Her mind was on how her story would be shot and edited, not on remembering details for the police.

"You found the body. What did you see when you went into the room?" he had begun.

Sonya had tried to remember.

"Well, I saw Mrs. Franklin slumped over the dressing table. I turned and ran out to find Jefferson Tyler."

Again Sonya felt her panic on seeing Harriett lying there and realizing she was probably dead.

"Was there anyone else in the powder room?" Harris asked.

Sonya had been cautious. She had answered slowly, "I am sure the room was empty except for the body."

"What happened when you came back with Mr. Tyler?" the detective had continued smoothly.

"We saw Kim Kelly standing over the body. She appeared to be trying to pull out the dagger. At least I thought it was a dagger. It turned out to be one of the letter openers that were part of the table decoration."

"When did you find that out?"

"When I got closer to Mrs. Franklin."

The next question had been totally unexpected. "Why did you go into that room in the first place?"

Sonya had laughed nervously. "Detective, it had been for the obvious reason. I was looking for a ladies' room. I found one."

"And how about Mr. Tyler? What was he doing in the corridor?"

Sonya had never thought about that. What had Jefferson

been doing there? It was a dark corridor, and as far as she knew, no door along it was open. She drew a quick breath and paused before she answered.

"Honestly, I have no idea."

Harris wrote on his pad, then asked, "Did he say anything to you? Think carefully. He must have given you some reason to be in that corridor."

"I have no idea why he was there," she had replied.

The detective referred to an earlier note on his pad, wrote something again and then smiled broadly. Sonya was puzzled by his reaction. She knew he had spoken to Jefferson already. What had he said?

"Okay," said Harris. "Let's talk about the people at the Franklin table. I would like to know if anything seemed odd. Was there an argument, for instance?"

Sonya thought back. Anger, certainly, between people who disliked each other.

"Not an argument. Harriett Franklin was upset that her husband had left to make a phone call. And she was upset at Leonard Novelli's speech, but there was nothing I would call an argument."

She added, "I wasn't at the table the whole time. I went to talk with my cameraman."

"Okay then, just one more thing for now. Where was everyone just before you discovered Mrs. Franklin's body?"

"I don't know, Detective. After the award ceremony, everyone got up and moved around the room to chat before the entrées were served. It was nothing unusual. That's what happens at these dinners."

"So you don't know where your table companions were at the time of the murder?"

"No, I don't. I went to see my cameraman and then headed for the ladies' room. All I know is that when I left the table, everyone there was getting up. When I came back into the room to find Isaac, some people were seated at our table, but not him. He was standing alone a few yards away. He seemed to be looking for someone. That's all I know."

Harris had written a quick note.

"Thank you. What you said will be helpful. We will probably need to talk again later this week. In the meantime, call me if you think of anything you missed telling me."

Relieved, Sonya had thanked him and started to leave. His voice had stopped her at the door. She had turned to see him smiling broadly.

"Good luck with your story. I like your show, and I'm glad to have met you."

Sonya had smiled back her thanks.

That was last night. But this morning, Sonya had to concentrate on getting the story together. She started to review all the elements she had collected. She looked at the list of shots she and Perry had gotten last night, shots that would give her piece for the *Donna Fuller Show* an in-depth point of view. That's what Matt always insisted he wanted.

She had tape on the arrivals, the awards presentations, the police arriving, Isaac Franklin looking desperate as he stood outside the powder room, a hysterical Kim Kelly walking out between two cops, Harriett's body being wheeled out in that gruesome black body bag, and interviews with two of the guests who had sat at Harriett's table.

Yes, she had done a good job covering the story.

And she had plenty of color of her own to offer Donna as background to the story. She had sat at Harriett's table, talked with the victim and perhaps even with the murderer.

You found the body, she told herself.

The only thing she didn't have was an interview with Harriett. She had deliberately walked away from it. But how could she have guessed Harriett would be murdered?

She sighed. Thirsty, she reached for one of the small bottles of mineral water in the center of the table. But they were too far away. She sighed again. Rick Carlton, a reporter, was sitting next to her. He handed her a bottle.

"Here" he said quietly. "You must be wiped out after last night. Matt called me to see if I could get there to help you, but I was still on the road after a weekend skiing."

Sonya smiled her thanks, and glanced up to see everyone in the room looking at them.

"Do you think some crazy struck her down suddenly, or was the murder premeditated?"

"No, it was certainly not premeditated," she said, half to herself. "That's obvious. I can't believe there was any fore-thought. The letter opener was snatched from a table on the spur of the moment. Her murderer was either a man or a strong woman. I think it was someone who suddenly became enraged with her."

"Someone who couldn't bear to have her alive for another moment?"

She smiled at Rick again. "Maybe."

"On the other hand," Rick replied, "I understand there were about 1,500 people there. Any one of them could have picked up the letter opener, followed her, and stabbed her. Maybe it was someone with a long-standing grudge. Or it could have been a total stranger, a psychopath on the prowl who killed her because of her beauty."

Sonya said nothing.

Rick had raised some intriguing questions. For reasons she didn't yet understand, she sensed that Harriett's murder was one of rage, passion, and revenge. Her murderer was someone who knew her well. And, yes, she had to face it, that someone definitely could have been sitting at the table with her last night. She may have sat and talked, even joked, with a murderer.

An icy shiver ran down Sonya's back. She forced herself to bring her thoughts back to the *Donna Fuller Show*. She had a great piece to do, and she would fight Matt if he tried to push someone ahead of her to produce it.

Sonya started as the door swung open violently. Matt walked in. He said nothing, just went to the coffee machine. He poured his coffee, added milk, and laced it with three packs of sugar substitute.

He stirred it with a red plastic stick and took a gulp. From the end of the conference table, he turned to Sonya.

"You sure upset the local news director, giving that inter-view about Kim Kelly to the competition. He's furious. And so is the network news department. Did you forget which network you work for? Didn't it enter your head? They are the opposition!" Matt was shouting.

Sonya searched her memory. At the end, it had all been so confusing. So many police, so many television crews, so many reporters. All of them anxious to get the story. She remembered the light in her eyes, blinding her, the mike under her chin, turned so she didn't see the identifying logo on the microphone. She had told the reporter, "Yes, I found the body, in the powder room. I went to get help and when I came back, Kim Kelly was standing over it."

She had thought she was talking to a reporter from her own network's local news department. He had pulled a mean trick on her.

Matt wasn't interested in her explanation. He waved his hand to silence her.

"Let's get down to the real business."

No one in the room moved. Sonya was speechless. He was so rude. Self-pity rose in her until she had to swallow tears. TV was certainly a man's business. If a woman had insulted an inferior in that way, she'd be up in front of human resources in a minute. She'd be rapped over the knuckles for harassment. God help the network if ever Matt took charge.

Did that conceited, 31-year-old male have any sympathy for what she'd been through? Any idea what it was like to discover someone dead in the powder room and then have to hang around for hours to see her body wheeled out?

And how about getting some sympathy for the way the police treated her? One officer seemed to think that she had arranged to have Harriett murdered just to get a story.

And how her face had ached in the cold.

No, Matt had no sympathy or even interest in what she had gone through. This was a business meeting, not group therapy. Sonya wanted to cry with frustration. But she was determined not to let everyone in the room know how vulnerable she felt.

She managed to smile at Matt. "So, what's the plan? We've got a lot of tape."

"We'll have to act fast. I'd like to make the story the second half of tomorrow's show. That's 22 minutes and 40 seconds of airtime. We'll tease it constantly through the first half." He paused.

"Okay, Sonya, I'll have to let you be the field producer. Rick will be the associate producer. He'll stay in touch with the police. Will that work for you, Rick?"

Rick gave Sonya a quick glance. "Sure, I'd love to work on this one."

"Okay then, it's set." Matt turned back to Sonya. "I know you were there the whole night. No one knows better than you what went on. But you look washed out. I want the best, and if you aren't up to it, let me know immediately."

He looked directly at her. For a second, she thought she caught a glimpse of concern in his eyes. But no. His concern was for the story.

Sonya murmured a quick, "I'm fine. I do know the people. I'll get interviews set up fast." Inside, she raged at the way he had put it—"I'll have to let you be the producer."

Then a wave of excitement put aside all her anger. "Half the show," Matt had said. That much time was saved for only the most important stories—and this one was hers.

Her mind moved ahead to what had to be done next.

Thank God for Mari, Sonya thought. Mari, who through the long night had remained her usual self: polite, efficient, keeping the press under control, solving problems quickly. Mari would help her get the interviews she needed.

"Okay," Matt continued. "This is roughly it. We'll open with the murder and the update from the police. Whatever that is.

"Kim Kelly was released early this morning without being charged. According to the cops, she says she was snorting coke in the john and didn't hear or see a thing. She walked out high as a kite and thought Harriett had fainted. Right now, it seems unlikely she did it. But who knows what will turn up in 36 hours.

"Here's how we'll stack it," he continued. "The first two stories of the evening will be from Washington. We are almost finished with those. Then Donna will introduce the

Harriett Franklin murder and we'll spend the rest of the show on that.

"The first few minutes should show the glamour of the evening. The arrivals, the show itself, interviews with the people at the Franklin table. Anything we can get that's exclusive. It must be exclusive."

"Matt, I think that to close the last segment, I can arrange for Donna to do an interview with Isaac Franklin," Sonya said. "I'll tell him we'll make the segment as positive as we can."

Matt jumped in enthusiastically, "Great, Sonya. From all accounts this morning, I hear Harriett Franklin was an interfering bitch."

"Well, from what I saw, there were problems between her and her husband."

Matt barely heard her. He was talking so fast, Sonya could hardly take notes. "All that negative publicity can only be bad for his business. He needs our help. We won't paint her as an angel, but we'll concentrate on the family life. The kids, the charities, her love of art and antiques. Whatever.

"I'd like shots of her home and the kids, if possible. But if he won't give us that, settle for shots of the studio, his office, her office if she has one. Sketches. Some of the fitting or the workroom. I want lots of color. Lots of background.

"Get as much as you can."

Sonya was excited, but replied as calmly as possible, "I'll start with the press conference Franklin is holding at his office this morning. I think I can convince Mari St. Clair, the PR, to let us stay and get extra shots after the other crews leave."

Matt nodded in approval.

"Right. Great. Do it. We'll back you up with a team here. We'll view all the tapes you shot last night. How far did you get viewing and logging them?"

Sonya paused. She was efficient when it came to making logs of tapes, carefully listing everything as the crew shot and noting exact time codes. Sonya was a favorite among the editors who put together her stories. The detailed notes were important because it was often difficult to remember everything on a 30-minute tape.

Last night, toward the end, it had become impossible for her to concentrate. Her adrenaline ran high and got her through most of it. Then exhaustion set in and her hands started to shake. She doubted she could even read what she had written after midnight.

She explained this and watched Matt for his reaction.

"Okay, Sonya. So you screwed up. How much did you log?"

"It's fine right up to the end," she said, unhappy with herself. "Then it got so chaotic, I'm sure I missed a lot. I know the last tape has interviews I did with some of the onlookers. I was amazed by how much they knew about her. And I got some good sound bites."

She paused, remembering.

"One girl was really freaky. She gave me a quite a scare. I thought she was Harriett for a minute. Then I realized she was a young kid dressed as a Harriett double. Same hair, same makeup, same skinny figure, even a black dress. She said she cut out every picture of Harriett she saw and tried to look exactly like her. She said she wanted to be Harriett."

"She wanted to be Harriett," Rick queried. "Could she have killed her?"

Sonya let the idea sink in. "No. I think she wanted Harriett to be alive so she could enjoy copying her. It gave her a kick when she saw how shocked I was."

"You've got all of this on tape?" Matt asked.

"Yes, of course," said Sonya.

"Good," said Matt. "You didn't get an interview with Harriett?"

"No. Unfortunately, no."

"Well, maybe we can open the piece with this kid. It could give it an unexpected twist—Harriett Franklin, Manhattan cult figure." Matt gestured, as if he were writing it in lights across a marquee.

"That's a good idea," said Sonya. "She was just one kid, but she could reflect the impact Harriett had on young people. But on the other hand, she may have dressed like Harriett in the hope she'd be noticed and get a job at Franklin." She could tell from Matt's expression that he didn't like this theory.

"Report to me every hour on your progress," he said. "We're promoting this story heavily and I want to know exactly what you've got. Now, as to the rest of you here—let's move on to the other stories for tomorrow night."

Sonya swallowed hard. She understood that Matt was testing her. This story could change how he viewed her. And that could change her life at the network. Whatever cards Matt dealt her, she had to play them well.

THIRTEEN

9:15 AM, Monday

Grace Tyler lay silently on the bed, the covers pulled up over her naked body, her blond head buried in the pillow. She put her hand up, brushed her hair from her eyes, and smiled contentedly as she looked at the clock. It was 9:15, Monday morning, and Jeff lay sleeping calmly beside her. They were together in the penthouse above the offices of the perfume business. The bed was small but still took up most of the tiny room.

She was reluctant to move, fearing that if she did, she would wake him. It wasn't often she had a chance to feel so close to him. To be quiet, to feel his warmth, and watch his chest move with each breath.

By this time on Monday, he was usually busy in the office, two floors below. She was usually at home in Connecticut, coping with the hundred and one problems of a mother of three and a large household.

But Harriett's murder had made this Monday different. So

different, Grace felt she was back on those first blissful days of their honeymoon. She was satisfied. Strange that something so violent had brought such peace and joy.

Last night, after the announcement at the party, Jefferson had scrawled a message on a page from his diary: "Take the car to the apartment and then send the driver back here to wait for me. I'll stay with Isaac—and the police. They want to get a statement from me, and that will take time. I'll call if I can't make it home. Don't worry."

She had wanted to speak with him, but could not find him. Finally, she'd left, feeling neglected and frightened, on the verge of tears.

She had climbed up the stairs of the outside entrance of the apartment while the driver watched to make sure she was safe. It had taken her 10 minutes in the bitter cold, fumbling with the keys, before she had been able to open the complicated lock he had installed on the door. Jeff had come in hours later.

Lying there quietly, she became more enraged with every second as she thought of Harriett. Yes, she was dead and could do no more harm. But the evil Harriett had spun in her life was impossible to forget.

Grace was glad to be rid of her. And now that she was gone, Grace had to put her out of her mind. Discipline herself to never, ever think of Harriett again. That was important. Get on with her life.

But what had been going on between Harriett and Jefferson? Grace knew he had been desperately worried about something that Harriett had said or done.

"She's a big problem and one that won't go away," he had told her. "She wants her name on that fragrance, and she says she'll pull every string she can to get her way. I believe that she would even resort to blackmail."

Grace had pressed him to explain, but he had refused. "Nothing, really. It was just an example of the kind of thing she is capable of. That's all I meant. She insists she's responsible for the success of the company and she demands that Isaac recognize it."

There was no doubt Franklin was one of the best known and most respected fashion houses in the country. And it was for this reason Jefferson had accepted the offer to manufacture and help launch their new fragrance.

Franklin's fashions, in many price ranges, were worn by millions of women across the country. It would be easy to entice these women to buy a new bottle of fragrance. But to keep them captivated, the fragrance had to have a surprise, an unexpected quality. It had to be young and sexy, of course, but also possess something unique. Just the sort of challenge that Jefferson enjoyed.

It was the repeat sales, and the sales from all the other products that stemmed from the original fragrance, that would make the millions. Not the initial purchase.

"The time is right for designer fragrances," Jefferson had told her. "And the name Franklin has to be on the bottle."

Grace had said, "Get out of the deal. Trouble with Harriett is trouble indeed. We don't need to have anything to do with it."

But Jefferson insisted there was no way he would let Harriett take over, and no way he would let Isaac down. He had signed the contract with Isaac and that was that. Grace remembered how determined she had been to stop the deal and get Harriett out of their lives.

And now it was over. And this morning had rid her of her doubts about Jefferson, Harriett, and the fragrance.

When Jeff had come in, at about four, he'd stripped off his clothes and crawled into bed beside her without a word. Before she could ask a question, his mouth had been on hers, his tongue curling around hers.

They made love more passionately than they had in years. Jefferson's excitement had been overwhelming, and Grace had responded to it with an intensity she had rarely felt with him.

"It was the shock of seeing her dead that crazed me," he said later, almost as if he were apologizing for something. "She was so fragile and she died such an ugly death. From the look on her face, she was afraid of whoever killed her."

Grace stretched, moving her body slowly. Harriett was dead, she kept telling herself. Out of the way. No more problems. She ran her hand under her breasts. Harriett had not taken much killing. Just a little strength and a paper knife. It was all over in a minute or two.

Jeff stirred beside her, turned, and put his arms around her.

"What are you thinking about, Mrs. Tyler?" he said as he nuzzled her ear.

She hesitated long enough to think better of what she had been about to say. As much as she loved him, she had to keep some things to herself.

Instead, she replied, "I'm so sorry for Isaac and the children, especially Jeremy. Isaac always said Jeremy loved her most. He was so proud that she was his mother. Isaac even said that at the table last night. Her murder could ruin Jeremy's life. I hope not. I would hate that."

"Grace, I think it may be the best thing that happened to him. Isaac told me he will bring him home to be with the other boys. At last he'll be part of the family. It'll take time for them all to adjust, but Jeremy will have a richer life. Now let's stop talking about her." He lightly kissed her lips.

"Harriett never wanted him near her. She was ashamed of him. She was heartless. I could understand her pain, but never her neglect."

"Well, you knew her for years, so you're entitled," he replied coldly. Jefferson abruptly threw back the covers, stood up, and went into the bathroom. He obviously didn't want to talk about Harriett. Before or after her murder.

Grace felt she was entitled to her opinion. She had known Harriett since they were students at Connecticut College, a small private school, 20 years ago. From firsthand experience, she knew what it was like to be Harriett's victim.

As a freshman, she had admired Harriett—the admiration of a rich kid for a girl who had to fight poverty all her life.

Grace remembered what she had said to her mother. "Harriett's got such courage. She has a scholarship, but she has to work as a waitress three nights a week to get extra money. She never buys clothes. All her money goes for books. Yet she always looks great. She's determined to have a fantastic career and she will."

But it was her father who became Harriett's greatest fan.

"She's just one spunky girl," he'd said. "She never takes no for an answer. She knows what she wants and she'll get it."

It was because of his interest that Harriett came so frequently to their summerhouse on Nantucket. Looking back, Grace realized the old man had been infatuated with her. Harriett must have known it at the time; she certainly took advantage of it.

"We should be kind to Harriett," he had said. "Make sure that instead of working through the summer she can spend time at the beach."

He even checked schedules with Harriett to make sure she came only during the weeks he was in from the city.

The summerhouse wasn't just a house, it was a family compound. Grace's grandfather had bought the beach cottages after the depression in the '30s. He'd given one to each of his three children.

Grace's father had the biggest home. It overflowed with friends, cousins, distant relatives. Harriett seemed to glory in its richness, its obvious "old money" atmosphere.

It was there in that house, during that last glorious summer, that Grace had fallen in love. Fallen in love for the first time, unexpectedly and desperately.

"You've known Robbie all your life. How can you be in love with him now? For God's sake, he's your cousin, your first cousin. How could you think of marrying him?" her father had screamed at her.

But it had all happened so naturally.

He'd gotten a small sailboat for his 23rd birthday. It was perfect for the two of them. Every afternoon they went out on the deep blue waters together. Tacking their way across the bay, they worked together in the silent joy of being young, alive, and free.

At first, they talked about the family. Then they talked about their dreams, plans, and futures. And after a while, they planned their future together.

Robbie was in his last year at Harvard Law School. Once he had his degree, he was not, as his father expected, going to become a junior member of the family firm. Robbie planned to join the district attorney's office.

"New York needs people like me in the public service," he had told Grace. "I have the education, the background, but most of all I love the city. I'm a lucky person. I don't want to plan my life around making money."

At 19, Grace understood wholeheartedly. Unlike Harriett, she was not interested in making a name for herself. She planned on teaching disadvantaged kids and hoped to get a degree in psychology.

Her dreams were close to Robbie's. Every minute they could be together, they were. And no one knew what was really going on between them.

Only Harriett. She noticed their love immediately. Grace and Robbie met her at the ferry the day she arrived. She saw their happy faces, the way they couldn't take their eyes off each other, how closely they walked together, his hand touching her casually now and again, as if it were an accident.

"What's going on between you and Robbie?" she had whispered when Robbie walked away for a moment to pick up her bag.

"We're just fooling around," said Grace.

"Fooling around?" echoed Robbie as he rejoined them. "We are madly in love, and if Grace is pregnant, which I hope she is, we'll get married immediately. If not, I guess we can wait for Christmas."

Harriett had turned pale.

"But you are first cousins. You can't get married. Think of the children." She paused. "Does your family know?"

"You're the first and only one to know," Robbie had replied cheerfully. "It's our secret. I'm telling you because you must stand by Grace when she goes back to school."

Grace shivered.

"Please, Harriett," she pleaded, "we are counting on you. You are my friend."

Harriett had agreed. But that night, she told Grace's mother about the affair.

"I had to protect you," she had explained later. "You're young and you know nothing about life. At 19, you can't be married and have a child. And this is a child that could be born with serious medical problems. You have to plan a career. You need to think about the consequences of what you call this 'great love,' and so does Robbie."

And so it ended. Robbie had been sent to Europe for the remainder of the summer. Grace and her mother went to Boston for an abortion.

It had been unbearable. For months, all Grace could think of was Robbie.

Robbie, who was now married with four children, was a partner in the family firm. He had given up his dreams. His last great gift had been to introduce Grace to Jefferson. In the end, Robbie had looked out for her.

But Grace had never forgiven Harriett. She would always hate her, dead or alive.

Jefferson came out of the bathroom with only a towel over his shoulders. Grace stared at him. He had the same slim athletic body, the dark hair, the easy grace of Robbie.

"I guess I'd better start thinking about the day," he said as he pulled on a pair of briefs and went to his closet. "And for that matter, the rest of the week. I think you should drive back to Connecticut to be with the children."

"Yes, of course," she said, sitting up in bed. "What are your plans?"

"I'll stay here. I've got a couple of quick trips to make. I may even have to go to Paris overnight on Wednesday."

"Don't you think you should be here?" she said, unable to hide her disappointment. "I mean for Isaac and the police and everything."

He moved to the bed, bent over, and kissed her forehead. "Darling, don't worry. I did all I could last night. The police will know where to get me if they need me. And they will find the murderer. You can be sure of that."

He moved back to the closet. Grace watched him, admiring his strong back as he reached up, selected a shirt, and removed it carefully from its hanger.

Without turning, he added nonchalantly, "Now that Harriett's dead, we haven't a worry in the world."

FOURTEEN

9:30 AM, Monday

The call came just as Leonard Novelli woke. He rolled over and picked up the phone on the second ring.

He knew instinctively it was Isaac. And just as instinctively, he knew Isaac was worried about Jeremy. When it came to the boy, business disagreements faded away. Aware of Leonard's compassion for his son, Isaac often called on him.

"Where are you? What's happening?" Leonard asked.

"In the office," Isaac replied. "I was up most of the night, first with the police and then with my attorneys. The police think Harriett knew her murderer, otherwise there would have been more of a struggle. They say she must have seen whoever it was in the mirror. But it's still too early to tell."

Novelli had no reply.

"My concern is the boys. And for them, I want to ask you a favor. Jeremy must come home, as soon as we can get him here. I spoke with Dr. Hoffman first thing this morning and he agrees. I suggested that when Jeremy wakes, Hoffman should tell him that his mother had an accident and that is the reason he is going home. Hoffman didn't like it, but I insisted.

"Leonard, I am asking you to drive up to the clinic and bring Jeremy back. When he gets here, I will try to tell him the truth, or something close to it. The doctor will give him some medication to calm him. The clinic will have him packed and ready for you.

"Jeremy loves you like an uncle. He's used to you visiting him. There's no one else I trust to take care of him now. Harriett kept him so isolated from our family and friends."

Isaac had let his anxiety pour out. But now he paused to wait for an answer.

Novelli swallowed hard, then rubbed his arm across his cheeks to wipe away sudden tears. Jeremy had so few emotional resources. He had fallen and hurt himself the day before. His falls, which had become more frequent as he grew older, always upset him. Now he had to face the shock of his mother's death.

"You'd better give me Dr. Hoffman's cell phone number so I can call and let him know when I'm arriving," he said. "Don't worry. As soon as we finish talking, I'll call the garage, so my car will be waiting for me when I get there."

"I can send a limo if you'd prefer not to drive," said Isaac. "The roads may be bad with this icy weather."

"I don't think so. The expressways are probably cleared by now. Anyway Jeremy is used to me arriving in my own car. He likes to sit in the front seat beside me. A limo and driver might frighten him more.

"I'll call you and let you know our progress."

Isaac gave him Hoffman's number. "Thank you," he said. "You know and I know marrying Harriett was the biggest mistake I made in my life."

Novelli hung up. There was nothing he could say.

He left the apartment house 10 minutes later, pausing to say to the doorman, "If Kim Kelly happens to ask for me, tell her I've gone out. But I'll be back in a few hours."

Leonard walked along the sidewalk, enjoying the crunch of the ice under his boots. He was glad to be doing something with a purpose. Picking up Jeremy would start to heal the bloody wound he had opened last night.

To Leonard, Jeremy had been a source of pleasure, despite the problems of Down's syndrome. But he had also been the start of the designer's troubles with Harriett.

Some 10 years ago, Isaac had brought Jeremy to the office one Saturday morning. They were working overtime on a collection. Isaac and the boy had come into the design room, where Leonard had been at his desk, contentedly sketching the last few outfits for the collection.

"Will you keep an eye on him for an hour?" Isaac said. "He's a good boy for a five-year-old. He's got his crayons and he'll be happy playing on the floor."

Leonard had looked hard at Isaac, trying to guess what pressures at home had forced him to take care of Jeremy. Isaac loved the child but was certainly not the type of executive to bring a toddler into the office.

"Harriett insists that I look after Jeremy during the weekend," Isaac explained. "Today I have an urgent appointment with the new merchandising manager at Saks. I'll be back as soon as I can."

Leonard had bent down and picked up Jeremy. The boy turned toward him and smiled.

"Okay." Leonard smiled back. "So now I've got a new task. I have to make a designer out of you. The way to start is to learn about colors. So just keep coloring your book."

Jeremy had played happily at his feet, occasionally turning his head up and giggling at him. Leonard had laughed back at him. He was happy to be with the boy. And so they had bonded. He became a surrogate uncle, visiting Jeremy regularly after he went to live at the clinic.

Harriett had only been too glad to find an office baby-sitter for the boy. She also quickly realized what an opportunity he had unknowingly given her. She had used Leonard's compassion for her son to worm her way into the design room.

How often had he told himself that if he hadn't let Jeremy come to play and sketch with him, Harriett would never have had the excuse to come so often to his office, and learn how the business operated.

It had all seemed very natural on the surface. Isaac could hardly object. In fact, he had been pleased to see Harriett take such an interest in Jeremy.

Leonard sighed. He had done what he had done. He had allowed Harriett to manipulate him. He had listened to her stories. Given her sympathy. Escorted her to parties when Isaac had been too tired or too busy to go.

He had acted as her sounding board while she reinvented herself. When she had finished her transformation, she wanted him to disappear. He knew too much. She didn't trust him. For that matter, she didn't trust anyone.

She had been, in spite of her beauty and her quick wits, a woman with little sense of herself.

She had grown up desperately poor. Her mother was Jewish but had married out of her faith. Harriett had once confessed to him that she hated being Jewish, even though being born of a Jewish mother had made her acceptable to the Franklins.

Music had brought her parents together. Her mother had a beautiful voice and wanted to study opera. Her father had been an aspiring pianist. He had worked at the local bank during the week and played with a band on the weekends. They had two children, Harriett and her brother Ben. But as soon as Ben was born, her father had left them.

The abandoned family had moved into the ground floor of their grandmother's two-family home.

"We had nothing. Absolutely nothing," Harriett drunkenly told Leonard one night after he escorted her to a charity ball and they had stopped at a club for a nightcap. In those early days after Jeremy was born, Harriett had liked to drink. Falling asleep as soon as her head hit the pillow was one way of stopping Isaac's insistent lovemaking, she had confided.

"My grandmother was stingy. She never stopped telling us that if it weren't for her, we'd be out in the street. She had a little money, but she could never spare us a cent.

"My mother was pathetic. She was terrified of losing her job, so she worked for practically nothing. She clung to this romantic idea that my father really loved her and would come back rich and famous one day. She had a fantasy that he would creep in one night while we were asleep and wake us with extravagant presents.

"She put on makeup every night before she went to bed, in case he arrived. Her pillow slip was always stained with lipstick. But he didn't give a damn about us. I think he changed his name. Anyway, we lost contact with him. I don't even know if he is alive or dead."

"Why don't you get Isaac's attorneys to find out?" Leonard had asked.

She had put her head back and laughed. "When we first met in Mexico, I told Isaac that my father was dead, just to put an end to his questions. He is the most insistent man I ever met."

She had immediately regretted what she'd said. "I didn't mean to lie, but he might as well be dead, and I couldn't bear to go into all that boring history again.

"My grandmother eventually forced my mother to get a divorce. But even though men were interested in her, my mother never considered remarrying. She really believed my father loved us and would come back to us. She was a fool."

Her lips had curled with contempt. For an instant, he had seen the real Harriett Franklin. The Harriett who was riddled with bitterness, filled with hatred for her family.

She had apparently never forgiven herself for telling him the story, and when he looked back, he realized that from that night on, she had planned to get rid of him.

And she had succeeded. She had done it with her subtle, miserable trickery. At first he hadn't understood what she was up to. Then he realized she had a plan and she used every chance to further it. She had been both brilliant and tireless.

His fault had been his confidence in Isaac. They had worked together for years, building the company, expanding it collection by collection, until there was hardly a woman in America who didn't either own some piece with a Franklin label, or want one.

It took Leonard a long time to believe Isaac would let his wife interfere in the carefully controlled, long-established family business.

Then he realized that Isaac was powerless against her.

"She wears me down," Franklin had told him one morning when Leonard walked into Isaac's office and found him gazing dispiritedly out the window at the gray Manhattan skyline.

"I keep giving in, even though I don't agree with her. I tell myself to ignore her, but I can't. She's at me night and day. She has no respect for my opinion, or for that matter, anyone else's. I find myself doing whatever she wants."

Isaac had stood by, seemingly powerless, as Harriett put her plan into action against the man whom he had so often called his most valuable employee.

But now it was different. She was dead. Dead with shame and anger in her heart. She had tried to destroy him, but he had won. And his speech had been brilliant. He laughed out loud when he thought of what he had said.

Leonard left the highway at the exit that led to the clinic.

As he had expected, traffic had been light leaving the city. He would be there early. He called Dr. Hoffman's cell to warn him, but there was no answer. Next, he called the office and asked that the doctor be told of his early arrival.

"Tell Jeremy I expect him to be waiting for me by the front door, so he can see the car immediately," he said.

Soon the boy would be home. Home, where he should have been these past years. If only his father had had the strength to stand up for him. Leonard turned up the long drive to the entrance of the clean-lined, modern building. He honked the car horn in three quick blasts, as he always did to signal to Jeremy that he had arrived. It was something they had worked out together when he first visited him.

Jeremy was always eager to get away from the clinic, and so he was always waiting for him. And he was waiting today. He could see the boy through the huge glass windows. It was a subdued Jeremy standing inside the front entrance beside the doctor. His head was bowed, his shoulders slack.

Leonard quickened his step. His heart flooded with pity, and yet once again he felt elated. Harriett was dead and Jeremy would be happier now.

He strode eagerly up the path.

"Jeremy," he called as he swung through the door. "Here I am. I've come through all the snow to get you. Are you ready for me?"

Jeremy looked at him, wide-eyed and distraught. In all the times Leonard had visited him, he had never seen the boy that way.

"It's okay, Jeremy," he said. "I'm taking you home."

Jeremy's chest heaved with sobs. He turned away and buried his head in Dr. Hoffman's chest.

Leonard reached for him. "It's all right. I'm here, Jeremy. I'm here," he said. "There is nothing to fear. We'll have hot dogs for lunch like we always do when I come to pick you up, and when we're back in the city, you'll visit me and we'll do some painting together."

But Hoffman held up his hand. "Jeremy had a fall last night. He bumped his head and bruised his shoulder and his arm slightly. When he woke up, he was still feeling upset," he said.

"I'm sure it is nothing serious, but I think the three of us should sit down and talk for a while. Then we'll call his father and decide the best thing to do."

FIFTEEN

10:00 AM, Monday

Sonya swung through the revolving doors of the Franklin office building on Seventh Avenue and into the vaulted marble foyer. She immediately felt the tension in the atmosphere. Groups of workers, carrying their morning coffee in stiff paper bags, gathered at the elevators. Their voices were low, their heads bent together as they gossiped. Sonya guessed they were all talking about Harriett's murder.

How many of these people, she wondered, work for the House of Franklin? How many knew Harriett? She might want to get reactions to include in the story.

There was only one way to find out. She walked to the guard standing near the elevator bank.

"Did you know Harriett Franklin?" she asked.

"We all knew her," he replied, eager to talk. "You couldn't miss her, she was a beautiful woman."

"Was she friendly?"

He hesitated before answering. He looked intently at

Sonya as if he were deciding whether to trust her. "No. Why should she be? She was married to the most important man in the building; she kept to herself—except for an occasional smile."

"Did she come here often?"

He laughed. "Too often, from what I hear. She poked her nose into everyone's business."

He paused again, and Sonya realized he felt he had probably gone farther than he should. "What do you want to know all this for? Who are you?"

Sonya opened her bag and took out her press pass.

"I'm here for the press conference Isaac Franklin is having this morning," she explained sweetly. "Mari St. Clair, the PR director, called my office, and I've been sent to cover it."

Before the guard could question her further, Sonya pushed past several people and squeezed into the elevator that had just arrived.

She didn't want to waste a second. She had left the office immediately after the meeting with Matt, jumped into a cab, and told the driver to head down Seventh Avenue.

She wanted to be early for the press conference. But more important, she wanted to talk to Mari. She needed to set up the interviews and she wanted to make sure her crew got exclusive shots of Harriett's office.

Mari had worried her when they spoke that morning about the press conference. Gone were her easy, friendly manner and her strength. Her voice was flat with exhaustion. Mari sounded distant, almost as if she had something to hide.

But then, she probably did have something to hide. Despite their friendship, Sonya was a member of the press. She wondered what had gone on at the company in the early hours of the morning. Surely Franklin had called his attorneys for advice, and no doubt they had drilled Mari on exactly what to do and what she could say.

Her change in attitude had nothing to do with friendship. She was doing her job, and a tough one at that. Probably she'd had no sleep, had gone home merely to shower and change clothes and now was hanging on to the last vestige of her energy. Sonya understood what Mari must be feeling.

The dissent at Franklin's had been going on for months. There had been so much bad press over the firing of Novelli and the sudden hiring of the young, relatively inexperienced French designer, Jason Sarnoff.

CAN JASON SARNOFF, THE FRENCH BAD BOY DESIGNER, GIVE AMERICAN WOMEN WHAT THEY WANT? FRANKLIN FASHION HOUSE FIRES TOP DESIGNER. REPLACES HIM WITH FRENCH PUNK. Those were just two of the headlines Sonya remembered.

Isaac had reaped columns of criticism in every New York paper. Mari had had to contend with that. And now the murder. All the glamour, the pride, the stature of the House of Franklin was at stake.

Sonya felt Mari would, in the end, deal with it all calmly and decisively. That, after all, was what she did best.

However, it was a very different Mari that Sonya found sitting in her office. She was bent double in her chair, her head buried in her hands, her blond hair tousled as if she had spent the night sleeping there.

"What's happening? Mari, are you all right?" Sonya gasped.

"What about you?" Mari replied, straightening up and pushing her hair back from her face. "You must have gotten as little sleep as I did. Are you totally exhausted? We have coffee outside. Would you like some?"

Typical of Mari, thought Sonya, answering a question with a question. She won't say what went on last night, not even to me. There must be plenty to hide.

"No, Mari, thanks. I've already had too much coffee."

Immediately, Mari was back to the business of the day.

"I'm so glad you came early. Isaac decided to have the press conference in the showroom. I'll show you. We've taken out the tables and put in extra chairs. There's space for just a few cameras, but you'll fit in. Come and see."

The showroom was a large, beautifully decorated space with racks to display the clothes to buyers. It was usually furnished with tables with chairs grouped around them, where the sales staff and buyers discussed the collection.

As they walked along the corridor to the showroom, Sonya asked about getting shots of Harriett's office and the design room. She also told Mari that Donna Fuller wanted an exclusive interview with Isaac as soon as it could be arranged. Donna would call and discuss it with him. But she promised the tone would be gentle, and that the last thing Donna was interested in was upsetting Isaac or his children. "You know you can trust her."

"Of course, it's up to Isaac," said Mari. "He was extremely reluctant to have the press conference. But I persuaded him it would be a way to get the press over and done with at one time. Since he knows Donna and admires her work, maybe he'll agree. But at this stage, it's only a maybe."

She turned to Sonya and gave her a quick smile. "You know I'll do what I can."

Sonya smiled her thanks. It was good to have Mari on her side. She was going to need all the help she could get. And she made up her mind to give Mari as much support as possible.

"How strange life is," Sonya said. "Harriett was so eager to be interviewed by Donna. And now that she's dead, Donna is anxious to get an interview about her."

Mari laughed harshly. "What's the old saying, 'Don't wish too hard for something—your wish may come true'?" She continued, "Isaac is so shocked, so drained. All he really cares about is protecting the kids from the press and seeing that any psychological damage is kept to a minimum. He's already called Dr. Hoffman about his oldest son, and Hoffman has recommended a child trauma counselor for the other two. A meeting with the counselor is number one on his agenda after the press conference."

They paused at the showroom door. The wintry sunlight filtering through the windows gave it a gentle glow. It was decorated completely in beige to offset the color of the clothes that were shown there. The walls were lacquered a gleaming beige, the carpet was a deep-pile beige tweed, and the chairs were white with white-and-beige-striped seating. The gilt-framed mirrors that hung between the alcoves holding the clothes reflected the lightness and beauty of the room.

"These are all from Novelli's last collection," said Mari, waving a hand toward the clothes. "We picked out the best outfits because we wanted to get the message across that it's business as usual, and that business is great. And it is. That's absolutely true."

Sonya was impressed. The room transmitted an immediate feeling of the company's important position in the world of fashion.

A few minutes later, so did Isaac as he walked into the room and stood behind the lectern to start the press conference. He looked every inch the CEO, dressed in a dark, superbly tailored suit with a white shirt. His tie was dark with little flecks of red in it. An almost perfect image for television, all supervised by Mari, Sonya assumed.

Mari had arranged the dozen crews in a semicircle at one end of the room. There were seats for half the reporters; the rest stood, notebooks in hand. Mari introduced Isaac, saying he would make a statement and answer a few questions. She briefly reminded the reporters what he had been through, and asked them to understand that this was a difficult time for him.

Isaac unfolded a single sheet of paper.

When he began to speak, his voice was calm and confident. But Sonya noticed he gripped the sides of the lectern until his knuckles showed white.

"I'm here to say just a few words," he read. "In exchange, I ask you to respect my family and leave them in peace. My three sons have suffered a devastating shock, and I do not want them hounded by photographers as they struggle to bring their lives back to normal—if indeed that is possible."

He took a deep breath and looked around the room, seeming to study the faces of every reporter, every cameraman. Then he sighed, and continued slowly and carefully. "My wife, Harriett, was a loving wife and mother. We mourn her deeply. She was also a brilliant, generous woman. She worked endlessly for charities in New York and helped raise millions of dollars. So her loss is a grievous one not just to us, her family, but to the city itself.

"I ask you to remember that as you report on the details of her murder. She was struck down brutally, her life taken while she was happily enjoying a party, surrounded by friends who admired and treasured her. We all pray that the person who committed this heinous crime will be brought to justice quickly.

"We will do whatever we can to help the police in their investigation. Thank you."

Isaac looked up, as if to see the effect of his statement. His eye caught Sonya's for a moment. After all, she had been at the table last night. She remembered how Harriett had treated him.

Reporters' hands went up, then fell as Isaac continued to speak.

"Finally, I want to assure our customers that despite my wife's murder, Franklin is a business that's open for business. That will not be affected in any way by what has happened."

Sonya was surprised to hear him dismiss his wife's murder so quickly and coldly.

"Now, I'll take your questions. But before we start, I want to impress on you again that I want you to leave my sons alone."

His love for his children was obviously deep and genuine. The room remained silent for a moment. Sympathy for Isaac and his sons obviously ran high. No one wanted to be the first to disturb his grief.

Mari stepped forward to break the tension. "Now what about your questions?" she asked. A reporter raised a tentative hand, and Mari nodded to her.

"Mr. Franklin, is it true that your wife had an office here, and contributed designs or at least ideas to the collections?"

"She did have an office here," replied Franklin, "but she used it only for her charity work. My wife was an extremely efficient and effective woman. She not only raised money for charities, but worked with the charities to make sure the money was well spent."

He paused and looked anxiously for another raised hand.

A strong voice came from the side of the room, "Are you saying that Mrs. Franklin played no role in the work of the company at all?"

"No, let's be quite certain about that. Harriett had no interest in the workings of the company. Like all New York fashion houses, Franklin has an experienced designer who is backed by a team of assistants. That designer, Jason Sarnoff, is responsible for every design we sell."

The room went silent again. Sonya felt the mood in the room changing. The disbelief in Franklin's statement was growing. But the reporters were still held back by sympathy for him.

"What about Novelli's statement at the party last night?" came a woman's voice from the back of the room. "He accused your wife of manipulating you and the business. And I understand that it was Harriett who had Novelli fired—and that you and your wife were having real trouble in your marriage. Is that true, and do the police consider you a suspect?"

Franklin stared angrily at the reporter. The room was hushed, waiting for his answer.

"I've said all I had to say," he said grimly, and with ice-cold determination. "My wife is dead, and my three boys are motherless. Leave us alone. I warn you, stay away from me and my family."

He turned, looked at Mari, and abruptly left the room.

SIXTEEN

10:30 AM, Monday

Sonya left Perry on the sidewalk to take exterior shots of the Franklin building, and walked into the Starbucks next door. She ordered a large, skim milk, decaf cappuccino, took it to the window bar, and pulled out her cell phone.

Mari had told her that Franklin was unapproachable in his current mood. Sonya would have to wait for an answer to her requests for an exclusive interview with Donna.

"Go have a coffee and call me in an hour," Mari had said as she ushered Sonya and the crew out of the showroom into the hall. "Maybe I can persuade Isaac to let you shoot Harriett's office. But right now, he's got to calm down."

Sonya knew she should phone Matt and tell him the bad news. At the moment, she had nothing exclusive and little chance of getting it. But maybe it was better to wait. The big thing in her favor was the way Isaac had stormed out of the press conference. That had badly damaged his image with the press. She was sure Mari could argue that being interviewed by Donna Fuller, who would promise to take a compassionate approach, could help. The *Donna Fuller Show* was well respected as well as highly rated. Even Isaac's lawyers might suggest that Donna's coverage would be an advantage.

Yes, things weren't so bad. She might well get the interview. Sonya put the cell phone back in her purse.

Clutching her coffee, Sonya climbed onto a stool. The window gave her a good view of the street. She could keep an eye out for Perry.

She wondered what to do next. Maybe she could grab a few people on the street or in the Franklin building and ask them what they thought of the murder. You could never tell what people would come up with.

Harriett's murder has to be a hot topic on the sidewalks right now, she told herself.

Sonya first saw the tall blonde as she pushed through the revolving door of the café. She was ravishing. From the way she carried herself, it was clear she was a model. Even with her hair under her cap and no makeup, she'd look great on camera. It was even possible that she had been at the dinner last night. She just had to be persuaded to stick around until Perry arrived.

Sonya got up and walked toward her, smiling. She'd try for an interview. Then she heard an unmistakable high-pitched voice with that odd French accent.

"What are you doing here, Sonya? Why aren't you at the press conference?" His face was hidden by a baseball cap pulled low and muffler wrapped high, but Sonya instantly recognized Jason Sarnoff.

"What are you doing here, Jason? Having a coffee break?" Sonya responded. She was relieved at finding someone associated with the Franklin office. Maybe Jason would do an interview.

Jason quickly introduced her to his companion.

"This is my friend, Leila Lopez. She was one of the models with me at the party last night."

"Remember me? I came up to the table to say hello to you all," Leila interrupted.

"Of course, I remember you." Sonya smiled at her, determined to make her a friend. "You looked so beautiful, how could I forget? Weren't you wearing one of Jason's dresses?"

The thing Sonya remembered most was that Sarnoff had called her an airhead.

But the designer wasn't interested in chitchat.

"I was told to work at home today," he said huffily. "That is stupid. There is no way I can work at home. I don't have my sketchpads, my colors, and my fabrics. They are in the design room where they belong."

"Who told you not to come to work?" Sonya asked.

"Franklin's attorney. He is a rude man. When I told him it was necessary that I come to the office, he wouldn't listen. He just told me I have to do what he said."

"Why are you here, then?" asked Sonya.

"He got cabin fever in that tiny flat they leased for him, so I told him to come here, have coffee with me, and talk," Leila broke in. "We're good friends. I worked with Jason at his atelier in Paris, and he sure as hell needs a friend right now."

Leila had worked hard to lose her Brooklyn accent. But when she got excited she forgot. She and Jason were an interesting pair, Sonya thought as she listened, both with wild accents but completely different.

Sarnoff was not to be stopped. He had a grievance and he wanted it out.

"I have other personal things in the office which I do not want touched. I have my rights. I want to get my things."

Sonya tried to calm him down. She wanted both of them to stay with her until Perry was ready.

"I would guess they will let you in by tomorrow. Isaac told us at the press conference that it's business as usual. I'm sure he means it. He's a man with good sense."

"His good sense, that is a new thing to me," sniffed Sarnoff. "The Franklin business is a mess. I've been there for weeks and I still don't know what is going on. Franklin cannot make a decision. In Paris, if I wanted to order fabrics, I ordered them. I didn't have to get permission. I am not a clerk. I am the creator."

"How many times do I have to tell you that was Harriett's fault," said Leila quickly. "Now that she's gone, it will be different. Franklin is a great business. You landed on your feet here, even if somebody had to get murdered for it."

Leila laughed at her own wit.

Without another word, Sarnoff took the two coffees he'd ordered and walked to a table at the back of the room. Sonya followed him, Leila behind her.

"Do you think they've closed the office so that the police can search for clues?" Leila whispered, "I think that's why Jason is so worried."

"I hadn't thought of the police." Sonya felt her stomach turn over as she realized that once they came, she would never get in. "I didn't see any sign of them at the press conference. And I haven't seen them go in the main door. I've been watching for the last 15 minutes."

Leila smiled ruefully, then said quickly, "Let's forget it."

But Sonya couldn't. Of course the police would go there and search. That made it doubly important that she get into Harriett's office and get some shots. Her mind raced. What could she do?

She turned to Sarnoff and said, "Are you absolutely determined to get into your design room?"

"Absolutely, I don't care what happens. I have my rights," Sarnoff replied. "I have personal things there that I must have."

Sonya wondered what could be so important.

"Well, my cameraman is over there right now. We could go across to the building and I could interview you. Then you could slip into the elevator and go up with me. The guard knows me. I've already talked to him. I'm just waiting for Mari to let me know when to go back. I'll tell the guard that we are going to get some shots of you in your office.

That way, you won't be breaking the rules. You'll merely be showing the press that it is business as usual."

Sonya knew she was playing a long shot. She might never get upstairs, let alone into Harriett's office. And if the police got here to search, she would be totally shut out.

But if she could get an interview with the locked-out designer in the foyer of the Franklin building, she'd have something exclusive for Matt. Better than calling him and reporting total failure.

And if she got into Harriett's office, she could shake off Sarnoff. What he took was not her business.

Sarnoff broke into her thoughts. "What questions do you want to ask me? I told you everything last night."

"Well, things have changed," she said. "I'll just ask you what you were doing after the presentations, and then what you are doing and feeling today."

"Well," said Leila, "that's easy to answer. Why don't we just do it, Jason? It never hurts to tell the truth. And honey, it will help you feel better."

"Okay, but I'll only answer two questions," Sarnoff answered stiffly.

"Fair enough," smiled Sonya. "Bring your coffee and we'll go next door. Perry is bound to be somewhere just outside with his camera."

As they walked out together, Leila gave Sarnoff an encouraging smile. "I'd tell it all, Jason. It's going to be okay. You're in the clear."

"Just wait here by the Starbucks, and I'll get you as soon as I have set things up with my cameraman," Sonya advised them.

She found Perry focusing his camera at the Franklin logo on the building wall. "Franklin locked Sarnoff out of the office," she told him quickly, pointing to Sarnoff and Leila by the Starbucks. "I want to do a fast interview with him in the foyer. It's too cold and too noisy outside. The audio would be unusable."

Perry understood in a second.

"The guard may object, but I'll give it a try in the corner near the door," he said. "Keep the questions short. And see if you can get him to take off his cap and pull his muffler lower. He's unrecognizable. I can't even see his eyes."

"I'll take care of that, Perry. You get ready."

Perry went into the building, checked the battery, positioned the camera on his shoulder, and rolled tape as Sonya motioned Jason to come toward her.

Jason and Leila walked into the building. Perry then positioned Sarnoff with his back to the passersby. He did not want him to be distracted.

"Style him a bit for me, Leila. We can't see his face," Sonya said, turning to the blond model and smiling her most encouraging smile. Leila was only too eager to get into the act. Like a mother dealing with a reluctant child, she reached forward, pulled off the the designer's cap, and unwound the muffler.

"There," she said, kissing him on the cheek. "You now look more like the boy I tried to woo in Paris."

Sonya took the mike and looked at Perry. After zooming in to get a closeup of the designer, he nodded that he was ready.

"Jason, where were you last night after the awards presentations ended? Say between 10:00 and 10:15?" asked Sonya.

"I was looking for my friend, Leila, who is now standing beside me." Perry quickly panned to Leila to get a shot of her.

"Did you catch up with Leila?" asked Sonya.

"No. I looked everywhere, but she went back to the dressing area to help her friend find a ring she had left there." Jason was shaking.

"And did she find it?"

"Yes."

Sonya saw Jason was getting wary.

"I said only two questions."

Sonya continued quickly, "So what are you doing here with Leila now—here at the Franklin offices?"

"I told you, I am trying to get into the design room." His high-pitched voice went even higher. "I was told not to come in today, to work at home. But I have no work to do there. And I have personal things in my desk that I need."

"Who told you not to come in today?"

"The lawyer called me this morning."

Sarnoff was getting more nervous with every question, but Sonya had to keep going. He crushed his empty coffee cup and dropped it to the floor. Then he began to twist his hands around each other.

"At his press conference this morning, Isaac Franklin said you were in charge of design. You okay every design. Is that true?"

"That is the job they told me I had. But in reality, Franklin is run by a committee. Harriett Franklin watched everything I did. She took my designs to her husband. She told him what he should make. It was impossible for me."

Sarnoff seemed to realize he had said too much. "Turn off that camera. I am finished. I want a cigarette; I'm going outside to have it. You said you'd help me get upstairs. Now do it. I'll wait for you."

His hands shook violently as he turned, grabbed his cap from Leila, and moved quickly through the door of the building. Perry's camera followed his movements.

Sonya felt sorry for him. She nodded at Perry to stop the taping.

"What in the world has he got upstairs that is so important?" she asked Leila.

"It's a bunch of slides," Leila replied. "Is that camera still rolling?"

"No," Sonya replied.

"Can I trust you?"

"Yes," said Sonya, "of course. This is off the record."

"Okay then," Leila began, "Harriett read a review of Jason's last collection in Paris in a French paper. It said something like 'he was doing line-for-line copies of Jacques Verne.'

"She went rooting through his drawers and found some slides of a Verne collection, then compared them with some of Jason's sketches. I guess she found some outfits that were pretty much the same. She told Jason she had found out he was a fake."

Leila paused. "I hope I can trust you. So don't quote me."

"Of course," Sonya reassured her. "What happened?" She knew what she was hearing was important.

"According to Jason, Harriett said she would take them to her husband and have him fired unless he did exactly what she wanted from then on. She was crazy."

Perry signaled to Sonya, pointing to the camera, silently asking if she wanted him to secretly tape what Leila was saying. She shook her head, no.

Leila saw them.

"What are you doing? Are you taping me?" Leila drew back and started to move toward the door.

"No. I said we are not taping. And we are not. Don't worry. Go on. What happened?"

Leila stopped, relaxed, and continued, "Jason found the slides in her desk and hid them. Now he wants to get them before anyone else finds them. He was so angry with her. And he told me and some other friends that he could kill her. So he is nervous about that too. Well, you can understand. 'Kill her,' he said. And now she is dead.

"He is not a copier. He just got caught up in a trend similar to Verne. It happens to designers all the time. He's too sensitive. And now he's scared."

The building door opened and Jason stepped just inside, held the door open, and shouted at them, "What is going on? What is taking so long? I am ready for my second cigarette."

Sonya called back, "We are just closing up the equipment. Hold on a little longer."

Jason stepped outside and allowed the door to close behind him.

Leila continued, this time more softly, "Harriett was the full bitch. Everyone hated her. She knew I was a friend of Jason's and at my last show she came backstage and chatted with me while I put on my makeup. Just as I was applying the makeup, she deliberately bumped my arm so the brush went into my eye. It hurt so much, tears streamed down my face. All my makeup had to be put on again, and my eye was bloodshot for hours. That's the kind of person she was. Crazy. Mean. I'm not surprised somebody murdered her."

Sonya nodded sympathetically. Leila seemed to have no more to add.

"Thanks, Leila. Now, I've got to call Mari and see if we can go up and get shots of Harriett's office."

Sonya pulled out her cell phone and dialed. Mari's voice came through loud and clear.

"Good news. You can come up and we can talk about shooting the office," she said. "Send the crew to the freight elevator. Tell them to wait by the fabric department until we've decided what to do. And I think I've got you an interview with Kim at 12:30. Also, Franklin is getting warm about seeing Donna late tomorrow morning. I hope that won't be too late for the show."

"Oh, Mari, you are great as always. Thank you, I'll be right up."

She closed the phone and turned to Perry and Leila.

"Perry, it's the penthouse again. Wait by the fabric department until we come for you. Leila, get Jason. I'm going up now, and I'll do my best to take him with me."

She stood waiting impatiently as Leila went for Sarnoff. Together they walked to the elevators.

The guard looked up and saw her. "Where are you going this time?" he asked.

"Back to Franklin to get more shots." Sonya smiled broadly at him.

The guard glanced at Jason.

"He's coming with me," Sonya said. "I'm going to shoot him working in the design room."

"Oh, no, he's not," grunted the guard. "We've got instructions only to let the press go up. Not the staff."

Sonya put her hand on Sarnoff's shoulder and he smiled weakly at her.

"It's nothing personal," she assured him. "I think that Franklin prefers not to have anyone around while reporters are here."

Jason snapped back, "I've got nothing to hide."

Sonya thought of the slides and was not so sure.

"I'm sorry, but I have to go," she said, trying to hide her relief. "Call Mari. Maybe she can help you. I'll talk to you later. And thank you so much for the interview, Jason."

She added, "Leila, what you said was interesting."

"What does she mean by that, Leila?" was the last thing Sonya heard Jason shouting as she entered the elevator and the door closed.

SEVENTEEN

11:05 AM, Monday

With an arrogant sweep of her hand, Lily Allen snatched up the messages from her assistant's desk.

The young blonde was quick to read Lily's mood. It was not good.

"The publisher has called twice already," she said quickly. "She says it is urgent that you see her as soon as you get in."

"I hope you told her that I had an early morning meeting," Lily snapped back, defensively excusing her late arrival as she slammed her office door.

She knew, and her assistant knew, she had no early meeting. Lily was meticulous about updating her appointment book and letting her assistants know where she was.

"I have no secrets to hide" was one of her tartest sayings, a saying that was constantly mimicked around the office.

She consoled herself with the thought that there was always the million-to-one chance that she had forgotten to mention a meeting. Or it could have been something she had set up over the weekend. She hated to be caught in a lie.

But what her assistants thought of her was the least of her concerns. They would gossip about her, whatever she did. And many times she acted a role to amuse them and herself. She firmly believed that her high spirits created energy. Energy spawned creativity. And creativity was essential for a fashion magazine.

She knew that when she came in dispirited it was a downer for the whole staff. And today the news of Harriett's murder must have whipped through the office.

Harriett was well known to the staff, and in most cases well regarded. The Franklin company was generous with samples, and young editors often borrowed outfits for special occasions.

The office's sympathies definitely would be with the Franklins. Only Lily knew what had been happening between Harriett and Isaac. She leaned against the back of the closed door. This morning especially, she must be sure to put on her best front. Everything she was feeling must be hidden.

"Don't explain and don't complain. Just get on with it." Henry's often-quoted advice slipped into her mind.

Looking at her desk, Lily smiled. They were there, of course. A sweet, fresh bowl of flowers. This time it was a mix of mauve and yellow tulips. The first promise of spring on a winter day.

Henry sent flowers every Monday morning.

"It's your birthday gift," he had told her when she was first promoted to editor in chief. "I want you to think of my love for you the moment you begin work each week."

Thank God for Henry. He cared so much for her. If it weren't for him, she would still be home, drugged, floating in that peaceful, lovely world of the unconscious.

It was the blinking light of the TV set that had eventually brought her back from sleep, sprawled across the queen-sized bed. Henry clicked on the TV the minute he rose. This morning he had muted the sound, but left the set on so the light would eventually disturb her.

The night before, he had given her two pills, instead of her usual one. Then he had hidden the bottle. He had told her to sleep as long as she needed. She mustn't fight the lack of sleep as well as the problems of the day.

Lily was glad for the rest. She felt surprisingly well. She would get through the day. She picked up Henry's robe and wrapped up in it, telling herself she was also wrapping herself in his love. She smiled as she walked into the library.

Then she stopped. CNN was reporting the story of Harriett's murder. She knew what it was without switching on the sound. There was Harriett's body being wheeled out. With a gasp of horror, Lily fled the room. Suddenly, the night before was real again.

Henry had left coffee for her in the kitchen. Lily glanced at the clock as she poured. She was late already and she knew she looked a mess. It took her 45 minutes to shower, shampoo, and style her hair, put on makeup, and arrive at the office as if it were an ordinary day. But now she was in the office, and knew it would not be an ordinary day.

The mellow tone of her private telephone line bought her back to her world of fashion. It must be the publisher. Once Hilda Gorin had an idea, she didn't let go.

"Yes," Lily said into the phone as brusquely as she dared.

"It's me, it's Henry," the voice replied. "No need to put on your businesswoman airs with me."

"Oh, darling, I woke up so late I just got here. Hilda's been hammering at my office door since early morning. I just don't want to face her yet. I need some time to compose myself."

"Then take some time." Henry's voice was calm. "Take 15 minutes. Sit down and slowly go over everything I said last night. Remember how you should act. What you should say. Nothing more or less. You'll come through. You always do. If things really get difficult, say you need to discuss the situation with Henry. It's natural. Everyone knows how close we are.

"We can decide later whether you need a lawyer or not."

Lily blew a kiss into the phone, then hung up slowly. Henry was the very basis of her life.

Hilda Gorin was something else again. As Lily put down the receiver, the fat blond publisher, squeezed into a too-tight Chanel suit, burst into the room.

"What a story," she exclaimed. "And we've got an exclusive."

"What do you mean?" Lily asked distrustfully. "What are you talking about?"

"Harriett Franklin, of course," Hilda responded. "On Friday, when you wanted to do a story on her, she was just another Manhattan socialite. Who knew she existed? Today she's headlines across the country."

"But she was murdered," said Lily, beginning to feel very nervous. "We are a fashion magazine, we don't deal in murder."

"You told me you had prepared an exclusive interview with Harriett Franklin for the launch of the Franklin fragrance," Hilda said patiently.

"That was for the April issue. It was a no-go. The fragrance doesn't exist. We're replacing it with an accessory story."

"But surely the Harriett Franklin story can be rewritten," exclaimed Hilda.

This was unexpected. Lily knew her voice was shaking as she replied. "Rewritten how?"

"Well," Hilda paused. "We could give it a cover line— 'The Harriett Franklin I Knew,' by Lily Allen. You could do a quick rewrite and we can run the story in the March issue. It could be a real boost for newsstand sales. And, as you know, they can always do with a boost."

Hilda smiled broadly, and Lily noticed for the first time how imperfect her teeth were. Strange, Lily thought, how those details flash into your mind at unlikely times. Like last night. What details had she neglected?

Lily paused for what seemed a lifetime. "I don't know enough about Harriett to make a good story," she said.

"Well, according to her, you did." Hilda was prepared to get tough. "She called me on Friday and asked me to have lunch with her. When I asked why, she said she wanted to talk about some problems she had with you."

"What do you think she meant?" Lily tried to sound casual, but felt her heart racing.

"Well, nothing that really matters now, I guess. She did say she had known you from the minute you got the job here. That she had supported you in every way she could. She said she expected to get a little support in return now that she had a problem with the perfume, but it wasn't happening. In fact, Lily, she told me that you were close friends, and she was bitterly disappointed in you."

Lily shrugged.

"Really, Hilda, you mustn't believe everything you hear. Everyone in the business wants to be seen as the close friend of the editor in chief of a fashion magazine like ours. And so often what they say is completely without foundation. There is not a grain of truth in Harriett's accusation. I rarely saw Harriett or Isaac in a social situation. It was purely business between us."

Lily turned and looked directly into Hilda's eyes. She was beginning to feel more confident, and went on in a strong and unusually loud voice. "You know what happened about the perfume story. Harriett tried to pull a fast one on the magazine. She was a wicked woman. Her ambition controlled her life. I look back now and wonder if she was mentally ill."

"Now, Lily, that's going a little too far," Hilda admonished. "We could never claim that in the magazine."

"Well, Hilda, I can tell you she knew her husband had no intention of naming the fragrance after her, and she came to us and deliberately lied. She placed us in an untenable position. I don't see how we can run any sort of story after that."

Hilda glared back at Lily, unprepared to give an inch. "I'm not interested in her lies about the perfume, or her relationship with her husband and the business. I'm interested in her position in the social world of New York. Harriett Franklin was a brilliant hostess.

"Whatever dirt the press digs up won't bother us. We will concentrate on one thing—her success as a party giver. When she entertained, it was magic.

"In fact, the article can admit she was frustrated, but you can take the angle that she turned that frustration into positive work. Work that helped a lot of people who were much less fortunate. We can get a rough estimate of how much money she helped raise for charities."

It was clear that Hilda was going to insist on the story. The fear of having to write about Harriett was overwhelming. The panic she had felt last night returned.

"Our story can list Harriett's secrets of the perfect dinner party, tell ways of attracting important guests to a function, show photos of her table settings," Hilda went on with increasing enthusiasm.

"It's too dangerous," Lily said, trying a new tack. "She was murdered last night. Anyone might be accused of her murder. It could turn out to be the most sordid ghastly mess. And by the time the article appears, it could be outdated."

"Of course we have to be careful, Lily. But who murdered her is quite inconsequential. No matter how *sordid* her death, she was a woman of great style." Hilda's sarcasm was apparent as she spat out the word 'sordid.' "Can't you get it into your head that we will concentrate only on the parties she gave?" snapped Hilda. "You are stalling deliberately and I don't understand why. I want you to do this.

"And as for saying you didn't know her socially, what about the surprise 50th birthday party she threw for you? People are still talking about it. You must have pictures of that."

Lily remembered the party. She also remembered her amazement and delight.

A month before her birthday, she had walked past a townhouse that had once been the Indian embassy. It was up for sale, abandoned, a pathetic relic of another time in Manhattan.

"How sad," she had remarked to Harriett. "I went to some of the most luxurious parties of my life there. My mother was a friend of the maharani, and at her parties I learned so much about India, its food, its customs, its way of life."

Harriett had said nothing. But she had quietly hired the townhouse for a month and prepared it for a surprise birthday party for Lily.

Lily had not guessed a single thing. Not even when Novelli had called her in for a fitting for an Indian-style dress that he had designed for her to wear to her birthday dinner.

"I've been to an Indian store in Queens, and done a little shopping," he said. He had found an Indian wedding gown richly embroidered with silver and gold thread. He had taken it apart and cut it into a simple sheath.

"It is so heavy because it is all handmade," he explained.

Lily had wondered why she had to wear something so extraordinary and so glamorous on her birthday, but she was so taken with its beauty, she said nothing.

On the night of her birthday, when she entered the old townhouse she was overwhelmed. It looked exactly as it did 30 years ago.

"I found photographs and asked a lot of questions," explained Harriett. "So many people remembered the house, it became easy."

The rooms were lit only with candles. Rose petals were scattered along the hallways to guide the guests. The air was fragrant with the scent of incense.

Each woman was given a golden sari to wrap around her shoulders, so her face glowed in the soft light. The men were dashing in white ties and tails. Slim, brown-skinned girls, flown in from New Delhi, ended the evening performing a beautiful Indian dance with layers of veils.

"It was a dream," Lily had written in her thank-you note to Harriett. "I will never be able to repay you for the pleasure you gave us all."

Now she wondered why Harriett had done it. Harriett never did anything without a hidden agenda.

Hilda's voice broke into her thoughts. "Do you have photos of the Indian party?"

"Yes, I suppose so," replied Lily. "But from what I remember, they were so dark we couldn't use them. You know we only had candlelight."

"Well, you have the exclusive shots you took for the perfume story. And you can start looking at our archives, and then call the photo agencies. The photos are important. But what is essential are your memories."

Lily started to object again, but realized she was trapped. Still, she had to fight for time. Perhaps farther away from the murder, it would be easier to do.

"I'll give it some thought and perhaps start with the photos later this afternoon."

"We'll have another meeting this afternoon," Hilda said with finality. She walked to the door and opened it.

Then she turned back. "Well, who do you think killed her?" she asked.

Lily grasped her head in both hands, shuddered, and looked at the floor, struggling to keep her composure. Her mind went back. It was not the frail body of Harriett she thought of, but that of her son Edward. Edward lying dead on a bed in a seedy Lower East Side hotel.

At 16, he had fallen in love with Kim Kelly and followed her everywhere. Lily had fought to end that love and the pain it had brought. But she could do nothing.

In the end, a drugged Kim had taken him to the hotel for what she called "a party." He had taken an overdose of heroin and she had watched him fall into a coma. Then she'd left him to die.

The police had tracked Lily down at the office. She had found him there lying on the bed. His body cold, his dirty blond hair sprayed across the pink coverlet.

"Well, do you have any idea who is the killer?" Hilda repeated.

Lily looked up. Hilda's expression was gleefully expectant.

"Kim Kelly," said Lily. "She was found with the weapon in her hand, standing over Harriett's body. It's open and shut."

"But the police released her this morning without charging her," Hilda snapped back. "The word is that she was too drugged to have had the strength."

"Believe me, Kim Kelly is capable of murder. She killed my son. And she killed Harriett Franklin."

Lily walked to the door and closed it on Hilda. Then she rushed to the phone. She had come through. She had to tell Henry.

EIGHTEEN

11:10 AM, Monday

Mari was waiting in the Franklin foyer when the elevator door opened. She looked up, quickly scanning the passengers to see if Sonya was there. As Sonya stepped out, the PR took her by the arm. They walked past the front offices and into a small room at the back.

"Let's talk in here for a moment." Mari smiled. "I just want you to know how happy I am that this turned out so well."

Sonya heard a false note in Mari's voice. She wondered what had happened since the press conference.

Mari went on, "Isaac realized he shouldn't have been so abrupt with the press. He wants to repair the damage. He likes you very much, and he knows and trusts Donna."

"Does that mean he's agreed to the interview with Donna?"

Despite the soft talk, Sonya felt Mari was hiding something. She was a friend, but she was also a public relations professional, and a very successful one at that. When it comes to business, Mari's clients come first, Sonya thought.

"Yes, don't be worried. The only problem is time. We can't possibly arrange it until tomorrow morning. He has so much to set up for the boys. He wants to get in touch with the trauma clinic for his two youngest sons, and then do everything the counselors advise to help them deal with their mother's death."

"But," added Sonya, still hammering her case for an early interview, "the business is important too. I don't mean to be cold about it, but you know better than I do that his image can have an enormous effect on his company. And the interview with Donna will help him."

Sonya wondered for just a moment if she should pass on the gossip she had heard downstairs, then decided Mari should know. "Mari, the rumor in the building is that Isaac murdered his wife."

"Isaac?" Mari paused. "Why Isaac? Kim was found with the dagger in her hand. She did it. Isaac? No way. That's crazy."

Sonya saw Mari was badly shaken by the rumor. She wondered how close Mari really was to Isaac.

"Then why did the police let Kim go?" Sonya continued.

Mari answered quickly, "They have her passport. They told her not to leave Manhattan. And they made the same thing clear to that hotshot attorney that the almighty Glam-Gals Agency provided. She called me this morning to tell me; she's too scared to move."

Yes, Sonya could see the thought of Isaac as a suspect had her rattled. This was not the time to tell her that Jason Sarnoff was downstairs, demanding to be let into his office. Let Sarnoff look after himself.

"Why would Isaac follow his wife into the ladies' room and stab her to death? All this with 1,500 people around— 1,500 people who knew him. They lived together for God's sake, they went on vacation together, and if Isaac wanted to kill Harriett, he had plenty of opportunities."

Sonya hesitated, trying to think of a way to calm her.

"Mari, I am just repeating lobby gossip. From what I heard, they are saying that he was angry because he knew what Novelli said in his speech was true. That part about Harriett's ambitions. You know, it's the tabloid-TV version of life. 'Husband murders domineering wife in fit of passion.' "

Mari tossed her head angrily. "I tell you, it is totally ridiculous. Isaac knew Harriett was upset about Novelli's speech. He thought Novelli's accusations were outrageous."

That wasn't exactly the way Sonya remembered it.

"Were you with him?" she asked Mari.

"Only for a few moments after we all got up from the table. I discussed Novelli with him briefly, and then we parted. I had press things to check on, and he had people he wanted to talk to. Why the hell are you going on about this? As you said, it's only stupid gossip."

Sonya was quiet. She had upset Mari and that was the last thing she wanted to do.

"Let's forget it," she said calmly. "I think that Donna's interview will help Isaac. After all, you know this is just the first of the rumors you'll have to cope with. That's not going to be easy, but as you told me with my face-lift, just take it hour by hour."

Mari laughed. "Well, it's more traumatic than a lift. But you're right. Follow my own advice."

Mari led her down the hall to Harriett's office. The door was locked. Mari took a key from her pocket and opened the door with a flourish.

"She really had extraordinary taste," Mari said. "This space is tiny, but she used every square inch. After his father died, Isaac moved into the old man's office, and cut off a corner to make a private space for Harriett. She insisted that her office be right next to his.

"Harriett chose furniture in the Viennese style of the early 1900s to decorate it. It's light and geometric and gives a marvelous sense of space. And you see the color scheme? It's so simple—red, black, and ivory. With her dark hair it was the perfect background for her. You have to agree, whatever her faults, she had a real eye and great taste."

Sonya looked around. The office was beautifully proportioned. More important, it would be easy to shoot. Perry would make it look dramatic on camera.

"It is really exquisite," she said. "I'd love the crew to get started. By now, they must be waiting at the elevator by the fabrics department."

Mari picked up the phone and spoke briefly. "While they're unpacking, let me give you a few sketches of some of our most dramatic designs. They'll look wonderful in the story."

And, thought Sonya cynically, they'll be great publicity for the company too. She admired the way Mari managed to keep doing her job, no matter what.

"Do you want Novelli as well as Sarnoff?"

Sonya nodded, unable to believe her good luck. Matt would be happy with this video. It was all exclusive.

Mari went to a file drawer, pulled out a folder, and handed it to Sonya. Sonya opened the folder and looked at the sketches.

"These are by Novelli?" she asked.

"Yes, you can tell the Novelli designs by the face," Mari said. "He always used Harriett as his model. He caught every expression she ever had and every hairstyle she ever chose."

"That's odd. He must have been fond of her," Sonya said as she sorted the sketches.

"Well, at one time they were the best of friends. Novelli took Harriett in hand shortly after she married Isaac and taught her an enormous amount about personal style and the business of design. Around the office, people say that Leonard created Harriett."

"When did they have the falling out?" asked Sonya.

"I'm not sure. But a few years ago, when Leonard's lover was told he was HIV positive, apparently Harriett didn't want to have Leonard around socially anymore. It was tough on him, but that's the way Harriett was."

Sonya remembered what Novelli had said at the awards, and there was no doubt in her mind that the difficulties involved more than that.

It was Isaac Franklin himself who ushered Perry into Harriett's office.

"Mari," he said, "I need you now."

"Okay," said Mari. She reached for another folder and handed it to Sonya. "I'm sure we have some of Jason's sketches here. After you've shot them, I'd appreciate your putting them back into the folder for me. I'm not sure how long I'll be with Isaac. Will you be okay?"

"Don't be concerned about us," Sonya assured her. "We'll leave as soon as we finish, and we won't take long. And if you are still busy, I'll give you a call later in the day. Thanks for setting all this up. And let me know when Donna can interview Isaac."

As soon as she was out of sight, Sonya heaved a sigh of relief.

"Let's shoot the office first, Perry," she said, "starting with the desk. Lots of still shots of the pieces on it, then pan across. I want to see the papers and pens she used just before she was murdered."

"You got it. We'll get some great stuff in this room."

"Then I want to get Novelli's sketches. Play with different angles. But whatever you do, hold the shots of her face. He used her as his model on all of them. I grabbed as many different colors, looks, and hairstyles as I could. Better shoot more than less. They'll give us a lot to play with in post-production.

"Just make it as fast as you can, so we can be sure to get everything we need. Everyone here is so tense, anything could happen."

"Including the arrival of the police to seal off this office and throw us out," laughed Perry. "Just let me start."

As he set up a light, Sonya fussed around the room. She tried not to touch more than she had to. It was not right to set up things for a news program. Everything should be just as it was found. Not that most programs bothered with that refinement. But Sonya did. And on the other hand, she was frightened to touch the books and papers in case the police might have some objection.

When Perry finished with the desk, she walked over and sat in Harriett's chair. The file of Jason's sketches was in her hand, ready to be checked and shot.

"This may be turn-of-the-century Viennese, but it is turn-of-the-century uncomfortable in New York. I'm tired and I need to relax," she told Perry.

"I finished shooting the Novelli sketches. We could use a few more if they'll give you some."

Sonya replied, "I think Mari took them out of this drawer. I don't think she'd mind if I take a few more. I want to be sure we get the best."

She opened the file drawer and looked at the titles on the folders.

"Yes, here's another one with his name and the date on it. From this year. Do the ones from Jason, and we can pick up these other Novelli ones if we have time."

Sonya sat again. She pushed the chair close to the wall, leaned against it, and closed her eyes.

"I don't care, Mari," she heard Isaac say. "If I have to drive up myself to get him, Jeremy is coming back tonight."

Isaac's voice came through the wall. Harriett, thought Sonya, must have been able to hear every conversation her husband had in his office.

She heard Mari's voice. It had regained its usual calm.

"Novelli loves Jeremy, and if he feels it is not safe to bring him back right now, perhaps you should let him stay," she replied. "At least let him stay tonight. It'll give him a chance to settle down."

"He won't settle down," Isaac said bitterly. "Jeremy loved his mother more than anyone. He idolized her. But his brothers and I can give him the comfort of the family."

"I'm not going to argue with you," said Mari. "Get the doctor on the line and get his point of view."

Sonya was surprised to hear the way Mari spoke to Isaac. They were like a couple discussing their son.

Sonya heard Isaac dial the number. "Put it on the speakerphone, Isaac. I want to hear this."

Sonya heard Isaac asking to be put on with the doctor.

"Dr. Hoffman, it's Isaac Franklin, and I want my son home just as fast as we can get him here."

Sonya could hear both sides of the call clearly.

"I understand how you feel, and I'm sorry. But I have to consider the health of the boy. He's my responsibility and my concern. I want to test him before he goes back to New York, to make sure we haven't missed anything."

"That's different from what you said last night," Isaac answered with just a hint of annoyance. "When I spoke to Jeremy last night, he was quite normal and happy. He'd fallen, true enough, but he told me he was feeling fine. He wanted something to eat, and even asked for photos of his mother at the party we were attending."

"Yes, but when he woke up this morning, he was irritable and overtired. As we agreed, I told him that your wife had an accident. That upset him and he became disoriented. The fall was slight, and he was only unconscious for a few moments, but there may have been some bleeding. I don't want him out of my care until he's had a scan."

"A scan?" Isaac's voice was shaking. "You believe he did serious damage last night? Why didn't you do the scan then?"

"Calm down, Isaac." Dr. Hoffman was obviously keeping himself under control. "If I had believed he was seriously injured last night, I would have had him tested immediately. I really don't think the fall harmed him at all. I just want to be certain that before he takes the drive to the city and faces all that he has to face, he is as fit as he can be."

Isaac was having none of it. "Then the sooner he gets home, the better," he said. "I can arrange for the scan this afternoon. He will have every test that is available."

"He'd be happier having them here," Hoffman came back. "He knows the nurses, the doctors, the hospital. You know we'll look after him and protect him."

"You cannot protect him from the other boys," said Isaac. "When they find out that his mother was murdered they will be at him. I dread to think what they could say to him. He is my son and I will protect him. I have the legal right. And it is the right thing to do. I want him home."

"It's your decision," said Hoffman. "We'll make the arrangements. Let me have the name of his doctor in New York and I'll e-mail his charts."

"Will Novelli bring him back?"

Hoffman was quick. "I'll get Mr. Novelli for you," was all he said.

Perhaps, thought Sonya, the doctor was relieved that the decision had been made. She was sorry for Franklin. Mari had been silent through all of this—was she whispering something to Franklin that Sonya couldn't hear?

She became aware of the folder of Novelli's sketches in her lap, but realized her concentration had been on the conversation in the next office. She handed the unopened folder to Perry to shoot.

"Novelli," she heard Franklin's anxious voice, "what's happening there?"

"Calm down, Isaac."

Leonard Novelli's unmistakable voice came through the speakerphone loud and clear. "Jeremy was confused at first. He turned away from me when I first arrived. He couldn't understand his mother's accident. Now he thinks she fell over and hurt her head, just as he did last night.

"I got his crayons out and he's been drawing my car. As soon as we get his things together, we'll head for the city. I'll call you as usual when we are almost home."

Franklin's gruff reply was nearly inaudible. The only words that Sonya could make out were "careful" and "important."

But Novelli's reply was slow and clear. "Isaac, I am taking care of everything. You understand—everything. Good-bye. I'll see you shortly."

"Thank you. I'm counting on you. Good-bye."

Sonya heard the phone click. Mari spoke. "I've got to get back to Sonya and the crew. They said they wouldn't take long, and I want them out of here before the attorneys arrive."

"Mari, I need you here," said Franklin. "First the doctors,

then the attorneys, and then you need to give me some real preparation for the interview tomorrow."

"I'll only be a minute," she said.

"No, stay here," said Franklin.

"Pack up quickly," Sonya said as she took the sketches from Perry and shuffled them back into the folder. She added quietly, "I think we're about to wear out our welcome."

"Well, I'm not surprised," said Perry, who moved close to her. "And I don't ever expect to be welcomed back. Every one of the sketches in that folder had BITCH printed across the face."

"What do you mean? Every one? On Sarnoff's sketches?" Sonya was aghast.

"No, on Novelli's. Every one you gave me. I thought you'd picked that folder purposely."

Sonya opened the folder.

"You're right. My God, I didn't even look before I gave them to you."

She quickly went to the drawer and replaced the folder.

"I'll have to check them on the tapes as soon as we get back to the studio. Don't mention this to anyone—and let me see the tapes before anyone else gets a look at them."

She put her hand on his shoulder. "Let's go. Now. While Mari's tied up. I'll go down in the freight elevator with you. Come on."

NINETEEN

12:30 PM, Monday

Kim Kelly lived in one of Manhattan's grand old apartment houses on Central Park West. When Sonya arrived and looked up at the façade, she wished she lived there too. Built in the '20s, its solid stone walls had all the grandeur of a medieval castle. She stepped inside and was impressed with the enormous foyer that seemed to run around the entire building. Overhead was an immense vaulted ceiling. The tiled floor was covered with rubber matting to protect it from the winter sludge, but Sonya still could see part of its bold geometric pattern.

She sighed. It was Manhattan living at its most elegant, just as Sonya had always imagined it during those austere Minnesota winters when she was a girl.

The apartments came in different sizes and configurations. All of them surely had interesting if heavy architectural details. And all, Sonya guessed, were expensively decorated co-ops.

The interview with Kim was set for 12:30, but Perry had wanted to get there a few minutes early and set up.

"Be kind to her with the lighting," Sonya told him as they walked to the security desk. "I'd rather she look beautiful than like a washed-out wreck."

"If she got home from the police station early this morning, she's bound to be a wreck," he said.

"If we want to get anything from her, we'll have to handle her with kid gloves," Sonya offered.

Perry agreed. "I like her; I thought she was great with the speech last night. She may or may not be a murderer, but she has guts. Don't worry. I'll take care of her. I'll keep the lights soft and warm."

Sonya relaxed, content to let him take over.

She smiled sweetly at the burly, uniformed doorman. She felt the muscles tighten uncomfortably in her cheeks. She realized it was her face-lift. She had almost forgotten.

"We have an appointment with Kim Kelly," she said. "We're a little early, but we'd like to go up anyway."

"You and all the rest. You'd think she'd be laying low after that murder, but she's had people coming and going all morning," he growled.

"Well, then, we'd better hurry." Sonya kept her tone easy. She didn't like his manner and she didn't want to hear his gossip. "We don't want to miss anything."

"It's apartment 12F at the back," he told her. "You have to turn right and walk down to the elevators at the end of the foyer. The elevator has a sign for the apartments on the E and F bank."

He looked closely at Perry and the TV equipment.

"As for you, with all that gear, you shouldn't be here in the lobby. You should've come in the service entrance in the basement. But I'll let that pass. Go around the back to the freight elevators. You can go up that way."

Sonya shrugged her thanks and walked down the matting. She was pleased it was there, forming a path for her to follow. The old building was labyrinthine. What dramas must have unfolded here during the decades since it was built.

The elevator opened on the 12th floor to a small foyer for the two apartments. The door to 12F was ajar, and Sonya could hear muted music as she walked toward it.

A pale, subdued Mari was talking on her cell phone. So was another competent-looking woman. Sonya knew her surprise showed. She had not expected Mari to be there.

"Yes," said Mari as she closed the phone. "I arrived this second. I managed to tear myself away from Isaac. He is so worried about the children. But once he had the appointments for the two boys at the trauma clinic, he calmed down.

"Let me introduce you to Wendy Sharp, who is Kim's booker at GlamGals. She's not here to do anything but listen. I hope you don't mind, but the agency feels it has to protect Kim."

Protect Kim, Sonya thought ruefully as she remembered her instructions to Perry. With these two coaching Kim on what to say, I'll be lucky to get the truth out of her. Then she felt a surge of guilt. Mari must have gone to extraordinary trouble to set up this interview.

"I'm thankful for your help," she said. "Perry is coming up in the freight elevator, wherever that is. This place is enormous."

As usual, Mari acted quickly.

"I'll get your crew. I've brought enough of them up in those elevators for Leonard when he was working with us."

"Leonard Novelli?" Sonya asked.

"Yes. He has an apartment in this same building."

Sonya wanted to ask Mari more about Leonard Novelli, but was distracted by the sight of Kim in the bedroom, having her makeup done by a young slim man in jeans and a black turtleneck.

The model sat patiently, her face turned to the light. Even from the distance, Sonya could see the dark shadows and the deepening lines under her eyes. She was exhausted and must be making an enormous effort for them. Sonya liked her even more.

"Find a seat, Sonya, and be comfortable," Kim called out. "I won't be ready for a while."

"Finding a seat is easier said than done," Sonya muttered despairingly as she looked around the drab, messy room.

How could Kim, a woman who worried so much about her appearance, care so little about the way her home looked?

The cheap furniture was stacked with magazines, many still in their plastic wraps. Unopened mail lay scattered near the door where it must have been since it arrived. The vase on the coffee table was filled with dry, withered roses. Next to it sat a plate of stale cheese and an ashtray full of cigarette butts.

"Doesn't she have a cleaning woman who comes in and looks after her?" Sonya asked Wendy.

"These top models never catch up. They work long hours and they're constantly traveling. At night, they party," Wendy replied with a laugh. "Kim had all sorts of plans to decorate this place, but she never got around to it."

"Well, I don't think she would want it to look like this on national TV," Sonya said firmly.

Wendy Sharp smiled at her reassuringly. "I thought I'd wait for you and when you decide where you want to shoot, I'll tidy that area."

"Great," said Sonya, looking around.

"I swear, I do more for Kim than her mother ever did. I've been her booker since she first came to New York from Holland. There isn't much I don't know about her."

"As soon as Perry, my cameraman, arrives, we'll decide on the best place," Sonya said. Maybe the interview won't be so tough, she thought. This woman knows how to get it together.

And so did Perry. He took over immediately and got the lights and the camera up and ready to shoot. The background was the mantel, tastefully arranged with books and the vase, minus the flowers.

Thirty minutes later, Kim walked out of the bedroom, striking poses, pretending life was fun and that all was well with her.

She looks good, thought Sonya. And remarkably fresh. The makeup artist had worked miracles.

Perry gave her a grin. "You're as pretty as the girl next door." Microphone in hand, he pulled out the chair for her.

Well, not really, thought Sonya. She's too sophisticated for that. But her makeup was natural, and her hair was brushed forward to soften her face. Instead of the revealing, sexily torn T-shirt she usually wore, she had on a pale salmon blouse. It gave her face a healthy glow.

"How about that?" she said as she sat down. "Lookin' good and just a few minutes late."

Sonya hoped that Kim was up to a long interview. Though the final story would have only a few words of Kim's, she needed to get as much information as possible.

Sonya hit the target with the first question.

"What did you and Harriett talk about when you left the table together?" she asked.

"She was furious with Novelli," Kim said. "It was the speech he made. She said that after all she'd done for him, he'd deliberately belittled her in public. That she'd find a way to get her revenge. She was raging. I'd never seen her that bad before."

"If she was so angry, why did you go with her?" asked Sonya.

"She had a tight grip on my arm and I didn't know how to get away from her. She was a strong woman. I didn't want to fight with her in public. When she wanted something, it was easier to give in than to say no."

"What happened when you got to the ladies' room?"

"I went into the toilet stall. It was the only way to escape from her. I sat on the bowl and held my head in my hands." She looked directly at Sonya. "It took a lot of courage for me to make my speech. And then everyone applauded. I was so happy. I thought I had done so well. Harriett terrified me. I needed to be quiet. To give myself time to recover."

"Did you hear anyone come into the room? Did Harriett say anything?"

"No, nothing. It was just as I told the police. I wasn't listening for anything. I was just trying to calm myself."

Sonya heard Kim's voice begin to waver.

"And then, Kim? How did you feel?"

Kim answered rapidly, rushing on. "I wanted to go back to the party and have a good time. I've worked with most of the people there. I wanted to spend some time with them. I've been through rehab and I want to get my life back."

"Why did you come out of the toilet?"

"I heard someone scream. Then I saw Harriett. I didn't know she was dead. I tried to help her by pulling out the dagger. That's what happened. That's all I know. I told the police. They believe me."

Kim's eyes began to fill with tears. She put her hand up and touched the mike as if she were going to take it off. She'd had enough.

Change the subject quickly, Sonya told herself. She had pushed too hard. And Kim seemed to be telling the truth.

"Tell me about working at Franklin's," she said. "That's where you started working in New York, wasn't it?"

Kim relaxed and her face lit up as she remembered.

"Yes, when I first came to New York, Leonard Novelli gave me a job. I was a kind of part-time house model. I was just a kid trying to make it in the Big Apple. He taught me so much. I have to thank him for everything."

"He loved to sketch, didn't he?" Sonya smiled as she asked the question.

"Yes. And he had the most fantastic sense of humor." Kim's mood had changed completely. She was happy, remembering those good days. "He could sketch anything and anyone. And he used to scribble words on his sketches to make them even funnier. We used to laugh all the time."

Sonya decided she should take the chance to find out more about Novelli's drawings.

"We found some sketches at the studio with the word BITCH written on them. Is that the kind of thing that he wrote?"

"Oh, yes, and even worse," laughed Kim. "He used to call

me his Dutch hooker, or sometimes the Amsterdam bitch. 'Bitch' and 'hooker' were his two favorite words."

Wendy stood up and motioned Sonya to stop.

"We've gone as far as we need to go," she said. "Let's wrap this up. I've got to get back to the agency, and Kim must rest."

"Fine." Sonya leaned forward and unclipped Kim's mike. "You were great and you looked great. Thank you so much."

"Whew," said Kim. "I did it. I said I'd do the interview and I did. And now I've had it. Everyone clear out. I'm going to bed and this time I'm going to sleep."

Wendy motioned to Kim to go into the bedroom. She did as she was told, but turned on her way to blow kisses.

"She knows when and how to turn it on," Perry said admiringly to Sonya as he unscrewed one of the light poles. "That's what it takes to be a supermodel. You have to love the camera. And the camera has to love you."

Wendy came out of the bedroom, closing the door behind her.

"Will you let yourselves out, please?" she said to Mari. "She's going to rest now. The phones are ringing off the hooks at the agency. I've got to get back. She's so relieved it's over, she'll go to sleep immediately. I'll check on her tonight, but I'm sure she'll be okay. She's a lot tougher than she looks."

"Okay," said Mari as Wendy left. "Sonya, I'll take the crew to the freight elevator and then come back for you, and we'll go down together. Is there anything more you want us to do?"

"No. I'm set," Sonya replied. She sat down, pulled out her notebook, and began to write a quick rundown of the interview. She had several good sound bites she knew could work into the piece. Perry waved as he followed Mari out the door.

"Are you coming in the van with me?" he asked. She nodded and waved him on.

Then she heard Kim calling for Wendy. She sounded weak, as if she were crying.

"Wendy, are you still there? I'm so tired, but I can't sleep.

I don't think I'll ever sleep again. Help me. Find the remote so I can turn on the TV. I don't want to think about Harriett anymore."

Sonya rose, went to the door, and walked in.

Kim was huddled on the bed. She hadn't removed all her makeup and her cheeks were smeared with mascara. The dark circles were back.

"Wendy has gone, but I'll find the remote for you," Sonya said.

"Oh, Sonya, it's awful." Kim reached out a hand to her. "I hear it every time I'm about to drop off to sleep. It wakes me with such a start."

"You hear what?"

"Harriett's voice. But it is so scary. She doesn't really sound like the Harriett we knew. She says 'No, no, no,' and then she makes a strange gurgling sound. I can't tell you just how it sounds, but I keep hearing it. I can't get it out of my head."

Sonya walked over to the side of the bed and sat down. Kim's eyes were wide. And afraid.

"Kim, if you can, tell me exactly what happened. There are no cameras and microphones now. Just us."

"Harriett attacked me. She put her hands on my shoulders and shook me and shook me. She told me I had conspired with Leonard to trash her. She said Isaac would never hire me again, and she would make sure no one else did. She told me I would never kick the drug habit. I would end up in the gutter. I tried to get away from her, and when I couldn't, I slammed the door of the toilet and locked myself in. She shut up then, but I could still hear her breathing heavily. I crouched there, too frightened to come out. Oh, Sonya, I hated her.

"Then when I heard her say 'No, no, no,' I thought she was starting again. But in my heart of hearts, I knew something had happened. I knew someone else had come into the room."

"Did you tell this to the police?"

"No, I didn't remember it until I got home and was trying

to sleep. I am not sure who it was. Sonya, maybe there's something else I don't remember. But I don't want to talk to the police yet. It would just mean more questions. Do you think I'm imagining the whole thing?"

Kim began to sob. "Oh, Sonya, I just can't talk about this anymore."

"I understand, Kim," Sonya comforted her. "We can talk about this again another time."

She reached out and took Kim's hand, then slipped her arm around the model's shoulders and propped her up.

"Let me arrange the pillows so you'll be more comfortable watching TV," she said. "Next, I'll find the remote. Watch something mindless so you can drift off to sleep."

As Sonya picked up the remote from under a pile of cushions, Mari appeared at the bedroom door, holding a shopping bag.

"Look what I've found," she said.

Kim's face lit up. "It's Leonard's award. He left it for me last night with a note that I should enjoy it for a few days. He said he wanted to thank me for the great speech I made."

Her eyes filled with tears and she reached for a tissue.

"Get a grip on yourself, Kim," Mari said harshly. "I'm putting this outside so it won't remind you of what has happened. Just turn on the TV and watch till you go to sleep."

"We have to go," added Sonya. "But Wendy will be back to check on you later. Kim, relax. It'll all be okay."

Mari was silent as they closed the front door and walked to the elevator.

"Will she be okay, do you think?" Sonya asked her.

"She's fine. She's a lot tougher than you think."

"Odd, that's what Wendy Sharp said too," replied Sonya quizzically.

"One day, Sonya, when we have a few hours, I'll tell you the real story of Kim."

TWENTY

5:15 PM, Monday

Jefferson Tyler, 42, naked, smiled at himself as he turned, checking the profile of his upper body in the bathroom mirror. He knew he was good-looking. All those hours at the gym were paying off. His body was almost perfect.

He'd inherited his Austrian mother's genes. Her slim build, narrow bones, low waist, and straight, long legs. It was a sensual body, almost androgynous. The kind of body, he thought with a smile, that looked equally as good in women's clothes as men's.

His problem had been his round shoulders, but now, after a year of working with an expert specializing in postural integration, he was where he wanted to be.

"I'm not interested in just building muscles," he had told Rick, his personal trainer. "To me, the sexiest guy is slim and elegant. Like Cary Grant."

The sleek black phone on the wall of the penthouse bathroom gave a low ring. Tyler picked it up and listened. It was his personal assistant.

He told her, "Well, if Sonya and the crew are there already, they'll have to wait for me. I'm just out of the shower, and I want to do a few breathing exercises before I dress. So it will be at least 15 minutes before I'm down."

"That's all right. They want to set up, so they will be ready for you when you come down," she replied.

"Is Mari St. Clair there?"

"No, but she's coming."

"Well, she suggested either my office or the conference room. Show them both to Sonya and let her make up her mind."

Tyler had thought he had plenty of time when he came upstairs to prepare for the interview. He wanted to be perfectly calm and in control, and with his mercurial nature that was never easy.

The way to get past it, Rick insisted, was to be and to feel physically fit. Jefferson believed that.

He had spent what little had been left of the morning, after Grace headed back to Connecticut, going over the problem of Harriett's murder with his attorney. Tyler was not a man who lived easily with uncertainties. He wanted to know exactly what to say. The attorney had advised him to do the interview. While Sonya had actually found the body, Tyler had discovered Kim with the knife in her hand. And he had been left alone with Kim for a good 10 minutes before Franklin and the police arrived.

It was important to make it clear he had nothing to hide. He would tell his story and he would protect his private life. No one must know his secret pleasures.

But, the lawyers said, most important was the image of the company.

Yes, it was important to establish that his involvement in the murder had come by chance. His relationship with the Franklins was friendly but based purely on business. Tyler was proud of the role he had played in building the perfume business that belonged to his wife and their children. He had to keep their name free from suspicion. When Grace's father had been killed in the plane crash, Tyler had been adamant about not taking over the company.

"I want nothing to do with it," he had told her. "There are plenty of competent executives to run it. I have a business of my own. I know nothing about fragrance or the industry. And I don't want to learn."

But Grace had had it her way. And as he worked, he found the industry and its long history fascinating. Fragrances had been used for healing and seduction since ancient times.

What had amazed him most was the discovery that he had a "nose." He could detect the different ingredients in a perfume as surely as professionals who had trained for years.

"You are a natural. It was meant to be." Grace had laughed in pleasure when he told her the news. "You have no excuse not to be one of us."

And now, as the CEO of one of the top three fragrance companies in the world, he had to face the TV cameras.

He slipped his hands into a "backward prayer" yoga posture, breathed deeply 20 times, and walked down the stairs.

"The crew is waiting for you in the office. Sonya says they are ready to start as soon as you are," his assistant told him.

"Is Mari here?" he asked in a low voice, following Rick's instructions about saving his energy. His anxiety must not show.

"No. She called and said she'd be delayed. Isaac wanted her to give him a list of questions that Donna Fuller might ask at his TV interview, and she had to go over them with him. But she won't be long, I'm sure."

Tyler nodded, opened his office door, and walked in.

The lights and camera were set up. Sonya was standing by the window talking on her cell phone. The cameraman was lounging in one of the easy chairs. He got up apologetically as Tyler entered.

Jefferson put out his hand.

"That's okay," he said with a smile. "Rest when you can. It's been a rough 24 hours for all of us. Mari hasn't arrived yet," he said to Sonya as she clicked off her cell phone and turned toward him. "I'd rather wait, if you don't mind."

He had dressed carefully in a perfectly tailored pinstriped suit, a crisp blue French-cuffed shirt, and a dark blue tie with small red geometric figures.

Sonya smiled at him. He looked directly into her green eyes. They were warm and friendly. There was nothing to be nervous about with her. She was a sexy woman. He remembered their meeting in the dark library hallway last night. He was attracted to her, and he thought that her warm smile meant she understood that.

He wondered if she would question him about why he was in that hallway so close to the scene of the murder. If she did ask, he had the answer ready. His confidence began to return. He smiled back at her, then added, "Okay, never mind. I guess we can start. Let's get it over and done with."

In minutes, he was seated at his desk, the mike attached to his tie, the lights switched on.

Sonya began. "Tell me what you remember when you came into the room and found Kim with Harriett's body. How did you feel?"

"Well, I was shocked. I've led an eventful life, I was in the Israeli Army and I've seen people die. You expect that in the military, but entering that room and seeing a beautiful woman murdered was something else.

"As you recall, Kim was hysterical, and Harriett was crumpled in the chair. All I could think of was to get help."

"But you did something," Sonya prompted. "What did you do?"

"Oh. Yes, of course. I checked to see if she was dead. I looked at the knife. I saw her blood on the floor and her makeup scattered everywhere. I knew she was dead, but I checked her pulse to confirm it. That's all. That's all I did."

He stiffened and took in a deep breath. Then he put his hand up and covered his mouth.

He was getting uncomfortable. He wished he'd waited for Mari. But Sonya was obviously determined to keep going and to keep his mind on the scene.

"The room was beautiful. It was the powder room reserved for the society women who donated money for the library, wasn't it?" she asked.

"Well, it was the first time I'd ever been inside a powder room," he said, smiling a little. "But the masses of orchids were beautiful. And of course the fragrance, I remember. It was the fragrance that my company put together, the one we are about to launch for the Franklin Company."

"Will that be soon?" asked Sonya.

Tyler looked around for his assistant, and seeing her, put his hand over the mike on his chest.

"Has Mari arrived yet?" he asked.

She shook her head.

"Sonya, if you want to know more about all that, Mari has material on the Franklin launch, and she'd be the best one to give it to you," he said with finality.

"I hope you won't mind our continuing the interview," she said. "While I won't use all of it on the air, I need as much background information on you as I can get. And, Jefferson, I would like to get to know more about you."

He looked into her face and saw her encouraging smile.

"Sure," he replied, returning the smile. He was definitely attracted to her. She had won him over.

"You say you have led an eventful life," Sonya began. "Where were you born?"

"In Israel, where my mother and father met and were married. But I don't remember very much about it all. They are both long dead."

He watched Sonya's green eyes fill with sympathy as she waited expectantly.

"It's a typical story. My grandparents on both sides were killed in the Holocaust. My parents moved to Israel. Then my mother died while giving birth to me. The only real memories I have of her are the photographs my father took when they went on vacation to some seaside resort. She was a beautiful woman, small-boned, and, at least in the photographs, always happy.

"My father was in the army. He was killed in a border skirmish and I was sent to live with a cousin in New York."

"How old were you then?"

"About seven."

"It must have been very sad for you." Sonya seemed genuinely sympathetic.

"Well, my cousin's wife had dark hair like the photos I had seen of my mother, so I used to fantasize that she was my mother. She was a kind woman, and although she had three kids of her own, all younger than me, she tried to help me."

Sonya seemed at a loss what to ask next.

He went on. "She was a good woman and certainly didn't deserve what happened to her."

There was an awkward pause.

Then he said, "She got cancer, and after a painful battle, she died. She had chemotherapy, she lost her hair, and got thinner and thinner. In the end, she was so weak she couldn't even kiss us good-bye. It was a tragedy for all of us. I took it pretty badly. When I left the house for the last time, I took the wig she had bought when she lost her hair."

He gave a sudden, embarrassed laugh.

"I know this will sound strange. But in my worst moments, I used to put it on. It made me feel connected to all I had lost. Sometimes even now, if I see a woman in the street and the way she dresses reminds me of her, it brings it all back to me."

He stopped, wondering if he had said too much. But without hesitation, Sonya asked, "Do you still see the family?"

He relaxed, realizing how affected she was by his story.

"Shortly after his wife's death, my cousin took us back to Israel. Then after a stint in the army intelligence corps, I got a scholarship to Amherst and came back here. I missed my family terribly. I still do. I'd been the big brother to those three kids. But then I met Grace, we married, and before we knew it we had a family of our own."

Sonya seemed relieved at the upbeat note.

"I'm glad the story has such a happy ending," she said.

Tyler took a deep breath. He had felt he was going to lose it. He wondered if Sonya was connecting something about his story to Harriett's murder.

He wished he had waited for Mari. He was convinced he had said too much. She would get no more from him.

Sonya added with a smile, "Did you and the Franklins spend time together socially?"

"Not really," he said. "Of course we met at parties and chatted. I believe that Harriett and Grace may have known each other briefly at school. But that's all. We lived in two different worlds."

Sonya turned her head as she heard the door open and saw Mari's face appear.

"Okay to come in?" Mari mouthed.

Sonya nodded to Perry and he stopped taping. "Sure, it's okay. You just missed the last question."

Mari walked across to the desk and smiled at both of them, then she turned to Sonya.

"How did it go?"

Tyler looked anxiously at Sonya, then turned quickly to watch Mari's expression.

"It was fine, we got what we needed," Sonya replied. "Some great sound bites."

"Great sound bites," repeated Tyler. "Mari, you should have been here on time. You promised me you would be. You know what I'm like. I got out of control and blabbed out my whole life story."

"That was fine," said Sonya. "It's a moving story. And it has a happy ending."

"No, it doesn't," interjected Tyler. "Grace's family hates anyone to know I'm Jewish. I changed my name from Titelbaum to Tyler so no one would know."

TWENTY-ONE

7:30 AM, Tuesday

Isaac Franklin strode into the sleek gray gym Harriett had had built next to her bathroom. The gym he had steadfastly refused to use when she was alive.

"Swimming is the only exercise I need," he had always said to her. The truth was he had wanted no part of her daily routine.

But the frustration he felt this morning was overwhelming. There was no time for a swim at the club. A run on the treadmill might ease his mind and give him the shot of adrenaline he so desperately needed to get through the day.

He flipped the switch, stepped onto the treadmill, and started to pace. As it picked up speed and he began to run, he went over the problems he had to face that day. Most worrying was his physically well but deeply depressed oldest son, Jeremy.

He sighed.

Jeremy had found out about his mother's death in the

worst possible way, just before he left Hoffman's clinic. He had seen the story of her murder on the television in the nurses' break room. He had run there to say good-bye before he left.

Dr. Hoffman told Isaac Jeremy had slipped away unnoticed while he and Novelli completed the discharge forms.

"Jeremy saw the whole gruesome story of your wife's murder on TV," Dr. Hoffman had said. "He believed his mother was still alive because I followed your instructions and told him she'd only had an accident. Then he realized she was dead. He saw her go into the party, and then he saw her come out on a stretcher with her face covered.

"You insisted I lie to your son. The result is, we now have an extremely disturbed boy on our hands. I realize how wrong I was to have followed your instructions."

Franklin had tightened his grip on the phone. Shouting at the doctor would do no good. He replied as calmly as he could.

"And I also insisted Jeremy was to be guarded at all times so he didn't see TV or the newspapers. How could you have let this happen? Where was Novelli? Where were the nurses? Where were you?"

Hoffman had ignored the questions and gone on coldly. "It is our policy to let the children feel free at the clinic. Jeremy behaved as he always did. He knew he was trusted to do the right thing. There is no blame to be placed here."

He's obviously covering for himself, Franklin had thought. He had listened attentively as the doctor continued.

"Isaac, you must consider the part you played in this," he said. "If you had let me tell Jeremy that his mother was dead, he wouldn't have had to face this confusion. The policy at the clinic has always been to tell children the truth. Gently, of course, but always the truth. I think you'll find that because of the lie, Jeremy no longer trusts you."

Franklin had swallowed hard to hold back the anger that was building in him.

"If so," he said, "it is because of your failure to supervise him. Now he must come back immediately with Novelli.

I've talked to Dr. McDermott, who has treated Jeremy here for years, and Novelli can meet me at his office."

"I understand," Hoffman had said dismissively. "You are his parent and I am obliged to follow your wishes. But I want to tell you officially that it is against my best advice."

"Put Novelli on," Isaac had said.

It was a mortified Novelli who had come to the phone.

"Isaac, I'm sorry. I was filling out forms in the doctor's office when he ran off," he had said. "Jeremy was saying good-bye to Nora, who is one of his favorite nurses. Apparently she left the room and he wanted to see her again. We didn't know where he'd gone.

"She was in the break room, watching the story of Harriett's murder on TV. She had the sound up and didn't realize Jeremy was standing behind her until the piece ended. She believes he saw Harriett arriving at the library, and then her body being taken out—and then my speech, where I warned her to stop meddling in the business."

Novelli had paused. Franklin had known he was hoping for some words of forgiveness. But he could offer none.

"He is one unhappy boy," Novelli had finally continued. "But I'll bring him back to you as fast as I can. And I'll keep him cheerful. He is okay. He's still our Jeremy, warm and loving. He'll get through this."

Franklin had known Novelli was desperately trying to reassure him—and to escape any blame for what had happened. But he had cut him short. He had no patience for a long explanation. Nothing could justify the boy's being left unprotected.

"Just bring him straight to Dr. McDermott on 73rd and York Avenue," he said curtly. "He'll see Jeremy as soon as he arrives. I'll be waiting there." Isaac's tone had softened slightly. "Leonard, call me just before you arrive, so I can go out to meet him."

Franklin stepped off the treadmill, walked into the bathroom, and turned on the shower. He wanted to be in the office by eight. Then he'd do the Donna Fuller interview and be back in time to have lunch with the three boys. He wanted to prepare them for Harriett's funeral the next day.

As he dried off and dressed, his mind went back to Jeremy. He had arrived early at Dr. McDermott's office and waited for Novelli in the parents' room. Too impatient to sit, he stood looking out the window.

As he had watched, the sun had sunk below the horizon. Deep shadows had crept over the East River. Soon the gray, flat water disappeared altogether. The city had turned dark, cold, and desolate. Isaac could almost smell the dank air that swept up the building.

The wait for Novelli to phone from the car had been endless. And in the end, no call had come. It was the receptionist who told him that his child was waiting for him. Waiting for him, white-faced and dazed, beside an impatient Novelli.

"Take him. I'm double-parked," the designer said, gently pushing the child forward and moving toward the door. "I'll be back."

"Don't come back," Franklin had said, suddenly outraged at Novelli's lack of compassion. "Leave Jeremy to me. Why didn't you call from the car as you promised?"

Novelli had stopped and turned on him, equally enraged.

"The phone was dead. I hadn't charged the batteries. I wasn't planning a long trip. And what does that matter? What is important is that you should never have forced the doctor to tell Jeremy his mother was in an accident. Even before he saw Harriett's body on TV, he sensed something more serious had happened to her. The looks of pity he got from the attendants, even from Hoffman's secretary, told him something was seriously wrong. He is sensitive; he reacts to people and their moods."

Jeremy had looked from one to the other, not understanding, tears beginning to fill his eyes.

"When you asked me to pick him up, I had no idea of the state he would be in. Hoffman told me he begged you to let him stay at the clinic where everything was so familiar to him. And I understand why. You were a fool, Isaac. You should have listened to the doctor."

Isaac had lost control.

"You, of all people, shouldn't judge me! You of all people have no right!" he shouted.

To cover his rage, Franklin had put his arms around his son and stroked his hair as he had done when Jeremy was upset as a child. Then he put his hand under the boy's chin to lift his face and look into his eyes. Jeremy turned from him, squirming, and stumbled trying to escape and get to Novelli. But Novelli was out the door.

"Let's get you into a wheelchair. You must be tired after such a long trip," came the comforting voice of Dr. McDermott. He was short and solid, with a brush of gray hair unexpected in a middle-aged man.

"We'll go into my office for a moment, Jeremy. I want to have a look at you. We might even take some X rays of that bruise you got when you fell last night."

Jeremy had slumped forward, his eyes on the floor as he climbed slowly into the wheelchair.

"Come into my office too, Isaac," the doctor had said. "You can wait there while I examine Jeremy, and then you can both go home together."

"You can't imagine what it has been like," Franklin had told McDermott apologetically as they walked along the corridor. "I tried so hard to do the best for him, and for Henry and Byron. I don't want Jeremy to suffer, he's had enough. But I can't control everything."

The doctor had turned and touched him on the shoulder. "No one expects you to."

That was a comforting memory.

Now as he stood in the kitchen and turned on the coffeemaker, Isaac said aloud, "I can't control everything, but no one really expects me to."

As he drank the hot coffee, it brought him back to himself. His driver was already waiting downstairs.

When the car stopped at a red light on Seventh Avenue at 44th Street, Isaac automatically looked out to check the condition of the huge Franklin billboard that seemed to take up half a block along Times Square.

It looked good, and so did Kim Kelly in a slinky mini evening dress. He and Mari had selected the dress for the advertisement because of its graphic qualities, and they were right. It had turned out to be the buyers' favorite for the coming season. It would be stocked in stores across the country.

Isaac began to feel better. He stretched his legs. It was time to pull himself together. To think about business. He'd clear his head by walking the last few blocks to the office.

"Thanks, Joe. I'll walk the rest of the way," he said to the driver as he opened the door and stepped over the icy gutter.

The wind bit into his cheeks. He turned up his coat collar and shoved his hands deep into his pockets. For a few minutes, he would be free of the pressure.

After yesterday, there could be no more outbursts of rage. He sighed. His sudden attacks of temper were a problem.

The first thing he would do at the office, he told himself, was go over the questions Mari had outlined for the *Donna Fuller Show*. He had to be very careful of everything he said. The list of questions was at the top of the pile of things on his desk. Mari would rehearse the answers with him. He would be gracious, courteous, relaxed. The interview would change the impression he'd created by walking out of the press conference.

When the elevators closed behind him on the penthouse floor, he took a deep breath. At least here he was safe. Everything was familiar. There was great comfort in dealing with the day-to-day routine, he told himself. It was what life was really about.

He walked slowly along the corridor to Harriett's office. Was she really dead? It was hard to believe she would never again sit at her desk, waiting to argue with him. He reached out and put his hand on the door handle to test the lock.

The door swung open at his touch. He stood looking at Harriett's bold red, black, and ivory color scheme and the furniture she'd received with such joy when it arrived from Milan.

He slipped off his coat, threw it over a chair, and walked to the desk. He had to go through her papers, separate the personal matters from those of the business. And there undoubtedly were files that would have to go back to the charities she worked for.

If there was one thing about Harriett he was sure of, it was her compulsive neatness. There would be no problem sorting the files. He felt odd about going through the possessions of his dead wife. It was almost abstract. He missed the feeling that he was violating her privacy.

Idly he opened the top drawer, where she'd kept her cosmetics and the magnifying makeup mirror. She had used it for the endless checks she needed to reassure herself that she was perfect. The makeup was a mess. Some hand other than Harriett's had been here. Someone had been searching for something. Harriett's perfect order, her powders, her lip glosses, her brushes, had been rudely pushed aside to see what lay beneath.

Isaac quickly jerked open the file drawer beneath it. Something was wrong here too. It seemed the folders had been taken out and searched, and then shoved back. Harriett's orderly system was destroyed.

Whoever had done the search had been in a hurry. A desperate hurry.

No member of the staff would have touched the desk without permission, let alone rifle through the files.

What could Harriett have had that someone needed so desperately?

He turned to the low cabinets that lined the wall opposite her desk and opened the drawers. Another mess. He looked at the books, sketches, fabric swatches, and jewelry pushed aside. Someone had gone through everything. Someone who didn't care what traces they left behind, as long as they found what they wanted.

Franklin's mind raced. He felt sick with rage. Whoever it was didn't care enough even to close the door behind them. Had they left in such a hurry because they found what they wanted? Had they been disturbed? How was he to find out? How could he discover who had been there?

He needed time to think. He sat at Harriett's desk and put his head into his hands.

"Harriett," he said out loud. "Harriett, will it ever be over? Will you ever leave me alone?"

He looked up and saw the silver-framed photo on the desk. Harriett, in full evening dress, at the White House party they'd been to a year before. Harriett was smiling at the First Lady in a way she had never smiled at Jeremy.

He picked it up to look at it more closely. His rage surged again, rage he could not control.

"You bitch!" he shouted.

That night, Harriett had been satisfied for once. She had looked like a star among the stars. And that was the only thing she wanted. He hurled the photo as hard as he could across the room.

"You bitch!" he shouted again.

The picture smashed into the full-length mirror, elegant on its stand of black lacquer. The glass shattered and sprayed across the carpet. The mirror was destroyed.

For the first time that day, he smiled.

He was calm.

TWENTY-TWO

8:00 PM, Tuesday

Sonya stood on the steps of the network's building watching the cars crawl along 57th Street. Usually by Tuesday night at eight most of the commuters had left and the streets had begun to clear. But tonight, the traffic was still tangled. It was often that way in Manhattan when the weather was uncertain. Snow was flaking down gently. The city was beautiful in a special way.

Sonya framed the picture like a movie shot: the big city, glamorous, the fast track. The New York of everyone's imagination.

The car she had ordered to take her to the Princeton Hotel was already 15 minutes late. But, she consoled herself, the chilly air was refreshing and would probably ease the swelling in her face. And by the time she arrived, Mari would have that first golden glass of white wine waiting for her.

She fantasized about the alcohol slipping into her bloodstream, relaxing her shoulders and eventually her whole tired body. It was an escape like no other, an escape she rarely took, but tonight she needed it.

Why did she feel such an urgent need to let herself go? To forget everything? There was something about Harriett's murder that she was missing, and at the same time, she had the feeling that she knew more than she realized.

She stamped her feet, partly to warm herself, partly to bring back reality. She'd had worse days, and bigger problems with Matt.

After all, Harriett's murder was a breaking story. She'd gotten exclusive interviews. The shots Perry had taken at the party were unbeatable, especially the ones of the Franklin table. No one else had them. And at Matt's insistence, Sonya had even taped a sound bite saying how horrified she was when she found Harriett's body. The *Donna Fuller Show* that was due to run in two hours was as good as it could be.

The problem was Donna Fuller herself, and what she had said to Sonya when they were at the Franklin offices. The trouble had started when Mari phoned early in the morning and said she would have to cancel—or at least postpone— the interview with Isaac Franklin.

"Mari, you can't," Sonya had pleaded. "We're building the whole show around it. We've run promotions on it all day. The network is expecting a ratings boost. Franklin's got to give us half an hour of his time."

Mari had paused for a long time. "I've done what I can. He is absolutely adamant. And there is the funeral tomorrow that he has to plan. Anyway, Sonya, if he does do the interview, he won't say much. He is really wound up. I've never seen him this way."

"What if Donna herself calls him?" Sonya had come back. "He knows her and trusts her. She's been to a lot of Harriett's charity dinners. She's been very supportive. Maybe she can talk him into it."

"Go for it," replied Mari. "I've done as much as I can at this end. I told Franklin he needs to do the interview. If he cancels it at the last minute, the press will grab the story. 'Husband of murdered socialite suddenly refuses Donna Fuller.' And the tabloids will be worse. It won't do him any good and it certainly won't help business. It just looks suspicious."

Donna did call. She'd talked Isaac into giving her half an hour for the interview. "I used every trick I know," she said as she walked into Matt's office where Sonya was already waiting. "And I had to promise him the world. He wants no mention of suspects, let alone of the murder. He just wants to talk about Harriett's love of her children and her work for the charities. I'll try to draw him out as much as I can, but it will be tough going."

The interview with Isaac Franklin had been close to a disaster. If it hadn't been such a hot story, and if "The Franklin Exclusive" hadn't been so heavily promoted, Sonya doubted that the program would even include it. Despite Donna's skill and charm, she had failed to draw out any new information.

Franklin had answered her questions in guarded monosyllables. He was reluctant to look at her, and kept glancing down at his clenched hands. Sonya took out her notebook, watching him closely. He was tense, almost frozen with fear, a changed man.

Donna's first question was about Jeremy. She knew he loved the boy and she thought talking about him might help Isaac relax. But instead, his face hardened.

"He is well enough," Isaac said.

"Where is he now?"

"He's at home with his brothers."

"I understand he was at a clinic. When did he come home?"

"Yesterday."

Donna waited, hoping Isaac would say more, but he merely pursed his lips and stared at his hands.

And so it had gone. Donna kept getting sweeter, her voice low and controlled even as she became more and more frustrated.

At last, she gave up. There was no way she could penetrate the icy barrier. Someone had done something or said something to Franklin. Sonya shuddered as she took his clammy hand in a farewell handshake. As they walked into the elevator, Donna turned to Sonya.

"You know we can't make him look as bad as he was. I promised him we would be very gentle with him. This piece must be edited with extreme care."

Sonya had nodded. "Of course."

Donna put her hand on Sonya's shoulder and looked directly into her eyes.

"I feel nervous about it all, Sonya," she said. "Be careful. Don't get too close to anyone here. There is a police investigation going on. You may have found Harriett's body, but you mustn't get any more involved than that.

"And Mari. I wonder about her. She's obviously very close to Franklin. I watched them together while we set up for the interview. From the way she fussed over him, I'll bet their relations are more than professional."

They reached the lobby, and Donna took Sonya's arm and moved her to a corner. It was obvious to the crew that the conversation was private.

"I knew Mari's mother briefly," Donna confided. "She was a strange woman, and she had a strange relationship with Mari. From what I gather, there was great animosity between them. It was, as they say, a dysfunctional family, and the children of dysfunctional families carry a lot of baggage.

"Just keep your distance. I like Mari and I can see she is your friend. But you have no idea what's really going on here, and you have no idea what will happen. So for your own sake, just do your job. Don't get too involved. This is a murder and the murderer has not been caught."

Sonya was taken back, surprised at Donna's apprehension.

Donna was a brilliant woman. She could walk into a room full of people and gauge what was going on in seconds.

Matt often joked that she was psychic and could make a lot more money telling people's fortunes than she could as a TV star. Sonya admired Donna's uncanny ability to see into a situation, though she overdramatized things at times. That was part of what made her exciting on television.

Most important to Sonya was that Donna had proven herself to be a friend. Or, if not a real friend, a mentor. Donna's advice had so often steered her on the right course. Donna's talk was well-meant. She had to be taken seriously. And Donna was right. If for no other reason, as a producer Sonya had to avoid any personal involvement.

Still, Donna seemed to be implying that Sonya could be in danger.

Could that be true? She had found the body, but did she know any more than that?

Just stay cool, she told herself. But she was not able to shake a twinge of fear.

Anyway, the show is finished, she thought with relief.

Sonya had worked with the editors on it for hours and had argued with Matt about the final cut. In the end, neither of them had been completely satisfied. That was the way it always was.

She was tired. She had slept little the night after the murder, and last night she had worked late, viewing tapes. By the time the program was finished, the glass of wine and bed were almost all she could think of. But she still wanted to see and thank Mari.

Without her, the *Donna Fuller Show* would never have gotten the interviews it had. Yes, Tuesday's show was wrapped up—but what about tomorrow? Who could tell when the police would solve the crime? Who could tell what follow-up stories Sonya might be asked to do? And who better to help her set up the interviews than Mari?

In the end, Sonya was only 20 minutes late for their date at the Princeton. She stood at the door of the bar and looked around for Mari. The dark paneling softened the dim light even further. It was a convenient place to meet if you didn't want to be observed.

She saw Mari sitting comfortably in a dark leather banquette at the side of the bar. A glass of red and a glass of white wine stood on the table in front of her.

How does she do it? thought Sonya. Mari was sitting there with perfect posture, perfectly groomed, and perfectly composed. All on what must be only a few hours' sleep. She was dressed in a winter-white suit. The jacket was cut to show her slim figure. It took a confident woman to wear that light a shade in a January blizzard.

But Mari knew the colors that suited her blond good looks and never wavered from them.

She saw Sonya walking toward her and welcomed her with a slight wave and a smile. Sonya thought of Donna's warning.

"Don't be concerned. I got here just a few minutes ago," Mari said as Sonya arrived at the table. "The traffic is in such a snarl, no one is expected to be on time."

Sonya bent down and kissed her on the cheek. "Thank you for everything," she said as she slid into the seat beside Mari. She picked up the glass of chardonnay and added, "Also for this."

"I'm on my second one already. It's been quite a day." Mari raised her glass of red in a mock toast. "Well, how did it go? Are you happy with the show?"

"You were right about Isaac," Sonya answered. "He said very little. Not one new thing. That interview was one of the toughest editing jobs I've ever faced. I'm just so glad we had three cameras there; they gave me plenty of cutaway shots.

"What upset him, Mari? Am I allowed to know?"

Mari touched her on the shoulder.

"No, I can't tell you," she said quite formally.

Then, as she took a deep draught of wine, she added, "But you can be sure of one thing. Whatever upsets Isaac has something to do with Harriett. She really knew how to get to him. And even now that she's dead, the story goes on. I used to be amazed at the effect she had on him. We'd agree to do something and then Harriett would 'pop in,' as she used to say. Before I knew it, Isaac had changed his mind.

"In the first few years I worked for him, I don't think he knew what she was up to. Then, when he knew, he found it impossible to fight back. He just grew more and more resentful of her manipulations. In a way, I think Isaac is frightened of women and their power."

This was a new Mari. Despite her perfect exterior, she was obviously tired and stressed. For the first time, she was willing to talk about her clients. She had never done that before.

What was Isaac like as a man? He seemed to easily lose his temper, going from calm to violent in a moment.

"Was their marriage ever happy?" asked Sonya.

"Yes, I suppose in the beginning. Harriett was a strong woman, determined to control Isaac. And perhaps that's what attracted him to her. She was what I call a 'no, no, no' woman. 'No, no, no. Do it my way.' I'm not surprised those were the last words she uttered."

Sonya nodded sympathetically. "What's Isaac's problem with women?"

"It all stems from his mother. She committed suicide when he was a teenager, and he's never forgiven her for it. Isaac found the body. It took him a long time to work through her death. I don't know if he will ever get over it. First the guilt, then the anger.

"That terrible anger. When he's that way, he could do anything. I've seen him smash a hotel door when we got back late from a conference and found that Harriett had locked him out."

"I didn't know his mother committed suicide. That must have been awful." Sonya was shocked.

Mari lifted the glass of red wine to her lips and smiled. The glass was empty and she ordered another. "Well, we all have problems with our mothers. Harriett was very like my mother. I found I had to deal with her in the same way."

"Donna knew your mother, didn't she?" asked Sonya, with some reluctance. She wanted to encourage Mari to go on.

Mari continued as if she had not heard the question. The wine was making it easier for her to talk.

"I was an only child and my mother had very high standards for me.

"I remember when I was a kid, I desperately wanted a pet. Then a school friend gave me a mongrel kitten—a sweet little tabby. I fell in love with it and raced home to show it to my mother.

"She was furious. A mongrel was not to be seen in our pristine household. After a few days, the kitten disappeared. Mother told me that she had wandered off. Later I learned that she had killed the cat and thrown its body in the trash. Harriett was the same kind of person. I guess that's why I was able to get along with her. I had been trained by my mother." She laughed.

Sonya frowned in sympathy. She wondered if this was what Donna had meant about Mari's mother.

"How awful for you," Sonya said.

Mari laughed again. "I guess it toughened me up. Just what you need in the public relations business. Anyway, we all have stories about our mothers and fathers."

"But your mother was a brilliant woman, wasn't she? I remember you once saying something about your mother's interest in French history. You remember, when I was working on that story about the costume institute's show of French design through the years. Didn't you say that your mother was something of an authority?"

"Actually, mother was fascinated by Maria Theresa of Austria." Mari twisted her wineglass in her hand. "Maria Theresa's daughter was Marie Antoinette, the Queen of France—the poor woman who is most famous for being beheaded during the revolution. That's one hell of a way to get famous!"

Sonya laughed with Mari.

"She even named me for Marie Antoinette. That's where my name came from. Mari. My real name is Marie."

"Marie Antoinette?"

"Yes. How do you think it would go over if I called myself Marie Antoinette—Marie Antoinette St. Clair?" Mari laughed.

"Anyway, this Maria Theresa had 12 children, married most of them off well, and through them she controlled Europe. One smart lady!

"I think that was what my mother wanted. Five or six

sons. Maybe one could be president of the U.S.A. If my mother couldn't have the palace at Versailles, then at least the White House, was the way she looked at it.

"Instead she got one child. Me. What a disappointment. No matter what I did, I couldn't please her. She was a woman with no compassion or mercy."

"That must have been difficult for you," offered Sonya.

"I was glad when she died." Mari's eyes glistened with tears. Sonya reached out to touch her, but Mari pulled away.

"I'm okay," she said. As she moved, Mari splashed the contents of the wineglass on her jacket. The red wine spread quickly, staining the pale fabric.

"Damn, damn, damn," she said angrily. "That's something I don't do very often," she said as she picked up the napkin and started dabbing at the stain. "But when I do it, I certainly choose the wrong time.

"I'm going on to the party Lily is having to watch your show. That's something, isn't it? A party to watch a murder story. Late as it is, I'd better go home immediately and change. Sorry to have to rush out."

She waved to the waiter and motioned that she wanted the check.

"I can't be seen looking as if I've spilled Harriett's blood on me." She laughed again, and Sonya joined her.

TWENTY-THREE

4:00 AM, Wednesday

It seemed Sonya had been sleeping for just a few minutes when the phone rang. With her eyes only half open, she reached out to pick it up. Instead she knocked the receiver onto the floor.

She quickly switched on the light and retrieved it. As she did, she heard an annoyed voice saying, "Hello, hello, are you there, Sonya?"

Fear gripped her. She had been dreaming of Mari, her mother, and the dead cat. Despite the warmth of the room she started to shiver. She looked at her clock: 4:00 AM. Something serious had happened.

Sonya pressed the phone hard against her ear. "Who is it?"

"It's Matt."

"Yes, Matt," she said. "What is it?"

"Kim," he said. "Apparently she killed Harriett and the guilt and the investigation got to be too much for her. She jumped out of her apartment window into a small courtyard at the back of her building. The night watchman found her body half an hour ago. The report has just come in."

"She committed suicide?" Sonya was skeptical. "I can't believe that. I did the interview with her on Monday afternoon and she was okay. A little rattled, but getting herself together."

She paused to think and let her gut feelings come through.

"No, I'm sure. She didn't kill Harriett and she didn't kill herself."

Matt laughed. "You can tell that to the cops. Get over there fast. I've ordered a car for you. It will be waiting for you outside the building. Get as many interviews as you can. We don't know which way this will go, but I want to keep on the story."

"Is Perry coming?"

"Yes, I've arranged for your favorite cameraman. Call me when you connect. You've got my cell number."

"I'll do that," Sonya said calmly.

But as she put the phone back, her hand shook. She felt sick to her stomach. Her body seemed numb. Her face began to throb. She doubted if she could get dressed, let alone stand on the pavement and do interviews in the freezing cold.

She walked to the mirror. No, her face was not swollen. It was just nerves.

Kim dead? It was impossible to believe. That lovely oval face, the slim, graceful body lying on the ground torn and broken. Sonya's mind began to race. She was fully awake.

Kim had just turned 25. Her whole life lay ahead of her. She'd had problems, but none so grave that she would kill herself. Perhaps she had taken drugs and when they wore off, she became depressed.

But she had been trained to deal with that. She had the whole support network of the rehab system. She had to make only one phone call and help would pour in.

If she did kill herself, the decision must have been instant. Something dreadful must have happened to make her feel life wasn't worth living.

"No, not suicide. Murder," Sonya heard herself saying aloud.

One thing seemed certain. If Kim had been murdered, it must have been by the same person who had stabbed Harriett. And that person had to have had the strength to throw Kim's body out through the French doors.

Sonya walked slowly into the kitchen and pushed the start button on her white electric jug, opened a jar of instant espresso, and heaped a spoonful in a mug. She needed that rush of caffeine desperately. The taste was bitter, but the warmth of the drink revived her as it slid down her throat.

Cup in hand, she went back to the bedroom, pulled on black pants, a T-shirt, and then a warm sweater, boots, a heavy jacket, and finally a red wool cap. Red for Perry. How often had he said, "Wear something red, then I can always find you in the crowd."

She closed her eyes. Perry was a constant in her life. When she was with him, she would feel safe. And feeling safe was becoming rarer these days.

As Matt promised, the car was waiting. There was no traffic, and in minutes they pulled up a block below Kim's building.

Sonya walked stiffly past the police cars lined up along the street, bracing herself against the cold as it whipped around the corner and into her face. Tears ran down her cheeks and she pulled her hand from her pocket to wipe them away.

It was bitterly cold. It seemed worse than she had ever experienced since she left Minnesota.

How despairing Kim must have felt to open the French doors and jump out into the storm. How could she have done it? No, surely it was impossible.

Sonya reached the entrance to the apartment house and groped in her bag for her wallet and press pass. A sudden, unexpected blast of wind-driven sleet lashed against her and she stumbled as she climbed the narrow steps into the building. A uniformed arm reached out to steady her. Not the police. Sonya looked up to thank the doorman of the building.

"It's you again, you with the red hair," he said. "You came

with the TV crew to interview Miss Kim the other afternoon. Well, now she's dead, lying wet on top of the garbage
cans in the court at the back."

"You found her body."

To Sonya's surprise, his eyes filled with tears.

"Yes. I didn't hear her fall. If I had, I might have been able
to help her. It was just by accident. The wind was gusting
hard and whistling around the outside of the building. It was
blowing so hard, I walked around to check if it had done any
serious damage.

"I shined my flashlight through the window and saw her."

He took out his handkerchief and blew his nose loudly.
"She shouldn't have done it. She was just a kid. And she was
so kind. She always asked after my wife and family, and always bought something for them at Christmas."

"The police are here?"

"Yes." He waved his hand toward the courtyard. "You'll
see the yellow tape. Just turn along the corridor over there."

"Did she have any visitors last night?"

"I think a couple of people came by, but she wasn't
available."

"My cameraman will be here in a few minutes. Will you
tell him where I am, please?"

"Sure."

Sonya started to walk away, but she sensed the doorman
had something more to say.

"That woman—her booker from the agency—came in a
few minutes ago. She wanted to see the body and go up to
Miss Kim's apartment."

"Where is she now?"

"I don't know. She knows the building. She came here a
lot. She could have gone up by the back elevator."

Wendy was at the lobby door, looking out onto the courtyard, held back from going out to Kim's body by the yellow
police tape. She was arguing with a policeman.

Sonya stood behind her and listened.

"I just want to see if she left me a note," Wendy pleaded. "I am her representative here in New York. I have her power of attorney, I am her friend, the closest person she has here. Her parents are in Holland. She must have left me a note, and I must be the first person to read it."

"Her apartment and the courtyard are closed until the investigation team gets through with them. I'm sorry, but I can't let you or anyone else in."

Wendy turned away from him. She put her hands up to cover her eyes. "What can I do? What can I tell her parents? Her brother?"

Sonya stepped forward, put her arm around Wendy, and drew her close.

"It's too awful to accept," she said. "I don't believe she committed suicide, Wendy. I don't believe she killed Harriett."

Sonya surprised herself with the strength of her conviction in what she had just said.

"Yes, Sonya. Yes. I know, even in the worst times, when she was really low, she never talked of killing herself. I talked to her two or three times last night and she was okay. She had a fight with Leonard Novelli. It upset her. But she was okay after it."

"He lives in the building, doesn't he?"

"Yes, he has a big apartment on the other side. Kim told me he invited her over for dinner and to watch the show. He was so good to her. And she was grateful to him. This is a fight that should never have happened."

"Why did they fight? What was it about? Something in the show?"

Wendy hesitated. She looked anxiously at Sonya.

"I don't want to get you involved in this," she said. Then she nodded and took a deep breath. "I didn't catch the show, but I'm sure it wasn't your fault. Apparently, you showed some of Leonard's fashion sketches. Ones that he drew with Harriett's face and figure. Some had the word BITCH written across them in red.

"Then Kim came on and said Leonard always scribbled words on his sketches. The show implied that Kim knew who had written BITCH on the sketches, and although she wouldn't say it, it was Leonard. Leonard believes the police will use the sketches to prove he had a motive for murdering Harriett.

"He got furious at Kim. Threw a real fag fit. Kim hadn't realized what she had done. She said she didn't mean it that way. She told him that when you interviewed her, you mentioned the sketches. But she never said Novelli wrote the words on them."

"That's right," Sonya agreed.

"As a matter of fact, Kim believed it was someone else," Wendy continued.

"Who?" Sonya asked urgently.

"She didn't tell me that. She said she picked up the phone to call the police and tell them she knew Novelli was innocent. She would also tell them who she thought was guilty.

"But he grabbed it out of her hand and said he would get Mari to deal with it. And he would tell the police he had nothing to do with it. He told Kim to get out. That he'd had enough of her. And so she went home and called me to tell me all about it."

Sonya thought for a moment. It was easy to see how a nervous Leonard could react that way. She was sorry she had used the sketches in the story. But she knew she had to.

"Wendy," she said, "I can understand how he jumped to that conclusion. But if you listen to the tape, it just doesn't hold up. Besides, Novelli hasn't been in the design room for weeks and the sketches were right on top. Meant to be seen. Maybe someone had done it so Harriett would see. Who knows what went on in that place?"

Wendy motioned to the sofa by the lobby wall. They sat down.

"I told her all that. I said the network would give the police the full interview and that would clear both Novelli and her. So she calmed down."

At that moment, Perry walked in, his camera on his shoulder. Sonya rose to greet him.

"Meeting at crime scenes is getting to be a habit. But next time, let's make it in the middle of the day," he joked.

"That's okay with me," she said. "Kim's body is in the courtyard. We have to wait. When they finish photographing, they'll bring out the body and we can get a shot."

Tears filled Wendy's eyes. "Our beautiful Kim, what a dreadful final shoot. We had such plans for her. She could have been a star for another five or ten years."

"Yes," agreed Sonya. "You believe she could have made it back to the top?"

"Yes, and so did Mari. That's what Mari said to Kim last night."

"Mari saw Kim last night?" asked Sonya.

"No, she was at Novelli's, after Kim left. Mari phoned Kim from there and told her not to be concerned about anything. She said Leonard had calmed down and they would have a meeting to clear everything up."

"So Mari poured oil on the troubled waters? She's great at that."

"Apparently. I spoke to Kim at about eleven at the latest and she was upset, but in no way suicidal."

Sonya motioned to Perry.

"Would you say that on TV for me?" she asked Wendy.

"Oh no, I can't," Wendy sighed. "I've been crying, I'm so upset, I look a wreck."

"Please, for Kim's sake. If you don't believe Kim committed suicide, then someone murdered her. It's up to us to spread the word so her killer can be caught."

"Okay, you're right. I'll do it for Kim. But I'll only say what I believe. Kim was on the way to recovery. She didn't kill herself. Things like that."

Wendy reached into her bag. She took out a mirror and brush and began to smooth her hair.

Sonya said. "I'll only ask a few questions now, but where can I reach you during the day?"

Wendy put her brush and mirror away and pulled out a business card.

"Here are my phone numbers. When we finish the interview, I'll go back to the office. I need to reach Kim's parents. I dread having to do it. But they must hear it from me rather than some reporter."

Perry put his camera on his shoulder, switched on the light, and handed Sonya the mike.

"We're rolling," he said.

TWENTY-FOUR

6:00 AM, Wednesday

Jason Sarnoff lay sleepless in bed, tormented by the thought of more questioning and of his own stupidity.

He turned over and switched on the light. Just 6:00. He rose and put on his black silk bathrobe.

Six o'clock meant noon in Paris. He thought of his mother. As soon as he'd left Franklin's office yesterday he had called and told her as much of the story as he dared. As always, he had received her support and the comfort he so desperately needed.

But even her soothing words did not long ease the mix of fear and guilt that filled Jason's mind and body.

Like a pathetic schoolboy before a grim school principal, he had sat face-to-face with the two detectives and admitted he had searched Harriett's office.

"Explain to us exactly what it was you were looking for?"

It was Harris, the large detective with the smooth, round face who asked the questions. His voice was calm, but Jason could feel the authority it held.

"One of Harriett's red folders. In it were some of my sketches and some photographs of outfits taken in Paris at a fashion show last November. The Jacques Verne spring show."

"And why was this so important to you?"

Jason swallowed hard. He looked at the two figures in their crumpled suits. How could he explain to these tough men the nuances of high fashion?

He went on, feeling naked and defenseless.

"I got slides of Verne's last collection from a photographer I know. I liked Jacques's work, so I studied it. Then I sketched a few of his ideas in some outfits for my collection. Harriett had been spying on me. She had searched my desk, where she found the Verne slides and my sketches. She put them in the folder and said she would take them to Franklin and complain that I had copied Verne's ideas."

"Who is this Jacques Verne?"

"He is a young designer in Paris. He received rave reviews for his last collection. Fashion editors went wild about it. They call him 'the new global trendsetter.' Naturally, I wanted to see what the fuss was all about, so I got some slides. That is all. It is not a crime."

But the detective looked at him so intently, he felt forced to continue.

"Looking at other designers' collections is a must in this business," Sarnoff explained. His voice got higher in spite of his attempts to keep it low. He knew this often irritated people, but it left the men opposite him unmoved. "It is not a matter of copying their designs, but interpreting what is happening, what is the mood of the moment."

This time it was the silent, note-taking detective who spoke.

"You wouldn't call it industrial espionage?" he asked.

Sarnoff spread out his hands in a gesture that begged for understanding.

" 'Industrial'?" he said. "High fashion? No. Never. It is not anything to do with industry. Designers are creative. We are artists. Even Picasso and Matisse watched each other's work."

"So why were you so frantic?"

"Harriett made me frantic. She told me she would use the slides and sketches to convince Franklin that my work was just copies of other designers' ideas. She said she would discuss it with him on Monday morning.

"She said I was too young and inexperienced to be head designer here. That she would take charge of my work and that of my design staff. She would take over my job."

He paused, hoping they would consider the enormity of Harriett's ambitions.

"She was a scheming woman. She had encouraged me to give up my business in Paris and come here. I trusted her, but now I know I was wrong. I think she had a master plan, a plan to take over the whole business and run it her way."

The detectives had looked at each other. And although he watched them closely, Sarnoff could not guess what had passed between them in that fleeting glance.

"Can't you understand what Harriett wanted to do to me?" He bent toward them as he pleaded for sympathy. "She wanted to break my contract, to control my work. She wanted to choose the fabrics with me, to go over my color range, to tell me what sketches I should put in the collection."

His voice trembled as he remembered her demands. Then, in an effort to calm himself, he settled back in his chair, grasping the arms with his hands.

"When I made the agreement with this company, I made it with Isaac, not with Harriett. Harriett had nothing to do with it.

"Isaac wanted me to develop a luxurious style for rich, young women. Young women who want fashion, but who lead increasingly casual lives. I was happy to agree. Between us, we decided that was the way to renew the Franklin name as a leading fashion house."

The big detective interrupted. "Okay. But what about Mrs. Franklin? She must have had some influence?"

"She was a society queen who had never worked in her life. She was a woman who dressed to kill, to make the entrance, to be the star of every event. What she wore was not for the women of today."

He paused again, wondering if the detectives could understand him. They stared at him silently. The note taker had even stopped writing.

"It all was becoming impossible. I knew it, and I knew I would have to do something. Perhaps," he nodded his head, "perhaps leave."

Sarnoff slowly uncrossed his legs, then nervously crossed them the other way.

"But I had signed the contract. A contract that brought me more money than I have ever had. And also, a huge amount of publicity. To walk away from it seemed impossible."

"Well, I don't know much about your business," Detective Harris said. "But I wonder if you didn't feel it was honorable to fulfill your contract and work with your own original ideas?"

"What I did was not dishonorable." He wanted to scream his denial, to make them understand, but he held his temper and went on.

"Trends develop in many ways. It is important to watch what other designers do, if only to *avoid* the appearance of copying. Fashion shows are huge media events. The designer collections are shown immediately on TV, in newspapers, in magazines. If a designer copies another, the press is only too quick to point it out."

"So why did you use Verne's ideas? Or interpret them, as you say?"

"I didn't *make* the outfits. For God's sake, all I did was do some sketches. Don't you see, it was Harriett who was the problem, not my designs?"

His hands started to shake. The detectives had gone on relentlessly.

Sarnoff told the men how, when he found the slides, he had taken them home and destroyed them ruthlessly. Yes, he had cut them into small pieces, until they had been unrecognizable, then thrown them out with the garbage.

"I know I have been very foolish," he said, fighting back tears. "And I knew I would have to tell the truth."

In the end, he told them everything. His dream of becoming the Yves Saint Laurent of the 21st century. The joy of starting his business in Paris and receiving rave reviews from the press. The struggles of never having enough capital to expand the way he wanted.

Then, finally, Franklin and his offer. The move to New York that held so much promise.

He would sell his business to Franklin and pay off his debts. His name would be used on the major Franklin collection, but he would have influence over much more. With his team of assistants, Sarnoff would produce the less expensive lines as well as a range of accessories. And of course there was the perfume, to be introduced shortly. It had been all that he had dreamed of. The break of a lifetime.

Now all he had was the taste of death in his mouth.

"My mother. I did it all for my mother," he lied to the detectives, hoping for sympathy. "Now everything is gone."

With that he had completely broken down. He put his hands over his face and sobbed. Then the detectives had let him go—but not without a final warning. "You are free to go now," the tall one said. "But not to leave the city. We will want to question you further."

But it wasn't all gone, he told himself as he wandered aimlessly around the apartment. Harriett was dead now. He would put his faith in Isaac.

His thoughts were interrupted by the low murmur of his slim black phone.

He picked it up. At this hour, it could only be one person—Leila.

"Kim's dead," she sobbed before he could say a word.

"She can't be. I spoke to her last night. She was perfectly all right. She was going to sleep."

"What do you mean you spoke to her?"

"When I watched the show, I got upset about her comment on the sketches with the word BITCH on them. She implied that Leonard had scribbled BITCH on them. I know for a fact he didn't. He hasn't been anywhere near the design room. Someone did it to set him up—or me. Me, Leila. Do you think someone did it to me?"

He stopped short. Could it have been Harriett herself? Harriett, setting another trap for him? It was a dangerous thought. He couldn't discuss it with Leila.

"I looked through those sketches a few days ago," he continued. "There was nothing written on them. If Leonard wrote BITCH on them, he must have done it in the middle of the night. He fitted Kim's dress for the award dinner at Mari's office. Then I had it picked up from Mari so our workroom could alter it. Harriett wouldn't let Leonard in the Franklin door."

"So what did you do?"

"I called Kim right after the show ended, but her line was always busy. I decided to walk around to see her. I wanted to tell her the truth. When I got to her apartment house, the doorman called her. But she didn't want me to come up.

"I spoke to her over the house phone. She listened to me and said she was glad I'd come. They were having a meeting in the morning to discuss everything. But she was tired and wanted to sleep. I caught a cab and went home."

He paused. "You are sure she is dead? How did she die?"

"I heard it on the radio just now. Early this morning, she jumped out the window. She killed herself." Leila began to sob again. "Jason, you must have been the last person to speak to her."

He sank down onto the sofa as if his legs had given way. "Leila, I have to think. Let me talk to you later."

He hung up and tried to compose himself. He would escape to Paris. The police had told him not to. But his mother would find a way.

TWENTY-FIVE

7:20 AM, Wednesday

Mari St. Clair put the seven-pound weights precisely into their slots. Thirty reps—not bad after a late and troubled night. She glanced around the health club. Almost empty.

She looked at her watch—7:20 AM. She was satisfied to see that as usual, she was right on time. Twenty minutes to shower, dress, and catch the elevator to her office on the 22nd floor.

Mari paced through her company offices as she did at exactly 7:45 every morning. It was a routine she had started 12 years ago when she first moved in. The offices were being decorated then, and she had wanted to make sure the work was on schedule.

Now that walk was almost as necessary to her as breathing. She had to know the office was in total order before she could focus on the day's work. Every morning, she checked every desk in every office to make certain all was neat and orderly. As neat and orderly as she insisted in memo after memo to her staff.

Her shrink told her she had an obsessive-compulsive personality. She knew it caused her problems. The worst were the panic attacks that sometimes surged through her and left her almost paralyzed. If she concentrated on her early mornings in the silent office, usually she could control them.

On the other hand, Mari was convinced that the very same obsessive-compulsive behavior had made her a woman of substance. She owned and ran a company that controlled much of what went on in the world of high-fashion public relations. She did as much work as any three of her account executives. She fine-tuned every piece of copy that left the office.

But she was most proud of the space her offices occupied. Decorating it had cost her a large piece of the money she had inherited from her mother. The look was exactly what her mother would not have wanted. The décor reflected nothing of the past, instead looking toward what the future held. It was a high-style office in a high-tech building.

And how right she had been to spend the money. The elegant offices, looking across midtown Manhattan, had set her business apart from her competitors. The contemporary art, the orchids, the subtle shadings of color spelled money, taste, experience, power.

"My company is about promoting creativity. I represent the best of New York fashion and design, and I want my offices to reflect that," she had told the designer. A designer it had taken her months to select, with whom she had spent hours working out the details.

Her morning walk, as always, started in the washroom. She swung open the door, sniffing the air. It was fresh, although the cleaning woman had too heavy a hand with the French spice spray Mari insisted be used to hide the odor of the cleaning fluid. As Mari sniffed, she could still catch a whiff of it. She would mention it next time she saw the woman.

She often joked to her staff that she was a stickler for tidiness. She watched their faces as they laughed. She knew what they called her behind her back: "Tight-assed, controlling bitch," and worse. Let them.

Mari could feel her anxiety ease as she left the washroom and turned to the offices. Inspecting them was simple. The only office that had a door was hers.

Each desk had to be bare, or at least have the papers on it piled with precision. The wastepaper baskets were to be placed perfectly parallel to the desk.

She was pleased this morning.

Her message had gotten through at last. There wasn't a single untidy surface. There were photos of family on some desks, all of them simply framed so as not to detract from the décor.

She would e-mail the staff and congratulate them on their compliance with her instructions.

She liked to think of her office as a command post. From it emanated the press releases with their myriad photographs, fashion show schedules, brochures, and statements that made the fashion world buzz.

From her command post flowed fashion images and ideas that spread like spiders' webs across America and the entire world.

This morning, the first call Mari would make would be to Leonard Novelli. That was imperative. She went into her office, stopped at the mirror, and fluffed her hair. Fifteen minutes since she'd left the health club and it was almost dry.

When she turned to her desk, the message button was flashing on her private line. She pressed it to check the messages just as another line rang.

"Mari." Sonya's voice was tense. "Are you okay? You

seemed so tired last night. And now this dreadful news about Kim. I can't believe she committed suicide."

"Suicide? What are you talking about?"

"Surely you must have heard—it's all over the news. She jumped out of her apartment window. The doorman found her body early this morning. I got there about four-thirty."

"Sonya, where are you now?"

"At work, waiting for the morning meeting to begin. Matt is still with the local news director. Everyone assumes Kim killed Harriett and because she was guilt ridden, or because she was afraid of getting caught, she killed herself. I don't believe it, Mari, and neither does Wendy Sharp."

"You've talked to Wendy?"

"Yes, she was there this morning when I got to Kim's. She gave me a good interview. Wendy said when she talked to Kim about eleven last night, Kim told her that she was tired but fine. She told Wendy she was planning to meet with you and Novelli this morning."

Mari was surprised at Sonya's naïveté. It was amazing to her that Sonya had failed to realize that Kim had not been fine. How could she be? She had gone on TV and deliberately implicated Novelli about the sketches. Kim was a manipulating bitch, an insecure woman who was out of control.

But even Sonya, like most journalists, had been taken in by Kim's beauty and supermodel glamour.

And now that she was dead, Sonya and the rest of the press would elevate her to the status of a saint.

"The police are sure it was suicide?" Mari asked.

"It's too early to say, but that's what it looks like. We should know more later today. Wendy called Kim's parents in Amsterdam and they're on their way. I'm so sorry for them. They must be devastated. It's tragic, Mari. She was so young."

Mari could take no more. She stood up and walked around her desk to release the tension.

Then she protested, "Sonya, I appreciate how you feel. It's terrible. But I knew Kim. She was not an angel, believe me. Of course, I'm sorry she's gone, but I am not going to fool myself about her. I knew her for what she was.

"Take a good look at some of the clippings about her. Of course Wendy has nothing bad to say about her—she can't afford to. She's Kim's booker, after all, and she made a lot of money from her. But the people who worked with her saw the real Kim. She was a user, she was narcissistic, and she did a lot of harm to innocent people."

"Mari, I had no idea you felt this way. I know she had faults and problems, but she struck me as a basically decent woman."

"Oh, Sonya. I knew her better. Remember the designer Robert Robinson? When he first showed, she promised to be there, but didn't turn up. When he gave up waiting for her an hour later, most of the press had left. That's just one example. Wendy prefers to forget those incidents."

Wendy, Mari thought bitterly, had only two things on her mind. Protecting the reputation of the agency and generating income.

Models and drugs were a major preoccupation with the press, and Kim's recent trip to the rehab clinic had made headlines that caused the agency problems. Of course, Wendy would do anything, say anything, to accommodate Sonya and the powerful *Donna Fuller Show*.

"Of course, you're right, Mari. I can guess what happened last night," Sonya said after a long pause. "I know she had a lot to answer for. But I don't believe she killed Harriett."

Mari replied quickly. "Well, keep me posted," she said. "I'll be out of the office part of the day. But they'll know where I am and I'll have my cell with me. You've got the number. I can see I will have a lot to deal with today."

Mari hung up the phone and sat at her desk, thinking over what Sonya had said. Thinking about Kim.

No, Kim was no angel, she thought bitterly. Novelli had every right to be furious with her. He would never forgive her for the implications she had made on the show last night.

And who would have thought Kim was capable of what she had done? That sweet young girl with the charming Dutch accent. Mari remembered when she had first worked for Novelli. Kim had been an inexperienced 18-year-old, sharing an apartment with two other models from the agency.

Novelli had looked on her as a daughter and she had been almost pathetically grateful for the help he gave her. But you had to give her credit. She had worked hard to succeed.

When Kim's parents had first visited New York, Novelli had been almost as excited as the young model. He had arranged everything, with Mari's help: the car and driver to take Kim to Kennedy Airport to pick them up; the flowers in the hotel room. How proud they had been when he took them all out for dinner. Mari knew he had liked them— Kim's mother, who owned a boutique, and her father, the tall, already stooped professor.

Mari put her hand on the phone to call Novelli. But before she could lift the receiver, it rang again. It was a call she expected. She smiled when she heard Jefferson Tyler's voice.

"I'm glad to know you haven't abandoned your routine," he joked. "I can always catch you at your desk at 8:30. No matter what happens elsewhere. Good old reliable Mari."

"Not so much of the old, thanks," she answered. "Where are you? Still in Cincinnati?"

"No, I got home late last night. I'm in the city and just wondering how I'll make it to Paris. If the blizzard that is pounding the Midwest hits us later in the day, nothing will take off."

"Nothing would surprise me." Mari looked out the window. "It's driving, freezing rain. There's no way to get around town. And I was planning to spend most of the day at outside meetings."

"How about Kim?" Jefferson said, his voice becoming serious. "Mari, I might have been the last person to speak to her."

Mari felt her heart quicken. "When?"

"I spoke to her on my way back from the airport. I was in Cincinnati talking to a client about getting the right image for a new line of bath products they are turning out. I knew Franklin was planning to drop Kim now that Novelli's left. After all, she was Novelli's girl. So I mentioned to my client that Kim might come a little cheaper these days. I told them she was okay now and had gotten a standing ovation at the fashion awards on Sunday night. They were interested, so I called her. I told her it would be a national campaign. Not high fashion, mass market. Excellent exposure for her. And extremely professional people."

"How did she take it?"

"You can imagine. She was really delighted. Said she'd talk to Wendy first thing in the morning."

"Well, no matter how you build it up, it would have been a comedown for her. Can you just see the slinky, stylish Kim selling cheap soap? I'll bet your call just put it in perspective for her. It might have made her see just how much she needed help. How bad things were for her. Maybe that's why she climbed out the window."

"Mari," Jefferson's voice was grave, "I don't believe she did. I know how she sounded when I talked to her. I don't think we know what happened."

He paused. Mari knew him well. He was thinking of all the angles.

He went on. "I tell you, when I spoke to her she was in good shape. She told me she was turning on the answering machine to make sure she got a good night's sleep. What in the world could have happened to make her suicidal?"

"Drugs," Mari shot back quickly. "You've seen how fast she could swing from manic to depressive. It has happened time and time again. Remember how crazy she was when she was on them? Turning up hours late for a sitting, if she turned up at all. Promising never to do it again, and breaking those promises. It's so easy to forget and forgive now that she is dead. But it was the drugs that ruined her life.

"And you were one of her victims yourself. Remember what it cost you when she disappeared in the middle of that campaign? You had to start all over again. What was it? Tens of thousands of dollars?"

"Yes, I remember. I remember very well. But that's past. We'll know more when the coroner's report comes in." Jefferson's voice was becoming detached. Mari picked up on it immediately. He was about to change the subject.

"I'm concerned about Grace," he said.

"You're always concerned about Grace. You treat her as if she were a Ming vase. She is, in reality, one capable lady. She'll survive. We've talked about that before." Mari laughed.

"Well, she drove me crazy last night, talking about the *Donna Fuller Show*. She says there was a shot of Franklin taking something from Harriett's handbag. You were with her at Lily's—what was that all about?"

"Yes, she asked about it. Frankly, it was over so fast I'd have to get the tape and pause it to see clearly. I don't think it was anything. Maybe just a movement of the hand. But don't worry. If it's anything, the police will check it out soon enough."

"Soon enough may not be fast enough." Tyler was only half joking. "You know Harriett was after me to push for her fragrance. She said she would bring me some labels for the perfume bottle she had made up. Maybe that was what he took out of her purse. But I don't know why he would do that. Do you know anything about it?"

"No more than you."

"I'm off to Paris tomorrow. I don't want anything to blow up while I'm away. Can we get together before I leave?"

Mari reached out and looked at the schedule her assistant had printed out neatly the evening before. It was in its place at the top of her in-box, in the clear lightweight folder.

"Maybe later in the afternoon. I'll have to see."

Mari hung up. Then she straightened the papers on her desk, making sure the schedule was back exactly in its right place.

TWENTY-SIX

9:00 AM, Wednesday

Sonya sat impatiently at her desk, drumming her fingers. It was time for the meeting to start.

The staff of the *Donna Fuller Show* occupied half of the 14th floor of the network building. Sonya's office was one of five allotted to the show's producers. Small and compact, the offices were strung out along a narrow corridor that banked high, wide windows. Light streamed in, but the view was only of the glass-fronted building that soared into the gray sky opposite.

The 14th floor was too low to catch the panorama of the city and too high to offer a glimpse of the trees that lined the street. The best thing that could be said about the view was that the glass walls often reflected the patterns of the passing clouds.

Sonya was anxious, restless, but most of all—hungry. And while she was determined to not put on an ounce until her face was healed, she opened her top drawer and searched for a packet of the low-cal mini bagels she kept there for moments such as this.

Then she remembered she had used up the last three late on Sunday night when she had come back from the library. After seeing Harriett's body, she had lost all interest in dinner. But at one in the morning, when she had finished viewing the last videotape, she was famished. Knowing how little food she had in the fridge at home, she had wolfed down the bagels.

Sonya considered walking to the vending machine on the other side of the building to get more. But the meeting could be called any minute, and Matt liked to have them all waiting for him in the conference room. She knew it was a matter of power with him. She thought through the morning's work and went over the events since Sunday night. Was it really only Wednesday? So very much had happened.

The latest news bulletin reported that Kim had died early in the morning. Between one and two on that stormy night. She could have jumped, of course. But if she were sleepy and drugged from the pill she had said she was going to take, it would have been easy for a man to push her through the French doors and lift her over the rails of her tiny balcony.

Of two things Sonya felt certain: This had been no accident and no suicide. And somewhere on her tapes might be a clue as to what had really happened. She had interviewed most of the people at that table. What really was Kim's state of mind? Mari's view of Kim was very different from hers.

The thought of the interviews brought her back to the work that she had ahead of her. Another program was what she hoped for, and not just a segment. She wanted a whole program devoted to her story. That was rare, but she thought she could make a case for it. It would be a career maker.

The only new interview she had set up was with Kim's parents. And that lay in the hands of Wendy, who had promised to call and let her know when their flight was due from Amsterdam.

It was one tough job to plan the hour-long show for Thursday night. Harriett's murder and now Kim's suicide. Or possible murder. Either way, it meant that the story would be breaking news nonstop. And in the 36 hours they had to put the show to bed, anything could happen.

She opened her office door and stood resting her arms on the windowsill, looking out over the bleak, gray buildings. In the background, she heard a door close, and then muted footsteps as someone approached.

"If you're planning to follow Kim, forget it. Those windows don't open."

Sonya shuddered. Matt's humor was intolerable. Joking about Kim, that pathetic broken body lying so helplessly in the courtyard.

"Let's go to Donna's office," he said as he walked toward her. "We have to go over our plan of action for the next show. Kim's death is the mystery of the moment, but the police are rushing the coroner for a report. They're expected to issue a release later this morning."

He mimicked Donna's voice, "Don't go away, we'll be back with more of this story later."

Sonya turned quickly. "Is Donna in already?"

"Yes," said Matt. Sonya knew he was not happy about it. He disliked it when Donna came in early. To Matt it was his show, not Donna's, and he fought against her input as a matter of course.

"She heard the news on the radio and graciously rose from her bed and came in. The ratings were up two points on last night's show. We could top that if we can come up with a winner for this Thursday."

He pushed open the door to Donna's office and let Sonya walk in first.

"I haven't looked at this morning's tapes, but I understand you got an interview with the doorman who found the body and with Kim's booker from the GlamGals Agency," Donna said as they entered.

Sonya nodded, "Yes, Wendy from GlamGals was great. She's convinced that Kim didn't kill herself, and said so in the interview. She's promised to let me know when Kim's parents will arrive from Holland. With luck we'll get first go at them."

Donna Fuller was sitting at the desk, a mug of coffee in front of her. This was the first time Sonya had seen her without full makeup. She looked drawn and thin. Without the highlighter, the shadows under her eyes were deep purple. And without the blush, her cheeks were pale and hollow. There was no doubt Donna had come to the office in a hurry.

"How did Wendy get there so fast?" Matt broke in.

Sonya was equally quick with her answer. "When the doorman found her body, he called Wendy and then he called the police. Kim was a major GlamGals star. I'd guess that Wendy tipped the staff big time so she knew what was going on in Kim's life. She got there barely after the police, and she had to take the time to dress and find a cab. In fact, the doorman more or less directed me to talk to her to get any information I wanted."

Without taking her eyes from Matt, Donna said, "In reality, GlamGals was so concerned about Kim that they had a 24-hour watch on her."

"Yes, in a way that's true." Sonya hesitated. Then, thinking that she had been too hard on Wendy and GlamGals, she added quickly, "But remember, Kim had just gotten back from the rehab clinic, and of course they were concerned that she might slip back into drugs. If she did, they wanted to be there to help."

She went on, although she could sense Matt's impatience. He was shifting from foot to foot. She had often seen him move that way, and it always meant he was unhappy.

"I'm sure Wendy was genuinely fond of Kim. She'd been her booker for years. She got there so fast because she wanted to be on top of what happened, but she also wanted to salvage what she could of Kim's reputation."

"What was the use of protecting Kim's reputation if she was dead?" asked Matt. "Come on, get Wendy to come clean. Why was she so worried about Kim? Did Kim tell her she killed Harriett? How much does she really know? She might give us an exclusive. Tell her it's the living that count, not the dead."

Sonya murmured a protest, and then answered firmly,

"Wendy's no problem. She was totally professional with us when we interviewed Kim on Monday. She did what she could to help me this morning. She honestly doesn't believe Kim committed suicide. She says it on tape. She arranged for me to get first go at Kim's parents when they arrive. I'm not going to ask her for more."

This time it was Donna who interrupted.

"Sonya, you have to distance yourself from this story," she said. "You are a producer for my show. I warned you not to get involved with any of these people. I warn you again. This is a murder we're facing. I agree with Matt that Wendy could be lying to protect Kim's reputation. Kim was not some young innocent. The police believe she was on something, probably coke, on Sunday night. She was smart enough not to talk to them until her attorney arrived. He refused to let her give a urine sample. I know they found nothing in her handbag. But she had plenty of time to flush away the evidence."

Sonya started to reply, but Donna cut her off again.

"Kim was wily—a drug addict who knew all the tricks, how to hide her stash, how to lie, how to manipulate, to put the blame on other people. If she killed Harriett, which seems likely, she has left a family motherless. Isaac Franklin has three young children to bring up by himself. Their lives will never be the same again."

Sonya sat silent. She felt Donna was being harsh, even unrealistic. Then she remembered the bitterness and pain of her own father's death. As usual, Donna was right. At least about that.

But whatever Donna or Mari or anyone else said about Kim, Sonya was convinced that Kim had not killed Harriett and that she had not committed suicide. Sonya knew her own instincts. She respected Donna, but trusted herself.

"As for Wendy," Donna went on, "yes, she probably had some feelings for Kim, but the reality is that at heart she is a tough businesswoman. She has to be, to get where she is."

Matt spoke. "Did Wendy get into Kim's apartment before the police arrived?"

"No, she was too late. The apartment was taped off along with the crime scene. The police weren't taking any chances."

"Did Wendy know Kim's reaction to the show?"

"Yes, because Kim phoned her and told her about it. Kim watched it with Leonard Novelli at his apartment. He was upset with her. So she got upset. They had a fight and he told her to leave. That's what Wendy said."

"Why?"

"Apparently, and I'm quoting Wendy again, he thought Kim had pointed at him as the person who had written the word BITCH on the sketches we showed. So he felt the police would suspect he was Harriett's murderer."

"Do we have Novelli on tape?" Matt broke in.

"Yes," Donna said, before Sonya could answer. "There's the interview Sonya did at the party on Sunday night. It was pretty innocuous, just talking about the award he got. But I'm sure somewhere in that interview there's a sound bite we can use, if we can't get anything else."

Matt turned to Sonya.

"Can you get hold of him?"

"Yes. And of course I can ask Mari. The interesting thing is that he lives in the same apartment house as Kim. It's an old building, with several elevator banks. He could easily have gone to her apartment and killed her without anyone seeing him."

Sonya was making a wild, half-hearted guess to tease Matt. She knew he would take the bait. Anything for ratings.

"Wow," said Matt. "Suspect number one."

"Don't jump the gun, Matt," Donna cautioned, her irritation plainly showing. "I agree we should get an interview with him, and as soon as possible. But we have to be extremely careful. If the guy's not guilty, we can't make out that he is. We can't leave ourselves wide open to a lawsuit."

"Don't worry, Donna," Matt said condescendingly. "I've got the chairman on my back already. When in doubt, I'll send the interviews to the attorneys."

Sonya smiled. But she had to admire the way Matt handled himself. He was a master at shifting positions.

But Donna wasn't having any of it. With great seriousness, she lectured Matt. "Just remember, whatever we run, it mustn't smear the show. Our reputation is too good for sensationalism to hurt it."

Sonya felt the tension mounting. She changed the subject. "How soon will the coroner's report come in, Matt?"

"They're rushing it through. That's what I learned from the news department. With luck, they'll release a statement this morning."

"Then we'll just have to wait and see," Donna said. "For now, Sonya, what about the rest of the guests at this round table? Let's have a quick run-through and see what we come up with."

"There is one thing," Sonya offered. "One of the detectives told me most murders are committed by family members. The one family member at Harriett's party was her husband. I think the guy was trying to impress me and maybe get into the story. He didn't offer any proof, of course."

"Franklin?" queried Donna, "Murder his wife? I don't think so. He was devoted to her and the children. A family man."

"That doesn't mean he wouldn't kill her."

"No," replied Donna, "you're right. But he doesn't get my vote."

"Actually," added Sonya, "from what I saw of Harriett at that dinner, there probably were lots of people who couldn't stand her. And I'll bet most—or even all—of the people at that table had a motive to kill her."

"A round table of ten. Two of them dead. You, of course, Sonya, then seven others. Seven men and women who knew Harriett Franklin."

"Right, Donna. Seven people who'd seen her absolutely despicable behavior at the table, and watched her go to the ladies' room. Seven people who could have picked up the letter opener and stabbed her to death."

Matt spoke: "Let's talk about the ones we haven't interviewed."

"Lily," mused Donna. "A magazine editor known for her

corrupt approach to her work. She took everything she could from the Franklins. She doesn't earn all that much and neither does her husband at that political magazine. The rumor in the trade was that Franklin gave them a loan to buy that house in Connecticut. No proof, of course, but it was obvious at a glance it was above their means. And who else would lend them the money?"

"Then there's Grace Tyler, Jefferson's wife," Sonya picked up.

Donna continued, "Tyler was there with you at the murder scene, wasn't he? You left him to walk to the ladies' room where you discovered Harriett's body."

"Yes. He was on Franklin's side in the feud over the new fragrance that Harriett wanted named for her. He is tough, but I found him flaky at the same time. He is an Israeli and was in their army. I looked up his bio. He ran a parachute school. He looks smooth, but he's a strong man. Probably capable of murder."

"And his wife, Grace?" Donna asked.

"I don't know much about her, but I don't think she is the docile suburban wife she appears to be. I understand she's the one who actually owns the business her husband runs. She knows how to get what she wants."

"Well, I do know something about her. We have a mutual friend who told me she decided to marry Jefferson the moment she saw him. She fights tooth and nail to keep him. He's very attractive, as I'm sure you have noticed," said Donna with a smiling nod to Sonya.

"It's my impression she and Harriett have known each other for years," Sonya added, ignoring Donna's suggestion. "I understand they rarely mix socially. But I am not sure what is behind that."

"Don't forget Mari St. Clair. She was at that table too," added Matt.

"A force to be reckoned with," said Donna. "I don't trust her. Her mother was my godmother."

"Really?" asked Sonya. "That's odd. Mari never mentioned that to me in all this time. Does she know that about you?"

"Yes, but I don't know her well. I grew up hearing tales of Mari's misbehaving. Everything from deliberately breaking her mother's glasses to killing a cat."

Sonya had just heard that story from Mari. "I thought it was the other way around. The way I heard it the mother was the problem."

Matt laughed. "Whatever. Let's get an in-depth interview with her."

"Okay," Donna said. "Maybe it's time to hear her side of her mother's stories. But the other three come first. I don't think we should interview Mari in her office. It may be the latest thing in contemporary architecture, but it will look as if we are pushing her business. Do a fast one in the studio."

"Yes," said Matt. "She'll be the easiest to get, so do it later, in the studio. It will save us time in editing. Maybe we'll be lucky and hit the jackpot with one of them. Leonard Novelli, Grace Tyler, Lily whatever her name is . . . or Mari St. Clair. Which one would you pick?"

Matt looked directly at Sonya, but she avoided his eyes.

"It could have been anyone. Anyone in the room. Or for that matter a crank, a fashion groupie, a friend. Anyone," she insisted.

But Sonya knew it was someone at that table. Harriett had assembled them as if for the final scene of a play.

"We may know as soon as the autopsy comes through," said Donna. "If Kim was killed, it was by the same person who murdered Harriett, and it is very likely that person was sitting with you on Sunday."

"The round-table murders. Sounds like an Agatha Christie thriller. Or like that old party game where you pick a person that you dislike and describe how you would kill them if you got the chance. You know the old game, 'One Die, Two Die,' " said Matt, laughing.

Then he added, "Do your interviews, Sonya. I want Novelli, Grace Tyler, and the magazine editor today. Tomorrow, Mari St. Clair. We are going to devote the whole Thursday show to this story, Sonya. Your story, Sonya. So work fast. We have to be covered, whatever breaks."

"Yes," said Donna intensely. "But be careful. I have an eerie feeling, Sonya. The killer could strike again."

But Sonya wasn't listening to Donna. She had only heard what Matt said. Her story. A whole program.

TWENTY-SEVEN

11:00 AM, Wednesday

Frustrated, Sonya slammed down the phone. She had only reached Mari's voice mail. Ditto Novelli's. And Lily was out of touch—at a meeting with her publisher.

That left Grace. And by all counts, Grace was the least interesting interview of the four she had to do. In fact, Grace, the suburban socialite with her little-rich-girl background, was the least interesting of all of those sitting at the table on Sunday night. A night that seemed to Sonya to be eons past.

She called the Tylers' apartment. No answer. At the office, the same sweet-faced blonde with the Midwestern accent answered the phone.

"Mr. Tyler returned very late last night. He left a message that he will be in late. He is not to be disturbed. I believe Mrs. Tyler left to go back to Connecticut," she said. "Do you want the home number there?"

Sonya thanked her and scribbled it down. "Does Mrs. Tyler have a cell phone?"

"I'm sure she must have," came the smug, corporate reply. "But I don't have it and in any case we are not permitted to give out cell numbers. They're private."

Sonya quickly dialed the Connecticut number. Grace had not yet arrived and the maid did not know when to expect her.

It seemed the whole morning would pass before she could even make a connection, let alone get one of the interviews Matt had so freely ordered. But she was determined to have them for her program.

If she could get hold of Jefferson, she was sure he would set up something for her. But where was he? Anywhere, she told herself. He was a man who liked to keep moving. The thought of him flirting with her as they walked toward the powder room brought a smile. Donna was right. He was attractive.

The powder room, she remembered. Maybe she did have his cell number, after all.

He had scribbled a cell number on the back of the card he had given her that night. In the horror of finding the body, she had forgotten what he'd said as he'd written it. It was worth trying. What if she did disturb him? It was already past ten.

She quickly dialed the number. Two rings and the phone clicked on.

"Jeff? Is that you?" came an anxious pleading voice. "Jeff, I am so worried about you. I'm sitting here waiting for you at the apartment."

Sonya realized Jeff had given her Grace's number, not his own.

She pretended she hadn't heard Grace's plea. She kept her voice cheerful. "Hello, hello," she said. "Is that you, Grace? Grace, it's Sonya Iverson from the *Donna Fuller Show*. How are you?"

"Yes, of course. I recognized your voice, Sonya. I'm as upset as everyone over the dreadful news about Kim. Jeff spoke to her late last night and she seemed to be fine. But then she was only as okay as anyone can be when—you know," she hesitated, "when they've come off a drug dry out."

Sonya softened her voice. "Yes, I understand. I was there

this morning when the police were examining her body. It is so hard to believe that she committed suicide."

"Yes, Jeff finds it difficult too. He had talked to her and told her there was the possibility that she would be asked to do a national campaign. He said she was quite excited about it."

Grace paused, and Sonya heard her swallow as if she had taken a drink.

"But then," Grace continued, "we have to remember the drugs. She was seriously in trouble before she went to the clinic. They do wonderful work, but who knows how successful the treatment was for Kim. To be honest, Sonya, I don't want to think that she was murdered. If she were, it was probably by Harriett's killer. Who would be next? We weren't the happiest of tables on Sunday night, but we all knew each other. We knew each others' frailties, but everyone had a certain dignity. Now, my God, everything seems to have been stripped from us."

Grace's voice was thickening. She was on the verge of weeping. Sonya felt it was now or never. Grace was rambling and not making much sense. But her interview had to be part of the story.

"Grace," she said briskly, "I would be so grateful if you could help me out. Donna wants me to get a brief interview with the rest of the people who sat around the table on Sunday. Would you mind if my cameraman and I came to see you in a few minutes? It would only take a short while."

"Oh no. No, no," she stuttered.

Sonya waited. She heard Grace take another swallow before she continued.

"What do you want me to talk about?"

"Well basically, about Harriett."

"That's all?"

"Well, yes."

"Does Mari know about this?"

"No, not yet. I called and left a message, but she hasn't gotten back to me."

"Okay then, that's all right." Strangely, Grace seemed relieved that Mari wasn't involved. "There's not much to say.

Everyone already knows that Harriett and I knew each other. We went to the same college. She wasn't a close friend, but we did spend time together. After that we didn't see each other much. We lived two different lives. Me with my three babies, Harriett with her charities. That's all I can talk about."

"Thank you, that'll be fine. Save all of that for when we are there doing the interview." Sonya felt relieved. "We'll be over as fast as the traffic will allow. I hope we won't disturb Jeff. His secretary told me he was sleeping."

Grace gave a sudden harsh laugh.

"Not Jeff," she said. "He's out. Told me he was going for a walk. Told me to go back to Connecticut." Her voice slurred. "But if I do, I'm frightened I won't see him again."

Sonya paused. For some reason, Grace was desperate. She was drinking early in the morning. What was going on between her and Jeff?

"Not see him again?" Sonya was walking on delicate ground. She had to be careful and comforting. "You can't mean it. Jeff isn't in any danger, surely?"

Grace laughed in that strange way again. "You're right. Not Jeff. He knows how to look after himself. Maybe it's everyone else who is in danger. Come over. I'll be here. I promise."

The sun was struggling through the gray clouds as Sonya walked to Perry's van. The city was settling down after the storm. Even the traffic sensed that a thaw was on the way. The gridlock had eased. There was more movement. The horns were still honking, but to Sonya's ear they were less frantic. Or perhaps it was that she was not listening as carefully as usual. She was wondering what Grace had meant.

It was always quicker to go in the van with Perry than wait for her own car and driver. His press plates gave him the right to a parking spot. But even if he had to search, he would drop her at the building so she could get the interview organized before he came. Perry was waiting for her, his *Daily News* propped up on the steering wheel. He grinned at her.

"How's the face this morning? Be careful you don't get sunburn."

Sonya smiled back. He was a joy to work with. And as usual, he found a parking space. Sonya breathed deeply as they climbed the steps to the Tyler private pied-à-terre. She hoped Grace would not be too much of a mess for the camera. If she were, Sonya could call downstairs to the cool blonde and see if the Tyler business had a makeup artist on hand.

But when Grace opened the door, it was obvious she had made an effort to get herself together.

"Mari's not with you?" she asked tentatively. Sonya thought Grace looked relieved and wondered why. Grace pressed further. "Mari will call if she is coming, won't she?"

"I imagine so. As I said to you on the phone, I haven't spoken to Mari."

"Good," said Grace, in better control of herself. "Now, where would you like to do the interview?"

Sonya looked around the room. Contemporary furniture, contemporary paintings. Chic, but not very comfortable.

"The designer just finished," said Grace. "It reminds you of Mari's office, doesn't it? Jeff liked the look so much, he decided to hire the same decorator. I like it too. It's exciting to come here after our more traditional home."

"How long have you known Mari?" Sonya asked.

"A long time," replied Grace. "At first only slightly, but when Jeff decided to work on the Franklin's perfume, she became a much more important part of our lives. Now it seems she is always around, telling Jeff what to do and what not to do with the business."

"I know Mari is very capable, with definite ideas. You didn't have someone doing press relations before?"

"No, my father thought it was completely unnecessary. In a way, I suppose he was old-fashioned. Certainly a different generation. But he believed our job was to produce good-quality products and stay away from the hype."

This was a new Grace. Maybe it was the wine that had loosened her, or maybe it was the absence of Jefferson. But whatever it was, she was much more accessible. Sonya began to look forward to the interview.

Grace poured herself another glass of wine and took a large swallow.

When Perry was set up, he called, "Tape rolling."

Sonya decided to begin the interview by asking Grace directly about her relationship with Harriett.

"How long did you know Harriett?"

"My father was responsible for Harriett's marrying Franklin," Grace said. "I was supposed to go to Mexico with her after we graduated. She planned it for months, every place, every peso.

"I was forced to cancel at the last moment, and that left Harriett short of money. My father made it up to Harriett so she could do it alone. I'm sure Harriett didn't spend it rashly. In those days, that was one of the things I liked about her. She focused on what she wanted. She was determined to have a rich and a full life. To be someone important."

"And how did you feel about that?" asked Sonya.

"I just let things happen to me. It took Harriett to make me realize you had to go after what you wanted. If you like something, then grab it. Anyway, in Oaxaca, Harriett met Isaac Franklin, who took her under his wing. They were married when they got back to New York."

"You must have been close to plan such a trip together."

"Looking back, I suppose I was. But I was young and naive. I believed people too easily. I didn't realize what Harriett was really like."

Sonya looked at Perry, who had been working quietly in the background.

"How was that? What was she like?"

Grace laughed. She seemed to have forgotten the mike pinned to her blouse.

"It was my father who really had the relationship with Harriett. She was a beautiful woman, as you saw. But when she was young, she was ravishing. And she moved like a goddess. My father couldn't take his eyes off her. He encouraged me to keep up our friendship. Perhaps he hoped that I would pick up some of her poise.

"But Dad was fooled like the rest of us. She was a manipulator. She wanted everything her way and she didn't care what she had to do to get it. She was a vile woman. She had an angle on everything, a hold on everyone."

Sonya hardly breathed. She didn't want to do anything to interrupt.

"She had some hold over my husband. I know it. I know it. I believe she was using whatever it was to get my husband to help her. Help her to force poor Isaac to launch the Franklin fragrance in her name."

Grace looked away from Sonya. She stopped speaking abruptly, then called out, "Here's Mari." Her face twisted in anger. She raced on with abandon. "Mari, what was it that Harriett held over my husband? What's the secret? You know everything. Let it out. And what's more, do you know where my husband is right now?"

Sonya turned. Mari was standing at the doorway, a slim figure in a dark coat. As she looked, Mari moved swiftly past her and put her hand over the camera lens.

"Grace, you've been drinking," she said. "You are doing yourself and your husband nothing but harm."

Mari blocked the camera's view and reached forward to unpin the mike on her shirt.

"Sonya, I'm sorry to have to do this. But let's finish it now; I'm sure you must have enough. More than enough."

Grace began to weep softly.

Mari unbuttoned her coat, threw it over one of the Philippe Stark chairs, and moved to Sonya.

"Sonya, Grace is overwrought. She needs to rest. I hope you won't mind just packing up."

"Of course," said Sonya. She signaled to Perry, then turned back to watch the two women. Mari was standing near Grace.

"Everything is okay with Jeff. He called me and said he was going to take a walk to clear his head. He had an early meeting, and then had to go to a follow-up conference about the Cincinnati deal. He's there now. Why are you so upset?"

"Does he know where I am?"

"Yes. I checked my messages, and got Sonya's telling me she was about to interview you. I told him. He has to fix the final details before he leaves for Paris, so he asked me to come and make sure you got home to Connecticut. He is concerned about the children."

"You know Jeff spoke to Kim last night?"

"Yes, he told me."

"Did he tell you that she was hysterical?"

"No, he didn't. Grace, you are imagining things. I'm going to call the service and order a car and driver to get you home right now."

"No." Grace was adamant. "I'm waiting for Jeff. There is something going on. I don't know what it is, but I want to find out."

Mari bent over, took Grace by the shoulders, and looked directly into her eyes.

"Grace, you are just causing problems. Consider what Jeff has on his plate. This Cincinnati deal is enormous, and he has to be available for discussions whenever their CEO wants him.

"Then he has to work with Isaac to finalize the plans for the launch of the Franklin fragrance. That must go on. Isaac is a wreck. He needs Jeff's support both for the business and his boys. Jeremy is still an enormous worry. He is refusing to speak.

"And then there are the police. They are planning to interview everyone who spoke to Kim last night. He may have to face their questions today. All this, and tomorrow he has to be on the plane for the meeting in Paris. So, for God's sake, can't you just keep yourself together and cut him a little slack?"

Grace sank back into her chair. She closed her eyes and took a deep breath.

"Jeff is also the father of my three children. He has a responsibility to us. Business is not everything in life. But yes, I know. These are difficult times."

Grace seemed drained of energy.

"All right. Order the car. I'll go home like the good girl I am," she said sarcastically. "I'll take care of the kids. Maybe he'll come home later."

She reached for her drink, but Mari took it from her.

"Get your coat," she said. "I'll have the car here in minutes."

As Mari dialed the number, she waved Sonya and Perry to the door.

"Time to go," she said. "I'll call Novelli and Lily, if you like, as soon as I'm through here. I'll get you on your cell."

"Thanks, Mari."

As Sonya walked past her, on the way to the door, Grace reached out and took her hand. "Oh, Sonya. He is so troubled. I am desperately worried. I wanted him to come home and spend the evening with the children before he flies to Paris."

Mari moved toward them, rolling her eyes upward in exasperation. But nothing would stop Grace.

"I have a premonition that something dreadful will happen. That we will never again live together as a family."

TWENTY-EIGHT

11:15 AM, Wednesday

Ragú was, as always, the attention-getter on the sidewalk. For that reason, Leonard Novelli was protective of him. The small dachshund stopped to sniff at a tree trunk, and Novelli watched warily as a two-year-old boy waddled toward him.

"No, darling," Novelli said sweetly to the toddler. "He doesn't like being touched. He is a little dog and he gets frightened easily." The child hesitated, disappointed, then gained courage and took two more steps toward Ragú. Then he turned and ran back to his mother.

Novelli looked down at the dog. Ragú turned his head and gazed at him with devotion. Novelli's eyes filled with tears.

His voice was a whisper. "Ragú," he said. "Yes, Ragú, Harriett was buried quietly this very morning. So many deaths and so many betrayals. You are my love, Ragú, the only love left in my life. You adored Kim as much as I did. She found you for me. But we mustn't regret her death. She should never have done the things she did."

As if to protect himself from the despair he was feeling, Novelli bent and picked up the dog, holding him close to his chest. He stood with his face raised to the warmth of the sunshine, finding comfort in the wet licks Ragú slobbered on his chin and face.

Ragú was now eight years old. He had been born in Italy and brought here by Kim. Novelli's old dog had died while Kim was modeling in Milan. When she returned to New York three days later, she carried Ragú off the plane with her. He was jet black, his pointed face and inquisitive eyes wise beyond his three months.

A joyous, yapping bundle. Novelli had started to protest about a new dog, but one look at Ragú and he fell in love.

Still holding the dog, he walked to the end of the block, looking at the traffic moving slowly up the avenue. A wave of exhaustion swept over him. Life had no meaning for him. But he must gather his strength. He had decided what to do, and how to do it. He had the gun. He would go to his private studio a few blocks away. Few people knew about it, and his body would not be discovered for days.

He had made the decision late last night after the fighting with Kim had come to an end. That Kim was still on drugs had been so apparent. The pleasant dinner he had planned for her had turned into a bitter argument.

It had started when she had refused to eat the meal he had so carefully prepared.

"I'm just not hungry," she had insisted. "Stop trying to force me to do what you want. I'm tired of your nagging me. I've learned how to manage my own life. And I intend to do just that."

He had pointed out she was too thin, even for a model.

"I can never be too thin," she said. Then she had stood in front of the mirror, squeezing the minuscule roll of flesh on her hip. "See, I still have too much flesh here."

But the worst of it had been the *Donna Fuller Show*. It was malicious of her to have implied that he wrote BITCH on those sketches of Harriett. She knew it was just not true.

He was HIV positive. Despite all the drugs, ultimately he

was a man under a death sentence. What had he to do with petty maliciousness? He was long past that.

The old Kim would have protected him, whatever she thought. Whatever she knew.

When he came down from his apartment to take Ragú on his morning walk, he had desperately wanted to connect with Kim again. To see her. To say he was sorry.

He had walked along the corridor to see where her body had fallen. But the courtyard was cordoned off with yellow police tape. He had leaned across the tape, craning forward to see if anything was left to remind him of her. To have some memory of her last moments. But there was nothing.

She now lay in the still coldness of the morgue waiting for the autopsy. Mourn her passing. That was all he and the world could do.

Kim was the most beautiful and famous person living in the apartment house. Novelli felt the pall her death had cast over the building. Even the cleaner, vacuuming the hall, seemed to move more slowly and quietly. The doormen spoke more softly; footsteps clicked more gently on the tiled floors.

He reached the end of the block, still holding the dog in his arms. He leaned against the phone booth for a moment, and then slipped coins into the slot.

His plan was to call Mari and tell her he was going to the country. With luck, he would only reach her voice mail and spare himself her lecture on staying in the city. The police would want to question him. But enough was enough.

He dialed her cell number. He was in luck. Voice mail picked up after the eight beeps.

"Mari, it's Leonard," he said. "I have to get out of the city. I'm on my way to the house in the country. I'll call you from there."

She had one of those devices on her phone that enabled her to check the number he called from, he was sure. She might recognize it as a public phone. She would believe he had left his apartment. He had plenty of time to make the arrangements.

He went into the building and walked silently to the bank of elevators that served his apartment.

"Oh, Mr. Novelli," the doorman called. "Put the radio on when you go upstairs. Word has come through that Kim Kelly was murdered. She didn't commit suicide after all."

Novelli felt as if he had been hit in the stomach. His heart began to pound.

He waved acknowledgment to the man, clutched Ragú even tighter, and pressed the button for the 10th floor. How had they found out so quickly?

He sank into the bench at the back of the elevator. He burrowed his face into Ragú's tiny neck. "I will do it," he whispered. "And when I go, you will go with me. It will be painless. You will not know what is happening."

He opened his door, placed Ragú carefully on the carpet, and switched on the radio, tuning in to an all-news station. The doorman was right. After a brief commercial, the announcer said clearly, "Here is a news update. Police are now treating the death of supermodel Kim Kelly as a homicide. The 25-year-old, whose body was found early this morning, was at first believed to have committed suicide. In a statement released an hour ago, the police say a full murder investigation is under way, and until that is complete they will have no further statement."

Novelli switched off the radio and went into his closet. He needed to take nothing with him but he wanted the doorman to believe he was going to the country. He picked up the Fendi bag he usually took and threw a few sweaters in it. He put the bag on the dining room table and walked into the bathroom. He then went carefully through the rooms to make sure all was in order. It didn't matter, but that was his way.

The phone rang. He froze. It might be Mari, checking on him. Or the police. But when the answering machine picked up, he heard the voice of Isaac Franklin—a desperate Isaac Franklin.

"Leonard," Isaac said. "If you are there, please pick up the phone. Jeremy is sinking into a depression. He won't speak. I don't know how to help him. Call me. I am at home."

Novelli reached out and picked up the phone.

"What do you mean, he won't speak?" he said.

"Thank God you are there. It started yesterday. When he is not sitting slumped into a chair, he is wandering around looking for his mother. I think I made a terrible mistake bringing him home. He can't cope with being here. And I should never have taken him to the funeral this morning."

"You took him to the funeral?"

"Yes, I felt it was the right thing to do."

"My poor Jeremy. Has he eaten anything?"

"A little. Some soup last night and a mashed banana this morning."

"Have you called the doctor?"

"Of course. He advised me to get him out of the apartment for a while. He needs to be quiet, with someone he knows and likes. Someone who understands him."

"But surely the apartment will be overflowing with your friends paying their respects."

"Leonard, when it comes to Jeremy, you know the only person I can rely on is you. Could you come up and be with him for a few hours? Or better still, take him to your studio? Remember how he loves to go there and paint with you."

It was true that the boy thought of him as an uncle. In the early years he had taught Jeremy to draw, to recognize colors, to identify different fabrics.

Shortly after the Franklins had adopted Byron and Henry, Jeremy had been sent to the clinic. Novelli had been surprised at how much he missed the boy and had visited him often. And Jeremy had visited him too, the few times Harriett had permitted him to come to New York.

Novelli sighed. It was all too much. He had nothing left to give to this boy or anyone else.

He protested. "I can't, Isaac. Not right now. I'm on my way to the country. I've made my plans. Everything is set."

"Go tomorrow," Isaac pleaded. "Spend today with Jeremy. Remember, he is just a kid. He loved his mother. Now she's gone. He hardly knows his brothers. He doesn't have his usual routine, his playmates. He is at a total loss. He needs someone familiar to be with him. He won't have anything to do with me."

"Can't you send him back to the clinic?"

"I've talked it over with Dr. Hoffman, but he is not willing to have him today. He says Jeremy will feel even more rejected if he is sent back so quickly."

"What did the tests show? Did the fall do any damage?"

"No, he's okay. It is just his inability to understand and cope with Harriett's death. God knows why, but he loved her to distraction."

Novelli heard bitterness in Isaac's voice. He was remembering Harriett, remembering her neglect of her son. In that moment, Novelli wondered if their mutual hatred of Harriett was the bond that held him so strongly to Isaac. They came from different backgrounds and had few interests in common. But sometimes Novelli thought they were like brothers. Brothers who would come to each other's aid, no matter what angry words had passed between them.

But now it was too late. He had no more to give. He wanted to die.

"Isaac," he said. "I'm so tired. There is nothing I can do for anyone. Not even Jeremy."

"Oh for God's sake, Novelli. Stop it," Isaac retorted. "We are all tired. We are all depressed. There is plenty for you to do. You are a courageous, compassionate man. Turn your talents to Jeremy. Let me tell him you are coming. Can you be here in half an hour?"

Novelli glanced down at Ragú. The dog jumped up on his leg, his tail wagging. The man reached down and rubbed his head.

"Yes," he said. "Okay. I'll catch a cab there, but you'd better have a car and driver take us to my studio."

"Just get to my apartment," Isaac responded. "I'll drive you down myself."

* * *

Novelli believed that Ragú was responsible for Jeremy's short-lived happiness. The little dog seemed to know he had a job to do and greeted Jeremy as a long-lost friend. He ran in circles around the slumping adolescent standing sullenly in the hallway.

Then, in the car as they drove down to the 31st Street studio, Ragú left Novelli's arms and jumped onto Jeremy, his long pink tongue licking the boy's face. Novelli lifted him off and then raised his hand, pretending to spank him.

"Don't," murmured Jeremy. "He's a good dog. He didn't hurt me."

Novelli lowered his hand. "I wouldn't have hurt him, Jeremy. I'm just trying to teach him not to be so wild with people he likes."

Jeremy turned from his father when they arrived at the studio. Franklin bent down to kiss him good-bye, but the boy walked away. Novelli saw the pain in Isaac's eyes. The boy blamed his father for his mother's death. Would they ever be reconciled? Because of Jeremy's condition, it wasn't likely.

Isaac murmured a soft thank-you to Novelli. Then he added, "Call me on my cell when you're ready and I'll send the car to bring you both back to the apartment. I expect people to be coming by all through the evening."

Novelli let Jeremy carry Ragú inside. He watched him kiss Ragú before he put him down gently on the floor.

Jeremy settled beside Novelli at the small table he had come to call his own. He took great pains with his drawing. There was no doubt it gave him pleasure.

Novelli ordered hamburgers and French fries from a nearby coffee shop for an early lunch. Jeremy demolished the fries in minutes. Then he got sleepy. Novelli settled him on the sofa, covered him with a rug, and let him rest.

He looked down at him and smiled. Jeremy could give him a reason to live.

* * *

The phone shrilled, but Jeremy didn't stir.

"Novelli, at last I've found you," Wendy's voice was filled with relief. "It took me a dozen calls to track you down. I want you to do me a favor."

"Who told you where I was?"

"Franklin, but only after I told him why I wanted you. Kim's parents will arrive shortly. Because you were so important to Kim, they asked for you. I want you to meet with them tonight. Imagine the state they are in. And they don't even know she was murdered—that was announced after they got on the plane. I'll meet them at the airport and take them to Franklin's apartment. Then they will want to see the police."

"Wendy, why do you need me? After all I faced with your supermodel last night, I don't think I want to see them. I am through with Kim and her family."

"Leonard," Wendy almost screamed, "she is dead, murdered. We need to stand together on this. For all our sakes, for the industry, for what we once meant to each other."

"I can't face that craggy old professor and the overly made-up mother. And what about that brother—he despised Kim. Is he coming too?"

"No, as far as I know, just the parents. They were lucky to get two seats on the flight."

"Wendy, I just don't have the energy. She was a junkie, she sold drugs, she ruined people's lives. God knows what the police will find when they search her apartment. It terrifies me to think of what she hid there."

"The police will find nothing in her apartment. I can promise you that."

"How can you be so sure? You know how she stashed pills around the place."

"The police will find nothing. I searched every hiding place, and believe me the police will find nothing."

"When? You saw her late in the afternoon. You couldn't have searched while she was in the apartment. And even if you did, her drug-taking buddies could have dropped by and left her a load."

"I am sure. I was there early this morning, after she was killed."

"You saw her dead in the apartment?"

"No, of course not. Oh God, Leonard. Promise me you will never tell a soul. When the doorman called and said he had found her body in courtyard, I immediately assumed it was suicide.

"I wanted to make sure that if there was a note, I got it first. So I slipped up the back stairs and used my key to get in. I didn't find a note. Then I searched for pills. I'm not telling you what I found, but I took everything with me.

"Then I went downstairs and deceived the police, asking permission to go into the apartment. It wasn't easy. I know what I did was illegal. But I did it to protect Kim."

Leonard was silent.

"Now that we know she was murdered, I realize I have violated a crime scene. But Kim's name is safe. There'll be no stories about drugs found in her apartment after her death."

"Wendy, I won't say I approve of what you did. But I guess I'm glad you did it. Kim's parents will be spared."

"I loved her, Leonard. I tried so hard to protect her from drugs. But she traveled so often. Where she went, drugs were the done thing. She was only human. And she was really trying to lick it."

Leonard agreed to see Kim's parents. Then he hung up and he sat on the sofa beside Jeremy. The boy's deep breathing calmed him. Ragú jumped on his lap. The boy stirred. Then the phone rang again.

Jeremy opened sleepy eyes and watched as Novelli answered.

It was Mari. Sonya Iverson wanted another interview. Immediately. She wanted to talk about his relationship with Kim. Just three easy questions.

Novelli looked at the boy. "What about it, Jeremy?" he grinned. "Shall we let Sonya and her TV camera come here for an interview? You know Sonya. She's got red curly hair and she's pretty."

Jeremy looked up at him and smiled. "Yes," he said. "I like pretty girls."

TWENTY-NINE

4:30 PM, Wednesday

Sonya felt the change in mood as soon as she started down
the corridor toward Lily's executive suite. The offices on either side of the fashion magazine floor were strangely silent.
Instead of the bustle of the clothes racks being rolled from
one room to another, or glimpses of young editors busily going over layouts, doors were closed.

What had happened? She shook her head. For a moment
she had forgotten. Of course, it must be Kim's murder.

The staff here had worked with her, posing her for hundreds of photos. Dressed her up, changed her accessories,
and tried different types of makeup and hairstyles. Taken her
on countless trips. Kim's death must have given them, young
as they were, a sense of their own mortality.

Sonya turned the corner. Ahead lay Lily Allen's executive
suite. Everything was quiet there as well. The desks of her
two assistants were empty. Sonya got the eerie feeling that
Lily had been deserted.

She shook herself back to reality. There must be a conference going on. The staff would be dealing with the murder. In a few minutes, when Perry arrived, she would knock on Lily's red lacquer door and announce that she was here for the promised interview. Then, the all-beige sanctum would open up and she would go in to be greeted, even on this difficult day, by a charming Lily.

Everyone was responsive to the producer of an important television program. Everyone wanted to make a good impression. Especially Lily—good impressions were what she traded in.

This was the next to the last interview Sonya had to do that day. Kim's parents at six. Then the meeting with Matt and Donna. Another exhausting day. But, she told herself, an extremely satisfying one. She had the interviews they requested—Grace Tyler and Leonard Novelli.

Grace was so emotional, the tape would be difficult to edit. Leonard, on the other hand, was surprisingly calm, too calm. No matter what she asked, he only replied that Kim was wonderful and he loved her.

But both interviews were good. Well, good enough. It depended on what news broke. If the police arrested a total stranger for the murder of Harriett, then Sonya's interviews would be meaningless.

No, that wasn't possible. The two murders were connected. And one person had committed them both. Someone at that table, Sonya was convinced. All the pieces had not come together yet, but perhaps the answer lay somewhere in those interviews.

The police were making the rounds of everyone who was at the table, but Sonya already had interviewed most of them. She was ahead of the police.

In fact, they had not yet gotten around to her. She had given a statement on Sunday, but that focused on finding Harriett's body. She was scheduled to go to the precinct on Friday and make a formal statement.

Sonya thought about what she knew. First, Kim must have known much more about Harriett's murder than she had disclosed.

Yes, she had known something that would identify the killer. That Sonya was sure of. What had Kim said? What had she seen or heard in the powder room? Perhaps something she did not even realize she knew. But because of it, Kim was now dead.

Perry had dropped her off and gone in search of a parking space. Sonya was sure he'd soon join her on the 13th floor. Parking was never easy in midtown Manhattan, but Perry seemed to have a gift for it. Meanwhile, Sonya would wait in Lily's assistant's office.

The armchair for visitors looked cozy. She took off her coat with relief and slipped it on the rack. Then she looked in the mirror. Her cheeks were still swollen. Her eyes were tired; the dark circles under them were darker. Even her electric red hair had flattened under her cap. She fluffed it up. It was her saving grace in moments like this. It gave her energy.

She sat down on the chair next to the red lacquer door that opened into Lily's office. She smiled when she thought of how clever Lily was to put a chair like that next to her door. Even if she had to wait half an hour she wouldn't mind. She was obviously going to be the next person into the holy of holies.

Sonya reached into her bag to get the questions she had prepared. Then she stopped and sighed. Time enough for that. These had been long, difficult days, and she was still recovering from the face-lift. She leaned her head back on the wall and closed her eyes. The office was deadly quiet. Maybe she would take a quick nap. That always refreshed her.

But even with her eyes closed, she was not able to rest. Her mind ran over the guests at that table. She was about to interview another of them.

Lily, she thought, was one volatile woman. Early in the morning she had agreed to the interview, then, an hour later, said she didn't have time. After Sonya had called back to beg her to do it, she had agreed—and apparently agreed happily. It was as if she had a complete change of mind. Of course she had stipulations, but who didn't? Sonya wondered what was behind Lily's about-face.

As her mind drifted, she heard Lily's raised voice—without her usual charm.

"For God's sake, Henry," she said. "I know, I know, I know." Her voice kept rising. "You've told me a hundred times that I shouldn't have said those things. But I was Edward's mother, and I saw his body lying in that stinking, dirty hotel room. All because of Kim. Henry, you know that his death was totally unnecessary. We had the money, the connections to save him. Kim knew he was dying and she left him there, alone in that room, without calling the police. If he had help, he would be alive today."

Sonya heard a man's voice. "Lily, we have been over that—"

Lily interrupted shrilly, "She deserved what she got last night, and I will keep telling the world that I am happy that Kim is dead. Her death has kept other young people from being trapped into drugs. She was evil. I rejoice at the thought that she is dead."

Lily's voice dropped. Sonya shifted uneasily in her chair. She felt she shouldn't eavesdrop, but she wanted to know what was going on. Apparently, Lily had done something and now was justifying it.

She strained to hear Henry's reply, but this time all she could pick up were the deep gruff tones of his voice.

Then Lily: "Of course the editors were upset. They all knew Kim. Kim Kelly was one of our big stars. How many times have I told you how important she was to the magazine? She was on the cover. She was in practically every issue. She was at every important party we gave.

"Most of our editors had worked with her, and they could have understood why she committed suicide. They knew her for the junkie she was. I had no idea when I said those things about her at the editorial meeting this morning that they would discover she had been murdered. But I was only telling the truth about her."

"Lily"—Henry's voice rose with irritation—"you made me come racing over here just to tell me this story. I have work to do. I'm on deadline."

"Oh, Henry." Lily's voice revealed the panic she felt. "I had no idea the editors would react by complaining to Hilda. She is my enemy. She's using my feelings as a weapon against me."

"What do you mean?"

"She forced her way into my office and demanded that I run a story saying how great Kim was. She wants me to get some of the best shots and do a splashy obituary. 'Kim Kelly—one of a kind.' That's the cover line she wants."

Henry's reply was immediate. "Well, do it. It's a natural for the magazine. Hilda's right. Kim was certainly better known than Harriett Franklin. Kim Kelly will sell more copies on the newsstand. It might even get you a bigger bonus."

"You expect me to run a story praising the junkie who walked out and left my son to die in a disgusting hotel in the East Village? I won't do it. Never. That's what I told Hilda. Never, never, never." Lily was sobbing.

"Lily, you created enough of a scene at Edward's funeral. My God, Lily. You screamed at Kim, you pulled her out of the church pew and pushed her down the aisle and out the door. Isn't that enough? It was horrendous. Your son is dead. She is dead. You've got to get on with your life. Our lives."

Lily's sobs grew louder.

Sonya stood up and started to move away from the door. It wasn't right for her to hear this.

"But, Henry, it's worse than that," Lily cried. "Hilda told me the police were planning to interview her about how much graft I had taken from the Franklins. She called it 'graft,' Henry. She said she would tell them everything she knew. She said everyone on the staff believed my day at the magazine was over. She was going to make sure it was. She hates me."

"What can she really do, Lily? You are overreacting. Why would the police interview Hilda when they haven't even interviewed you yet? Now, try to calm down."

Lily's voice shook as she went on. "God knows what she is saying about me. She must have gone to the executive publisher. His secretary called and said he wanted to see me first thing tomorrow morning."

"What does that mean?"

"It means that I'm going to be fired."

"Why? How do you know?"

"He always calls me himself. If he had his secretary call, it is very bad news. Something he doesn't want to face."

"Then go in and say you're sorry. Rally the staff. Get the story on Kim together."

"Never." Lily's voice rose. She was adamant. "Never!"

"Lily!" Henry sounded infuriated. "Has it ever crossed your mind that Kim didn't force the cocaine up Edward's nose or push the pills down his throat? Or pump the heroin into his veins? He had control of his life. You can't blame it all on Kim."

"He was my son and he was a good person. Kim ruined his life."

Sonya heard a chair scrape back.

"You would give up everything you have—your job, your reputation, even your marriage—for something as stupid as this?"

"Yes." Lily's reply was quiet but firm. "Yes, I would."

Sonya heard the crash of broken glass and Lily's cry of dismay.

"Then it's over," Henry shouted. "I've had enough. Enough of you. I'm getting out of here. Do what you want. I'm not going to lie to the police. I have my own career to worry about. When the detectives interview me and ask about you, every word that comes out of my mouth will be the truth."

Sonya grabbed her bag. She rushed out the door and down the hall to the elevator bank. She leaned against the wall, gasping for breath.

How could she interview Lily after this? She closed her eyes. When she opened them Henry was standing in front of her, holding her coat.

"You left it behind," he said grimly. "I saw you run out of

the office as I was leaving. You heard our argument, didn't you?"

Sonya flooded with shame. She kept her eyes low. "Yes. I shouldn't have stayed, I know. Now I need to interview her."

Henry shrugged. "Give her a few minutes and then go right in and interview her as if nothing had happened. Being the center of attention gives her more pleasure than anything else. She'll put on an act for you."

Turning to leave, he took his gloves from his coat pocket and pulled them on. "But be gentle. You seem like a decent person, and my wife is going to need as many friends as she can find."

Sonya looked at his face, gray with fatigue, sweat gathering on his forehead. She pitied him.

"Henry, you don't think that . . . ?" She hesitated. Then she reached out and put her hand on his arm to steady herself. "You're not worried? You don't think she killed Harriett Franklin?"

Henry broke away from her without answering. He started to leave, then turned back.

"Sonya, that is for the police to find out." Then he looked directly at her. "But I don't know. If you'd asked me yesterday, I'd have said there wasn't a chance. But today, frankly, I just don't know. She's been a different woman since her son died. I don't understand her. I don't know what she is capable of doing."

When Sonya returned with Perry, some 15 minutes later, the red lacquer door was firmly closed. Sonya began to wish that she was anywhere else but in that chic office, where the only color was the splash of red that was Lily's door. She actually felt physically threatened—Lily had seemed that uncontrolled.

Sonya felt foolish, thinking that way. She was in no danger.

Still, she was glad Perry was beside her. He was loaded down with equipment, but ready to spring into action if Lily attacked her.

She thought of her mother. What would that quiet woman say about someone like Lily, a woman so different from those down-to-earth wives living in the small town in Minnesota. She doubted her mother would approve of anything Lily said or did.

Sonya composed herself, then moved to the bright red door. Within seconds of her knock, Lily was there, smiling and at ease, as if nothing were the matter.

"Come on in and let's get started," she said. "I'm a bit busy. As you can imagine, Kim's death has made us do a lot of thinking."

"Yes, I can imagine," replied Sonya, in awe of Lily's ability to pull herself together. "I won't take up too much of your time. Perry is very quick."

Lily sat down at her desk. "If you don't mind, I'm just going to skim through this report until you are ready for me."

"Sure," Sonya said with a wary laugh. "Then you'll be nice and fresh for me when I attack you with my questions."

"I'm not concerned about your attacking me." Lily smiled. "I don't think you're the attacking type."

Sonya looked around the room as Perry set down the tripod and unrolled the canvas bag that held the lights. On the far side of the desk, a water stain showed on the matte beige carpet. A few shreds of glass, stuck in the woven sisal, caught the light. On the desk, a few crushed tulips, mauve and yellow, were artfully arranged in a water glass.

The bowl of flowers going onto the floor must have been the crash she had heard. But Lily couldn't bear to lose them. Despite all that turmoil, she had gathered them together and put them in the glass. The flowers must have meant a lot to her.

Now, none of the upset showed. Lily sat calmly in her chair while Perry made the final adjustment to the lights.

"My reaction to Harriett's murder was complete disbelief," she said in response to Sonya's first question.

"Jefferson Tyler came to the table and told us. When I realized he was telling the truth, I became distraught. Why anyone would murder Harriett Franklin, a woman who did only good in her life, was beyond my understanding. It still is beyond my understanding."

"What was your relationship with Harriett?" Sonya asked.

Showing her first touch of nerves, Lily put her hands to her face and then pulled her left earlobe as if to make sure her earring was still there.

"I admired Harriett immensely. She was the most compassionate woman I knew. She helped raise millions for the charities of this city."

"You were fairly close? You saw each other frequently? On both a business and social level?"

"Hardly business," Lily came back quickly. "Harriett had little if nothing to do with her husband's company. I saw her mainly at charity events."

"I know she threw an enormous surprise party for you several years ago. It made the papers."

"Of course she did," Lily said, "and it was wonderful, but she did the same for many people. As I said before, she was a gracious, generous woman."

Sonya felt she was getting nowhere. She'd be lucky if she got one decent sound bite from Lily.

"Tell me about Kim Kelly. What made her so successful?"

"Kim was so photogenic. She didn't have a bad angle. That's what makes a model a superstar."

"What about her personality? Was she easy to work with?"

"Like all superstars, she was a dream. At first. Then when she became so much in demand, so famous, she found the pressure very hard to deal with."

"In what way?"

"Oh, the usual. She'd turn up late for a shoot. She'd forget to call when she had to break an appointment. All very irritating. And eventually bad for her reputation."

"Where would you list her? Say on a scale of one to ten?"

"I couldn't really answer that. She was once in the top three. But she'd been in rehab. All the publicity about her drug use was damaging. No. It's impossible to say."

Lily looked down at the papers on her desk. Sonya read that as a signal that Lily was finished talking. But she decided to try one more approach.

"Lily, at the party Sunday night, you were upset that Henry wasn't seated at Harriett's table. Why was that?"

Lily picked up the report from the desk, rearranged the papers, then set them down again.

"Sonya, dear, I think I told you that evening," she said sweetly. "He likes to be with me, so he can look after me. For instance, if I want to leave early, I just have to nod to him and he takes me home. Perhaps this is difficult for anyone to understand in today's world, but we have a perfect marriage. Henry is a political journalist, you know, and I am a fashion editor. But we understand each other perfectly.

"I can promise you, Henry and I have never had a cross word in all the years we've been married. And I promise you, we never will. You can count on that."

THIRTY

5:30 PM, Wednesday

Sitting in the van beside Perry, sipping hot milky coffee, made for one of the most comforting moments in Sonya's long and exhausting day.

"Lily is totally two-faced," she told him. "It would take me an hour to tell you about the violent argument she had with Henry, that poor husband of hers."

"Do you think that Lily Allen murdered Harriett and then Kim? She wouldn't have the guts. She'd be frightened she'd smear her makeup." Perry laughed.

Before Sonya could answer, her cell phone rang.

"Oh, maybe this is about Kim's parents. Here, please hold this." She handed her coffee to Perry, and then dug into her pocket to pull out the cell, answered it, and then listened. "Oh, Wendy, no," she almost begged. "I'm racing against a deadline. They've got to do the interview. You promised. They promised."

She paused to consider her best tactic.

"Yes, yes, I know they are just off the plane. But I'll deal with them gently. You know that."

"They want to talk to you," Wendy replied in a voice loud enough for Perry to hear. "It's the time and place. Harriett was buried this morning, so Franklin is sitting shiva at his apartment. You know, the Jewish gathering after a funeral."

"Yes, I know."

"Originally, I had it all set up for you to go to the Franklin offices. But everything has run so late, Franklin suggested they go directly to his house. His relatives and friends are coming to pay their respects. Kim's folks want to be there with him." She paused. "Sonya, there's no way you can take a television camera into a shiva."

"I agree. It would be an awful intrusion. Franklin and his family need their privacy."

Perry nodded in agreement beside her.

"But can't I grab Kim's mother and father now, before they go to Franklin's place? I'll meet them anywhere. On the street. In a lobby. Anywhere. And I'll be quick."

"No, they're already on their way. They'll meet you tomorrow morning, after they've been to view Kim's body."

"Wendy, no. That will tear them apart completely. You can't put them through that and then an interview. Anyway it will be impossible to get an exclusive. There'll be hordes of press waiting outside the morgue. All they'll be capable of doing is crying, believe me."

"Sonya, they really want to talk to you," Wendy replied. "They believe the press has been unfair. They want the truth out about Kim. They want to tell her story to a good, reliable journalist. But Franklin was so good to Kim when she first came to New York, they want to be with him at the shiva."

Sonya sighed. "Have you spoken to Mari?"

"No, but I'll try. Maybe she'll have a solution for you."

"Thanks, Wendy. I wouldn't do this to you, except that we have the show tomorrow night and this interview will be an important part of it. You know it doesn't just happen like magic. We need time to edit it, to write it, all the rest. And we need to do that tonight. Call me back after you speak to Mari."

Sonya disconnected the call, and took her coffee back from Perry.

"We'll wait," she told him. "There's nothing more I can do. I want an interview, not just a shot of them walking into an apartment building. I won't call Matt until Wendy rings me back with a definite turndown. Then we'll have to start rescheduling everything."

Perry shrugged, then said, "Call Matt right now and tell him the problems you're having. It's about time he learns just how hard you work. Let me tell you, none of the other producers work as hard as you."

Sonya pulled off her cap and fluffed her hair as if she were loosening up her life. Perry was right, of course. She did put too much of herself into her job. Matt knew that and counted on it. That was one reason she was doing so much of the work on this story.

"I'll wait," she replied almost defiantly. "Let's see if Mari comes up with something."

Perry must have realized he had upset her. "The magical Mari," he joked. "The solver of so many of our problems. She's one controlling broad. I wouldn't like to have her in bed."

"You're crazy." Sonya laughed. "She's beautiful, rich, runs her own business."

"That's just it. She scares me."

"You like your ladies more laid back." Sonya laughed and handed him her coffee once more as her cell phone rang. The call was brief, and Sonya ended it by saying, "Wendy, thank you, and thank Mari for me. Of course we'll be discreet. I'll go up the back entrance with Perry. We'll be ready in 15 minutes."

She took the coffee from Perry and took a long swirl. She needed that caffeine.

"You don't have to tell me you got the interview." He grinned as he looked at her smile.

"Yes, and it's pretty cloak-and-dagger. But Mari has set it up for us. We have to go up the service elevator to Franklin's apartment and set up for the interview in the maid's room. When you are ready to roll, Wendy will bring them in."

"The maid's room? Is that a suitable setting for the *Donna Fuller Show?*" Perry was only half joking. "How big is it? We have to fit in two chairs for them, one for you, the tripod, the lights. It's going to look awful."

"Well, it's the only place. Apparently, it's a kind of sitting room. We have to make do. Wendy will meet us in the lobby and look after us. The most important thing is that it is quiet and exclusive. And Perry, we've got the story first."

"Does Isaac Franklin know that we are doing this in his house?"

"Perry, stop it." Sonya was too excited to have any doubts. "He must. Mari must have asked his permission."

The maid's room was larger than Perry had hoped for, and with Wendy's help it was set up for the interview in 15 minutes.

"Their name is Dykstra. He is Willem, born and brought up in Amsterdam. He is a professor of mathematics at the university there," Wendy explained. "She is Helene, had a French mother and an English father. When Kim began modeling, she took her mother's maiden name, Kelly. Helene owns the city's most forward fashion boutique. They have a son, Dirk, but he couldn't make the early flight."

"Their English?" asked Sonya.

"As good as yours."

When Wendy ushered the Dykstras to the room, Kim was amazed at the difference in their appearance. Opposites surely attract, she thought.

Helene Dykstra was small, dark, and intense. Very French, thought Sonya, and every bit a fashion boutique owner. Her short black hair was spiked with gel, her lips stained dark red, and her almond-shaped eyes set perfectly in her oval face. It was the same sweet oval face that Kim had so obviously inherited. Sonya's heart turned over.

Willem stood tall and gaunt beside her. His mouth was pressed together into a tight line, his eyes dark and wary. He put his arm around his wife and guided her to the chair that Sonya pointed out. He sat down and opened his carefully buttoned jacket for Perry to clip on the mike. He was a thin man with narrow bones, and he moved gracefully. When he spoke, his voice was gentle.

"Everyone has been so kind and we are grateful. Our daughter Kim was well known in the Netherlands, and the people there are shocked and sad at her death. When we called the airline, they found seats for us on the next flight. We want to thank them all for their help."

Sonya swallowed the lump that rose in her throat. The sorrow on their faces was unbearable to watch.

"Thank you both so much for doing this interview. We'll only take a few minutes. This must be the most dreadful day of your lives."

She glanced at Wendy, who had taken a spot in the cramped corner of the room, and then looked up at Perry, who nodded that the tape was rolling.

Willem reached over and took his wife's hand. "Our beloved Kim has been brutally murdered. We must do everything we can to find the person responsible. We will cooperate with the authorities in every way."

Helene Dykstra looked at her husband as she spoke. "Of course we were concerned about Kim. The life of a celebrity, especially a beautiful woman, is difficult. But we never expected this. We knew, of course, of her problems with the drugs. So when we got Wendy's call, we could believe that perhaps things had gone very, very wrong and she had jumped to her death. But murder, never."

Sonya moved uncomfortably on the tiny stool Perry had squeezed in beside the tripod.

"You've seen the police?" Sonya asked.

"Yes," Willem answered gruffly. "They were at the airport

waiting for us. They tell us that there is no doubt Kim was murdered. They said she was killed by a single blow at the back of her head. Some sharp object fractured her skull and damaged her brain. But death was instantaneous. At least she didn't suffer."

"Did the police say they found the object?" Sonya pressed.

"There was a statue from the International Designers Association Fashion Awards on the table. It may have been the weapon. The police are testing it."

Sonya sensed he was relieved to share this frightening story.

His wife joined in. "The police say it was easy for the murderer to pick up her body and throw her over the balcony. She was so thin."

Sonya looked into Willem's somber eyes. He seemed to read her thoughts. "The police believe she knew the person who murdered her. The door wasn't forced."

Mrs. Dykstra took a handkerchief from her pocket and wiped her nose. "We were so proud of her success here, but trusting people in New York just brought her death."

Sonya lowered her eyes to her notes and then looked up directly at Willem Dykstra.

"Kim came home to Amsterdam after she left the clinic?"

"Yes, we wanted her to stay home and rest, but she was so concerned about her work."

"She was anxious to stay on as the model for the Franklins. But she was frightened that with Novelli gone, Jason Sarnoff wouldn't have the power to keep her," Helene added.

"Jason Sarnoff?" Sonya let her surprise show. "Kim knew Jason in Europe?"

"Yes, Jason was an old friend. He came to visit us in Amsterdam a number of times. Most recently he came to discuss whether he should go to New York and take the job at Franklin's. They spent the day together, and Kim gave him advice about the company. He said when he got that job, he would keep Kim as the Franklin model."

"Really?" asked Sonya. She was trying to sort out this new information about Sarnoff and his position at Franklin. Willem seemed to sense her uncertainty.

"You must realize my wife owns one of the biggest fashion boutiques in Europe. Many, many designers visit us in Amsterdam. We have a big house on a canal. It is always full of people."

"Of course," Sonya replied. "Kim was very much part of the fashion world. And beautiful. No wonder she decided to become a model."

"I didn't want her to model." Helene looked at Sonya for the first time. "I wanted her to design. Willem and I both urged her to go to London and study. She had real talent. I dreamed of opening a boutique for her. But no, she wanted to model."

"How did she get started?" asked Sonya.

"She got a modeling job when she was 15, at a department store. The photos made her famous. She had the look of the moment. It was all we could do to make her finish high school." For the first time, Helene Dykstra smiled. Clearly, she was remembering the excitement of her daughter's success.

"That is one reason why we decided to do this interview," picked up her husband. "We want to warn other parents against letting their daughters become models. It is a treacherous, dangerous world."

Sonya glanced at her watch. Fifteen minutes had gone by, but she still felt she had to ask the questions that might give her some clue to Kim's murder.

"What about drugs? When did she start?"

Willem looked at his wife, who nodded, giving him permission to continue.

"We have no way of knowing. But about a year ago, she brought Lily Allen's son, Edward, to Amsterdam for a visit. We learned then she had a problem."

Helene Dykstra continued, "At first she was very much in love with Edward. She did whatever he asked. But he was a selfish, spoiled boy. His mother gave in to his every wish, and he expected Kim to do the same. As you know, it is easy to get drugs in Amsterdam. One morning she came running to us saying he had overdosed."

"What happened?" asked Sonya, as gently as she could.

It was Kim's father who replied. "The doctor told us that Edward had a severe problem. Then Kim admitted that she was hooked on drugs too. She wanted to get off them. She wanted to leave him, but she didn't know how. He was destroying his life and hers as well."

Mrs. Dykstra continued, "I have known of Edward's mother for many years. But when I phoned her to discuss Edward's problem, she did nothing. Except blame Kim. Lily Allen has lied. She has done everything she could to place the blame on my daughter," she said with determination. "After his death, Kim went happily to the rehab clinic."

The couple stopped. It was obvious to Sonya that the painful memories of Kim's struggle with drugs were overwhelming. Sonya said softly, "I am sorry to keep you so long. But, please, could you just answer one or two more questions for me?"

After a moment, Helene Dykstra replied, "Yes, but please just a little more."

"Tell me more about Jason Sarnoff."

Again, it was Helene Dykstra who replied. She is the strong one. How sad that Kim didn't have the same strength, thought Sonya.

"We were so happy when Jason got Novelli's job. He promised to help Kim. When she came home after the rehabilitation, he called us regularly to report on her. He was looking after her." Helene sighed deeply, then continued. "But Harriett Franklin disliked Jason. Jason told Kim that he doubted Harriett would let him continue her contract.

"She was heartbroken. She appealed to Isaac Franklin, but got nowhere. If it hadn't been for the support Wendy gave her, she might have gone back on drugs."

Willem Dykstra reached over again and put his arm around his wife's shoulders.

"We have said enough," he said simply. "It is time for us to join Mr. Franklin and the other mourners."

Perry quickly unhooked the mikes and Sonya rose to say her thanks. Just then, Isaac Franklin appeared at the door. With him were his three sons. He had his hands on the shoulders of Henry and Byron, and Jeremy was close behind them. At first he saw only the Dykstras. He held out his hands in sympathy as they walked toward him.

Wendy stepped forward quickly, ushering the Dykstras past them. Then Isaac saw Sonya.

"What are you doing here?" he asked, his face stiffening with rage.

Wendy replied for her. "Isaac, I thought you knew. Mari arranged for Sonya to do a quick interview with the Dykstras. It was the only chance we had. We didn't want to intrude. Please forgive me. I would never have set this up without your permission."

Isaac turned to his sons. "Go back to the living room, boys. I'll be there in a moment."

As the boys left, he turned to Sonya. His voice was harsh and his jaw tight as he spat out the words. "Mari told me nothing about this. What was the interview about?"

Sonya stepped forward. "The interview was just background on Kim Kelly and her career. Just that."

"Just that?" His voice rose. "Are you sure? It doesn't include damage to the Franklin business? This is not the time or the place for muckraking. We are sitting shiva for my wife. My brutally murdered wife. My God, can't you people have some respect for me and my three sons?"

The strain was too much. Sonya could hardly control herself. She looked at him with tears in her eyes and a sob in her voice.

"I'm sorry. I thought I had Mari's permission, and your permission, to come here. I would never have intruded on you at this time. I am very, very sorry." She turned to Perry. "Let's go. There is nothing more I can say."

But as she stood by Perry, waiting for the elevator to take

them down, she thought there was a lot more to say. Where was Mari? Why hadn't she called Isaac? Why didn't she answer her cell phone?

Sonya grew frightened. Was Mari another victim?

THIRTY-ONE

7:45 PM, Wednesday

Perry was silent as they walked out of the building toward the van. He sensed Sonya's need to get control of herself. The blast of icy air coming off Park Avenue helped her get a grip on her feelings.

Once they were in the van, he switched on the engine and raised the heat. Then he turned to her, his anger clearly showing.

"That was a lousy trick your friend Mari played on you. She really set you up with Franklin," he said. "But you can take comfort. From the look on Franklin's face, she is likely to be fired when she does turn up."

"Oh, Perry," Sonya asked anxiously, "do you really think that's all it was? I can forgive her for the mess-up if I know she is safe. We've had two murders in three days, and both of them people I was with at that dinner. Could she be the third? Where is she?"

"You're letting it get to you. Mari is tough. She's more

likely to come after someone with a hatchet than be a victim." Perry laughed, then asked seriously, "What do you think we've got? A serial killer?"

Sonya turned to looked at him. He was extremely intelligent. She knew he was sensitive. She couldn't understand how he could be so lighthearted about it all. Why did he have to joke all the time? It irritated her.

But, she thought, he's been a news cameraman for years. He has learned not to let death and grief touch him. She wondered if she would ever be able to do that.

She was glad he was so strong. It had been three long days and nights of constant work since she had discovered Harriett's body in the washroom. She doubted she could have gotten through it all without him.

"Perry," she said, "you must be exhausted. Thank you. You're great."

"So are you. But I'll get away tomorrow. I won't do the last interview with you, realize that," he said suddenly and soberly.

"The last interview?"

"Yes, with Mari. You have it scheduled for the studio. That means robot cameras only. No way I can work in the control room. You know, it's a union thing. You'll have to rely on whoever is in there. Anyway, it's my day off and I'm going skiing."

"Oh my God, Mari's interview. I'd almost forgotten. I'm so worried about her, I didn't even remember she is set for an interview. I'd better start checking." She took her cell phone from her bag.

"Call her on mine," Perry said, handing her his phone. "You've been using yours all day and the batteries must be going. This baby is completely charged."

Sonya glanced at Perry. She wondered if he ever realized how good he was to her. He was as tired as she was but still with her, every step of the way.

Mari picked up immediately.

"Sonya, I am sorry." She spoke easily, but Sonya sensed her urgency. "I left a message for Franklin about the Dykstra interview. It was his assistant's fault, but this has been a difficult day for everyone at the company. If he'd received my message he would have agreed. He just felt left out."

"Where were you?"

"I had business to attend to. You know Franklin isn't the only company I represent. Other clients have problems too. I tried to get to you, but I guess your cell phone is dead. I called Wendy and she said she thought you were happy with the interview with the Dykstras."

Sonya felt tears at the back of her eyes.

"God, Mari, I was terrified; I thought something might have happened to you."

"That's not at all likely, but it is sweet of you to care." Mari laughed effortlessly, then continued in a low voice. "Part of the time I was being interviewed by the police. I guess my fingerprints were all over the apartment. Yours too, for that matter."

Sonya nodded to herself. "And Wendy's," she said, remembering what a mess Kim's apartment was, and how they had to clean it up for the shoot.

Mari was silent. Then she asked, "Were you happy with the interview with Lily?"

"Not so great. She clammed up on me, and mostly talked in the usual expected clichés. Her husband was leaving just as I arrived. They had some kind of fight. What gives with her?"

"There's a rumor that the new publisher is trying to get rid of her. I don't think it's going to happen. Lily is a brilliant editor and the magazine is going from success to success."

Sonya replied, "Well, there are always rumors."

"On the other hand," Mari continued, "she's in her 50s, and that's getting a little elderly for the youth-oriented fashion world. That could swing against her."

"What about you?" Sonya asked. "Are you ready to face the camera tomorrow?"

"Yes, as soon as I've finished checking everything at the office I'll be over. You know that because I'm employed by both the Franklins and the Tylers, I can't say a great deal on television about my clients. It won't take much time, will it?"

"No, but I think it would do you good to have Sabrina do your makeup. She's really good, and morning faces always need all the help they can get—even yours."

"That's great, thanks. It'll mean I look good for the rest of the day. I'll see you about nine."

"Where'll you be the rest of the evening?" Sonya asked, then added quickly, "Just in case I need to check something."

"Probably at the office," Mari replied. "Call me on my cell. I'll get back to you."

"Stay out of trouble then." Sonya meant it as a joke, but somehow, it didn't come out that way.

Mari's answer was hollow. "You too," she said. "And I mean it."

As she returned the phone to Perry, Sonya realized that she was afraid of something. Something that was not really clear to her. Mari was afraid too.

Sonya's mind raced. How much more did Mari know than she admitted? What had the police wanted from her?

And most important, what was it Sonya couldn't remember?

Perry pulled up alongside the network building entrance with his usual verve.

Sonya turned to him. "The Dykstra interview is only one tape. I'll take it up and log it in. Matt and Donna are anxious for it, I'm sure."

"They've got nothing to be anxious about as far as you're concerned," Perry replied. "You've done one fabulous job for them."

Sonya grinned her thanks, opened the van door, and stepped down to the pavement. Her legs refused to hold her steady. She leaned on the door, holding on for support.

"Are you okay?" Perry asked. Then he took one look at her drained face and said, "I'll take you and the tape upstairs."

"Oh, Perry. Just let me hang here for a few moments. The thought of going into the building, with all those empty, dark corridors, made me shaky. It's all getting to me. There's something important that I can't remember. Some connection. Something someone said."

Perry slung his camera over his left arm and offered his other to Sonya.

"Don't worry. It will come to you. It's been a tough day." He continued reassuringly, "There are plenty of guards around. My guess it is that it would be impossible to get into this building. So there is no real reason for you to be afraid.

"I'll walk you up to the conference room where Matt and company are waiting for you. If anyone tries to attack us, I'll turn the camera on and catch them in the act."

"That would make great TV." Sonya laughed.

Matt and Donna were sitting opposite each other in the conference room. Donna, a mug of coffee on the table in front of her, looked up as Sonya walked into the room. Displeasure was written all over Donna's face. Sonya guessed she had been arguing with Matt.

"Donna, I'm sorry we had to do the interview with the Dykstras in such a rush," Sonya said, the words flowing in an uncontrolled stream. "You should have been on camera with them. They were great, right up your alley. But I had no time. They'd just arrived. At one stage, I thought I'd lost the interview altogether. They went to the shiva at Franklin's apartment and the only place I could talk to them was in the maid's room.

"They were heartbreaking. They loved Kim so much. You can introduce the segment. It'll be great. You'll love them." Sonya stopped abruptly, realizing that she had been rattling on.

Donna shook her head.

"Stop apologizing," she said. "You're overwrought, and no wonder why. Sonya, you've done a sensational job. I'm not upset about missing out on the Dykstras. We're just discussing the lineup for the show. You've given us so much tape, it's taking a long time to settle, and time is the one thing we don't have."

At first, Sonya didn't grasp what Donna had said. She sank into a chair as fear flooded her again. She had discovered something dreadful, but she didn't know what it was.

She looked directly at Donna. "You were right, Donna, when you told me to be careful," she said. "But I haven't been careful enough. There is a killer loose. I'm too close to it all."

Matt, who had been listening, broke in. "We're definitely going with the idea we discussed this morning. 'The Roundtable Murders.' The whole show is outlined. We'll work all night on it."

"The Roundtable Murders," Sonya said, trying to think back over the day. "But surely the news lead is that Kim was murdered. That's hot. She was an international superstar. Young, beautiful, rich—she had everything and she got murdered. Not only that, but her body was thrown out the window in the middle of a raging storm. It doesn't get any better than that." Sonya's producer's mind was already writing Donna's anchor copy.

"Yes, but that story is all over the local news," Donna continued. "The only thing we have exclusive is your interview with Kim's parents. The theme of the roundtable murders gives us a chance to explore both murders. Who were those people at the table? What connects them? They were all invited by Harriett Franklin, the hostess who was murdered. Did she have some plan that went wrong? Or was it just fate? It will make a sensational show."

"We have the skeleton down," Matt added, "and producers are working on different segments. It's set; it's a go."

"We would have called you back to the office to discuss it," Donna said gently. "But you were on top of it all and we couldn't replace you in the field."

Matt chimed in impatiently, "Now the big question is the interview with the Dykstras. How strong do you think it is? Can we use it in the last segment? Tease it throughout the show?"

"It's strong. It's full of information and incredibly moving," said Sonya, taking the tape out of her bag and sliding it unsteadily across the table to him. "I got a good ten minutes, and with voice-overs you could stretch it to twelve."

She looked directly at Matt. "Any more news from the police?"

"Just that the cause of death was the blow she received at the back of her head. She died instantly, and the weapon was probably metal."

That confirmed what the Dykstras had been told. Sonya thought back to her interview with Kim, and what the model had said afterward.

"The only metal thing I can remember being there was the designer award that Kim gave to Leonard Novelli on Sunday night. Mr. and Mrs. Dykstra told me the police believed that might have been the murder weapon. Mari left it on the coffee table."

"What are you talking about?" Matt's interest was aroused. "How did the award get there? Wasn't it Novelli's?"

"Yes. But apparently Novelli left it for Kim on Sunday night when he came home from the party. The police had taken her to the precinct to make a statement. Novelli put a note with the award saying it would keep her company through the dreadful time she was having. You've seen his interview. You know he's the kind of person who is likely to do that sort of thing."

"You mean she could have been killed by the very award she presented to Novelli?"

"Yes," said Sonya. She sat at the table and rested her head on her hands. "Yes, I saw it there on Monday when we were leaving after the interview."

"We've got plenty of shots of it. I'll check with the police tomorrow. You're sure it was there?" Matt asked.

"Yes, I'm sure." Sonya sighed.

"Matt, have someone get this woman some hot coffee and some sandwiches," Donna interrupted. "She needs nourishment if we are ever going to get this show finished. Remember our deadline is tomorrow at 3:00."

Matt went to the phone and asked for coffee and food. Then he asked the senior producer to round up the staff and bring them to the conference room.

As they assembled, Sonya leaned back and closed her eyes for a moment's rest.

When she looked around the room, she saw that Matt had lined up the important members of the *Donna Fuller* staff. The two writers, the chief editor, and the two other show segment producers. She reached out and took a glass of iced water that was on the table and sipped it slowly. They were all looking at her. Enviously, she thought.

Once they had settled, Sonya took charge. It was a new feeling for her.

"What about the interview with Mari tomorrow? I lined it up for about nine. She said she'd be in makeup at 8:30. Is the studio booked?"

"Yes," Matt replied. "I want to feature every person who was sitting at that dinner table. I want to finish the skeleton of the show tonight. We have a lot of material, and still have Mari's interview to get. We'll allow two minutes for that. Do you think we will need more, Sonya?"

Sonya shook her head. Matt continued, "The people who sat at the table have to appear on the show."

"That also means you, Sonya," Donna added. "We'll get some shots of you while you are interviewing Mari. We'll use all three of the studio cameras."

Sonya started to protest, but Donna cut her off.

"I know it's unusual for a producer to appear. But you are part of this story. You were at that table. And don't worry, you'll look good."

Then, looking carefully at Sonya, Donna added, "But you'd better be in makeup at 8:00. Sabrina will be there to see that my top producer isn't looking too worn-out on camera."

"Yeah," said Matt, "if you keep this pace, you may end as our star crime reporter. We jumped in the ratings for Tuesday's show. We could even start a unit for you."

"The good news," Donna added, "is that I remembered that I once did a story on charity parties and interviewed Harriett Franklin.

"We found the piece, and although Harriett had changed

her hairstyle radically since then, she talked about the importance of charity in New York. It will be a nice way to set up who she was."

"That is super," Sonya said with a smile, remembering that she had not interviewed Harriett that night.

She reached out for the turkey on a roll that had appeared before her. She was feeling much better, more energized again. "Where do we start?"

Donna replied quickly. "There are a few points Matt and I want to discuss with you. But after that, I think you'd better go home and get a good night's rest. Tomorrow we want you to go over each segment. You are closest to the story and your judgment is crucial. But to do that, you've got to be fresh."

"Okay." She tried not to hide her disappointment. "Let me have the coffee and eat while we talk. I'll go home as soon as we've finished."

It wasn't fair, she thought. She had put in all that effort to make the show the best they could have. Now she was being cut out of the editing and writing process. That was the part she enjoyed most. That was the way she could control what went on air.

But to stay up until two or three would be impossible. Her face was achy and swollen. Better to go home, she realized. She would ice her face, have a glass of wine, try to forget the fear that still kept swamping her mind, and hopefully slip into sleep.

Tomorrow would be another day, and she would face whatever came.

"Thank you, Donna," she said as they finished. "It all sounds good. I want to stay, but you're right. I'm too tired."

"There's just one more thing," Matt said as she stood up. "Donna ordered a guard to take you home. She doesn't think you can take care of yourself."

"Yes, I want him to take you home—right up to your apartment and see you safely inside. He is to check every room."

"Donna, why?" asked Sonya, startled.

Donna reached out and touched her arm.

"I want you to be protected. I want to know you're safe. I'm worried about you. You *were* at that table."

Sonya put her cold hand over Donna's warm one.

"Thank you," she said. "To tell the truth, I am frightened. I know something at the back of my mind. I think I know who killed Harriett and Kim. I'm just too frightened to put it all together. Or maybe I'm just unwilling to admit it to myself."

THIRTY-TWO

10:00 PM, Wednesday

At last the children were asleep. When Jeff was away, getting them to bed was always difficult. Perhaps she was too easy with them. Perhaps it was Jeff's personality. His Israeli army training had left him a hard man to argue with. One word from him and they scooted off to their rooms.

Jeff, her husband. Jeff, the mystery man. Jeff, the man she had never fully understood. The man she probably never would fully understand.

She poured herself another glass of wine and walked through the living area into the wing that housed the children's rooms. She wanted to check on them. It was something she did several times before she went to bed.

Perhaps she cared too much. But the children were all they had. She was an only child and so was Jeff. Her parents had died in a plane crash, and Jeff's had died in Israel. The children had to be protected at all costs.

She stopped first in the room the two boys shared and

looked down at her sons in their twin beds. Travis and Peter, lying deeply asleep. They were totally different.

Peter was almost a teenager, blond with a strong nose and jutting ears just like his father. Grace smiled in spite of herself. Travis had darker hair. At eight, he was smaller boned, more delicate. But he was still a baby, she told herself, a boy who couldn't fall asleep without his teddy bear. Neither of them, she vowed, would ever fight in the Israeli army as their father had.

"Sleep well, my little ones," she whispered to them as she dimmed the night-light.

Patricia, the baby, had the adjoining room. Grace had long dreamed of a pretty, feminine daughter, but Patricia was having none of it. She was fascinated by everything her brothers did and ignored the dolls stacked up in her playroom.

Grace stood admiring her. The golden curls had a reddish tint. The green eyes were closed, and her narrow chest rose gently with her soft breathing.

She bent and kissed her.

"Stay safe, precious," she whispered. "You are my greatest love."

How proud she had been at Patricia's birth. The baby had made their family complete. Now their life would be perfect.

And so it had been for the first few months.

They had moved the business into the chicly renovated townhouse. The pied-à-terre on the top floor had its own private entrance. The tiny flat gave them the freedom of staying overnight in the city after going to the theater or attending parties. No more booking in at hotels or making the long drive to their Connecticut home in bad weather.

She told herself that the city apartment was their private love nest.

But as the months passed, she knew Jefferson used it for more than that.

"It's just too convenient to the office," he said, carefully overexplaining why she couldn't drive in and spend the night with him there. "We need to get an apartment that is farther away from the business."

"I don't understand what you mean. It's only a bedroom and a sitting room. There's no space for a lot of people to meet," she insisted.

"I don't have a lot of people there," he said. "But when I have an important meeting, it's great. To be taken up to our private apartment, with its high-tech furniture, means a lot to some executives. It makes them feel important.

"I can stay late to discuss problems. A lot of creative ideas have come up in that 'small space,' as you call it. It seems conducive to creativity. Sometimes we go on for so long, I call the caterer and get food. And sometimes, it doesn't get cleared until the cleaning woman comes in the morning.

"And that, my dear Grace, is not your style," he added with a smile.

Grace would argue she didn't have any particular style. She may have had servants all her life, but she liked running a home and she could do it well, with or without servants.

Who were these people that Jeff entertained at night? That was the point. When had they come into his life? Why were they playing such an important part in it? Mari was the key to it. That she knew.

Did Jeff still love her?

She forced herself to face the answer: "No." True, they had had great sex the morning after Harriett's death. But looking back, she knew his passion that day had not been for her. It was a passion for life. He had needed sex to bring him to reality. Any woman would have done.

Did he love his children? Yes, she told herself. But he didn't love them enough to come home and have dinner with them before he flew off to Paris.

Things had definitely changed, and the change had started when his company began working with the Franklin business.

That change, too, had been easy for Jeff to explain away.

"I have to give it a lot of my time. Isaac Franklin is the number-one designer business in the country. His fragrance, and all the things that can develop from it—the body collections, the bath collections, the treatment collection—could mean hundreds of millions to us.

"Remember what your father used to say—a business must never stagnate. Grow or die."

But it was more than business, Grace told herself. Something was going on between Mari and Jeff. She had watched them together, had seen what passed between them. A quick glance, a sudden smile. It was nothing—but it was everything.

And Harriett had known about it. Somehow, Harriett was manipulating Jeff. Just as Harriett had manipulated her own father.

She could not put her concerns out of her mind, even as she walked into the bar, opened the fridge, and topped off her glass. There was one way of finding out, and that was by driving to the city and surprising them. She looked at her watch. Nine o'clock. She could be there by ten.

Better give him one more chance. She quickly dialed the number of the apartment. It was busy, as it so often was. She guessed he had taken the phone off the hook.

Then she dialed his cell phone. The message service clicked on immediately. It was pointless to leave a message. Jeff already knew that she wanted him home.

She crossed to the maid's room and told Rosita that she was going out.

"Check on the children every couple of hours," she said. "I'm worried they may be catching colds."

Rosita nodded absently, used to Grace's anxiety.

Grace went into the bathroom and swallowed a couple of aspirin and some vitamin B capsules. She had to be sober. The roads were slick with ice, and snow was still falling.

The expressway was almost empty. The cold had kept people from going into the city. She drove carefully, keeping well within the speed limit. It would be disastrous to be picked up for drunken driving.

Manhattan was quiet. The streets were almost deserted except for a few taxis. Patches of snow spotted the sidewalks. The bare branches of the trees bent with the wind. It

looked like a glamorous Manhattan scene in an early Woody
Allen movie.

Grace parked opposite the townhouse.

It was completely dark, even the penthouse.

Grace put her head down on the steering wheel. Where
was he? Out? With someone? Asleep? Exhausted from the
day, as Mari had said he would be?

Did she have the courage to climb up the stairs and find
out what was going on?

She looked at the private entrance with its deep-green
awning. No. As Jeff liked to say, "It wasn't her style." She
would never barge in on a couple making love.

She could only go home to the children. That was her role
in life. She was a mother. The children must come before
any of her needs. She switched on the car lights, determined
to go back to the country.

Then she caught sight of someone coming out. Her head-
lights were shining on the figure. A man, but not tall
enough to be Jeff. She couldn't see his face clearly at the
distance.

She watched as the man adjusted his hat, pulling it down
over his eyes. Then he took his gloves from his pocket and
pulled them on. For a moment he looked directly at Grace,
but then, blinded by the car lights, he turned and strode toward the avenue and the taxis.

Grace could tell he was young and effeminate, a snappy
dresser in his fitted coat and well-creased trousers. Gay. That
was it. Jeff's secret life. He was gay and used their townhouse love nest to meet his boyfriends.

There was only one thing she wanted now. A drink.

Grace woke with a hangover. Her head throbbed as if there
were an electric drill inside. She turned and saw flashing
lights. She was in for a migraine. She had to get to her med-
icine fast.

She had driven home, carefully concentrating on the road,
refusing to think of Jeff. As soon as she had come in, she had

opened a bottle of vodka and sat in her favorite chair sipping. After two hours, she felt she had drunk herself to stupidity. She lurched into the bedroom she had shared for a dozen years with Jeff.

When she lay down, the horror of the night overcame her. A panic attack. She gasped for air, felt the sweat pouring down her body. She stumbled back into the family room and sank into the chair.

But she couldn't spend the night there. She couldn't let the children find her sleeping off her hangover. Never. She rose and felt her way slowly into the children's rooms.

The boys were sound asleep. Patricia stirred as Grace entered the room, but then turned and snuggled down into her blanket. Grace sat in a chair and watched her daughter sleep. Finally, she dozed.

Now it was morning and she had to face the day. She went into her own bedroom and put her hand cautiously under the pillow. Both phones were there. At least she had remembered to bring them. Jeff couldn't have called. But then she hadn't gotten home until almost midnight. And he never called as late as that.

Patricia climbed out of her bed and came into the room.

"Where's my daddy?" Patricia had always been his pet, and in return she had lapped up his love.

"Didn't I tell you? Daddy has gone to our farm in France where we grow all the flowers for the fragrances. He promised to take us all there for a treat next summer, remember?"

She opened her puffy, bloodshot eyes and looked at her daughter's innocent face. Patricia was sulking.

"Why didn't Daddy call me last night?" she pouted. "He promised he would."

Why indeed, thought Grace. Because having sex with his boyfriend was more important to him than the love of his only daughter.

But she said, "Daddy had a big meeting with some people who want him to make some perfumes from our flowers. When the meeting ended, it was so late he knew we would all be asleep."

Patricia was relentless. "Why did you come and sleep in my room?"

Grace could not hold back her tears. She swept the little girl into her arms and buried her face in her neck.

"What do you think?" she said. "Could it be that when I couldn't sleep with Daddy, I decided to be with the daughter I love so much?"

She hugged her closely, covering her head with kisses. Then, sensing that Patricia was becoming frightened to see her so emotional, she put the girl down.

"Get your dressing gown on," she said in a matter-of-fact tone. "I have to wake up those boys and get them off to school."

She picked up the phones and walked toward her bathroom. She would take the pills and then have a quick shower and change before the boys and Rosita saw her.

It was seven o'clock. The flight took off at eight. Jeff had to be on his way to JFK Airport. He had to check in by 7:15.

She dialed his cell phone number. Just voice mail. Well, after a shower she'd call the airline. He'd be waiting in the first-class lounge. He had to be.

In the shower, she followed her usual routine. Hot water first, to relax her aching muscles. Then cold, to bring her body to life and clear her head.

She slipped into her dressing gown and opened the door as the two boys raced through the bedroom toward her.

"Daddy, daddy, daddy," they cried as they flung themselves on her.

"Is Daddy on the phone?" She tried not to let her eagerness show.

"No, we want to talk to him. We've got a secret that you and Patricia aren't allowed to know."

"Oh." Grace smiled. "It couldn't be about Patricia's birthday next week, could it?"

"We want to talk to Daddy, and Patricia said he's gone to the flower farm."

"Yes, Daddy is flying to Paris this morning. He's very busy, but in a few minutes I'll call the airport and see if we can say good-bye. Now go and eat your breakfast. You've got school today. And for that matter, so does Patricia. She may not like kindergarten, but she's going."

She put her arms around them and walked them back to the kitchen.

"Don't take any nonsense from them, Rosita. Daddy may not be here, but the school bus will be shortly."

As soon as she left the room, the fear came back. She walked toward the family room. No, she couldn't call the airport from there. It was too filled with last night's anguish. The living room—the room they used least. It was calm, quiet, with memories of only formal evenings. That was the place to go.

She looked at her watch. Seven-thirty. He had to be in the lounge. The plane took off in half an hour.

The attendant was helpful.

"Yes, I know Mr. Tyler," she said. "He often flies with us. But he has not arrived yet."

"Is he still booked? We've had some family problems and he may have decided not to go. I must know."

"Oh, yes, Mrs. Tyler, I recognize your voice. He is still booked, but we are boarding and if he doesn't come in a few minutes he will miss the flight."

"Thank you. Please tell him I called."

Grace sank back in her chair. This was not Jeff. Something had happened. Jeff always called her before he left, and if he expected to miss the flight he would have contacted the airline. She had to find out where he was.

She went into the study and looked up the number of the car service. Jeff, she guessed, would have booked a car to pick him up at 6:15. She was put on hold for an agonizing 10 minutes. But at last, Grace heard a human voice.

"This is Mrs. Tyler," she said almost angrily, and asked to speak to the driver who had taken her husband to the airport.

"We put him down as a 'No-show.' Car 734 waited an hour for Mr. Tyler. We dialed the two numbers we have. One didn't answer and the other was busy. You'll be charged for the service."

"Okay, okay," said Grace. "Charge whatever you have to.

Do you have a car anywhere near me? I need to get into the city urgently. It is an emergency. I'm sure something terrible has happened to my husband. We are longtime clients. Please help me."

The operator said, "I'll talk to the dispatcher. Just be patient, Mrs. Tyler, and we'll do what we can."

Forty-five minutes later, Grace ran up the stairs of the private entrance to the pied-à-terre, slipped the key in the lock, and flung the door open.

She ran through the living room and opened the bedroom door. Then she stopped. Her knees buckled, the room went black, and she slipped to the floor, unconscious.

THIRTY-THREE

Sonya climbed into the chair in the makeup room nearest to the studio. She tilted her head back against the headrest and smiled at Sabrina. Having her face done by an expert was the best way to start a long day.

Sabrina switched on the bright makeup lights that edged the mirror, brushed Sonya's hair from her face, then bent over and examined her closely.

"For all the lack of care, your face is coming along nicely," she said. "In a way, you're lucky it's so cold. It helps keep the swelling down. In another week or so, you won't notice a thing."

Sonya sighed with relief. At times, during the last four days, she had almost forgotten about her face-lift. She hadn't iced her swollen, stiff cheeks as frequently as the surgeon had instructed. At night, instead of propping herself up on pillows, she had been so glad to be in bed, she had just fallen asleep.

"Well, it's true what they say about work keeping your mind off your troubles," she said. "I've been too rushed to even think how I looked."

Sabrina started to work, sponging foundation smoothly over her forehead.

"What's with the guard that took you home last night? I hear there's a serial killer loose. And it's your story. Are you really so scared you need a guard?"

Sonya smiled; Sabrina was obviously ready for a long gossip, but she wanted quick service.

"He was one big hulk, let me tell you. He insisted on coming into the apartment and checking every room and every closet. I felt safer than I had all week. I wouldn't mind having him around more often."

"Who ordered him for you?"

"Donna."

"I might have guessed. It's the kind of thing Donna would do. The kind of thing Matt wouldn't."

But Sonya felt too restless for the usual analysis of the motives of the network executives. The heat from the lights was making her skin prick and her face swell.

"I don't need much makeup, do I? I think they are only taking wide two-shots of me. And I want to go to the control room to check things out."

Sabrina bent forward and removed the makeup cape from around Sonya's shoulders.

"Have it your own way, sweetie," she said. "Just pop in and I'll put a little powder on you before you go on camera." The phone shrilled beside her. She answered, then looked at Sonya. "It's for you. Do you want to take it here or have it transferred to your desk?"

"Ask them to hold for a couple of minutes. I'll head back to my desk and take it there," Sonya said, anxious to get out of the hot room.

"If you're tied up when Mari arrives, I'll look after her for you."

Sonya was halfway out the door. "Thanks. You're a pal," she said. Then she stopped.

"Don't talk to her about the murders. I want her quotes nice and fresh when I get to her. Ask her something to get her mind away from them. Like—where's the best place to buy designer clothes?" She laughed in an effort to ease her tension.

Sabrina picked up one of her brushes and started to clean it. "This interview is really important to you, isn't it? I've never seen you so edgy."

Sonya nodded. "I'll come back and take Mari to the studio after you've finished her makeup."

Sonya walked down the long hall to the control room and put her head in the door. "Are we set for taping Mari St. Clair at 9:00 in studio 3B?" she asked.

One of the two operators looked up. "It's a three-robot camera setup in that studio. Do you need any help?"

"No, I'll be fine. Just give me someone to put on and test the mikes."

The other tech grinned at her. "Service as usual. And where is your bodyguard?" he teased. "We hear Donna won't let you go anywhere without him."

"That's Donna for you. He's at the end of the hall, outside the door to the studio, if you guys need protection," Sonya quipped.

They laughed. "Good luck. You're doing a great job."

"Thanks. Keep an eye on this interview. I'm hoping it may be just what we need to wrap the program."

Suddenly she remembered the call she'd left hanging and ran down to her office on the floor below. The voice on the phone was incoherent.

"Who is this?" Sonya asked quietly, "What do you want?"

"Oh, Sonya, I need help," came a faint whisper voice. "I can't do this by myself. Please come and help me."

"Grace?" Sonya pulled out her chair and sat down. "Grace, is that you? What is the matter?"

"Sonya, I didn't know who else to call. Jeff is on the floor. I think he is dead. He's cold. I've closed the window, but he's still icy cold."

Sonya was stunned. Another death.

"Grace," said Sonya, "you must call the police. If you can't, then I'll do it for you. Just stay there and try to be calm."

"No, no. You must come. You must help me. I can't do it by myself. I can't undress him by myself. For the sake of the children, please come and help me."

Sonya put her hand up to support her head. Grace sounded frantic.

"Undress him? You mustn't undress him. You must not touch him. You must leave that for the police."

"Oh, Sonya, I can't. He's wearing women's clothes."

"What do you mean 'women's clothes'? Jeff? Jeff, a cross-dresser? I don't believe it."

Grace took a gasping breath.

"He's wearing a bra and panties and an evening dress. Last night, I saw him with a man in a tux. The man who killed him."

"The man who killed him?" Sonya was unbelieving. "Grace, for God's sake, how do you know?"

"A slim young man wearing evening clothes. I saw him come out of the apartment last night about eleven. He must have killed Jeff."

Sonya's heart raced. "Why were you watching the apartment? Grace, what's going on?"

"He didn't call to say good night to the children. I thought something must have happened to him. I drove in, and when I parked I saw the man come out. Oh, Sonya, if only I'd had the courage to go up, I might have saved him. It's my fault. If I'd been more understanding, he would have told me and this would never have happened. Sonya, he's lying on the floor. Oh, God help me."

Grace was gasping again. Sonya feared she would collapse.

"Grace," she said, "hang on. I'm in the studio. I can't come and help you. But I'll call Isaac Franklin. He'll help."

Thank God for Harriett, Sonya thought ironically. Harriett had insisted she write down the Franklin home number at the party on Sunday night. She had entered it on her blackberry and there it was. She punched it out on her second line. Would Isaac take the call?

He had to. She had to get him to help Grace. If he refused, she would have to tell Matt. That meant an immediate call to the police. Grace would have to handle it by herself.

She didn't deserve this, Sonya thought. To find her husband, the father of her three children, murdered. And then to have the scene flashed around the world. Dead, and dressed as he was.

Franklin answered the phone with a curt "Hello."

"Oh, Isaac, thank God you're there," she breathed. "This is Sonya Iverson. Don't be mad at me about last night, just listen. It's Grace. She desperately needs help. She's at the apartment. She found Jeff's body there. She says he's been murdered."

"What?" Isaac sounded as shocked as Sonya felt.

Sonya suddenly wanted to cry. She fought to stop her voice from trembling.

"She says he's been murdered, and he's wearing women's clothes. She's trying to undress him so the police won't find him that way."

"Have you called the police?"

"No. Isaac, Grace doesn't want the kids to know he was a cross-dresser. She is begging me to go and help her."

"Sonya, do nothing," he said. "She may just be hysterical, he may not be dead. She's been drinking too much. Jeff wanted her to go to AA. I'll get over there right away. I'll call the attorney as I go. Leave it to me." He hung up.

Sonya clicked over to the other line.

"Grace, Grace?" she called. She heard nothing. "Grace," she said again as loudly as she dared. "Grace, hang in there. Isaac is on his way."

She put down the phone and started up the stairs to the makeup room. She paused on the landing and looked out at the morning's gray sky.

Now there were three murders. Harriett had many enemies. That was understood. But why had Kim Kelly been killed? And why Jefferson Tyler? What tied them together?

She put her hand on the railing to steady herself.

Of course. There was only one answer. All she had do was ask the right questions. Then she could prove what she knew.

Sabrina had just finished doing Mari when Sonya returned to the makeup room. Sabrina had used colors subtly. Mari's pale face was warm and glowing.

"Fabulous, Sabrina," Sonya said. "Mari, you'll look great on camera."

Sabrina smiled happily.

"I used a pink-toned foundation; I thought it would work with her navy dress and jacket. I'm glad you're pleased."

Then she picked up a brush and quickly dusted a covering of powder on Sonya's face.

"Off you go, my beauties," she said.

How casual all this sounded, thought Sonya. Casual, when Jeff lay dead only a short distance away. Casual, when a murderer threatened everyone at that Sunday night table.

Mari nodded her thanks and followed Sonya into the studio. "State of the art," she said as they entered. "But I don't think I'll ever get used to robot cameras." The technician sat her in one of the two chairs, pinned on a mike, and then handed her the heavy oblong battery pack that went with it.

"It's a long cable," he said. "We usually tuck the battery into the back of your pants so it won't show, but since you're wearing a dress, you can put it in the pocket of your jacket."

Sonya wound the cable into a soft ball and tucked it out of sight under the hem of Mari's jacket. "The battery pack is heavy," she said as she adjusted it. "It pulls on your pocket a little, but not enough to notice. You look great." Sonya settled into her chair and looked at her notes.

The technician said, "The sound checks out. The batteries are fresh. You shouldn't have trouble with the mikes." With that, he left them and headed back to the control room.

The red light glowed on a camera, signaling it was on-line.

"Mari, first let's talk about your relationship with Harriett," she said. "How well did you know her?"

"Quite well, although I worked for her husband's company, not for her directly. But I did assist her in charity work."

Sonya glanced down. Mari was giving her the usual Franklin company line. She wanted more.

"But, Mari," she said, "didn't Harriett have an office next

to her husband's? Wasn't that where she worked practically every day?"

"Harriett was a creative woman. She probably did want to have more power in the company. It is a family business, after all. It's natural."

"And she worked hard to get that power?"

"What do you mean, worked hard?"

"Mari." Sonya took a deep breath. "We know she was determined to choose the fragrance of the new Franklin perfume and have it named 'Harriett.' "

Mari shrugged. "As I said, it was a family business."

It was clear to Sonya that Mari was becoming uncomfortable. Her voice was growing colder with each answer. She had not expected this line of questioning.

Sonya continued, "You know it was a bitter struggle. Isaac Franklin was fighting her tooth and nail. He gave you the only sample of his choice for the perfume. Weren't you wearing it Sunday night at the award dinner?"

Mari did not reply.

"Didn't he tell you to put it on heavily so you could test it? To find out how women reacted to it?"

Mari said nothing.

"That's the truth, isn't it? You were the only one there wearing the perfume."

"Sonya, I don't know what you are driving at, but, yes, that is the truth."

Sonya looked at her notes.

"In his interview with us, Jefferson Tyler said that he smelled the fragrance when he first walked into the powder room and saw Harriett's body."

Mari stiffened. "So what?" she replied sharply. "I was in the room with the body that night. And let's remember that men don't recognize perfumes the way women do."

"Mari, you came into the room long after Jefferson. He was there guarding the body for a good 10 minutes. What's more, he is in the fragrance business. You know as well as I do, he is what's called 'a nose.' He can recognize a fragrance instantly."

Sonya looked straight into Mari's eyes.

"Mari, did you kill Harriett Franklin?"

Mari put her head back and laughed.

"What kind of interview is this? What's the matter with you? Of course I didn't kill Harriett. She was out to get control of the company, but it is not my company. As I said, I just work for them. Why would I want to kill Harriett or anyone else?"

Sonya watched Mari slide her hands into her pockets, her right fingers curled over the heavy battery pack. She wondered if the control room technicians were watching the monitor or chatting as usual. She felt alone—only the robot cameras seemed to be watching.

"Okay." She tried to smile. "Let's talk about Kim Kelly. How well did you know her?"

Mari looked at her angrily. "Are you going to ask me if I her killed her too?" Her well-modulated voice rose a tone higher. Before Sonya could speak, Mari continued, "The answer is no. I did not murder Kim Kelly."

Sonya leaned forward.

"How long had you known her?"

"As long as she worked for the Franklin Company. I knew her because of business. We did not have a personal relationship."

"You didn't go to parties? Or visit her apartment?"

"I don't socialize with models on drugs. I've been to the apartment once, and that was when you did the interview with her on Monday."

"If that's so, why did you tell me the police would find your fingerprints all over her apartment?"

Mari twisted in her chair. "This is ridiculous and insulting. You know I was helping you. The place was in a mess. The only other time I've been in that apartment house was to take some press people to Leonard Novelli's apartment. And I am not going on with this interview if you continue this way."

Sonya was relentless.

"Mari, you arrived late, and when you were in the room, you were sitting down most of the time." Sonya's voice was firm. "First, you checked the messages on your cell phone. Then you made calls. Wendy Sharp and I did all the cleaning up and rearranging. You know, and I know, that there is only one way your fingerprints got all over the apartment. You went back that night."

Mari dug her hands deeper into her pockets.

"Sonya, you are crazy to go on like this," Mari insisted harshly, nearly snarling. "When I told you my fingerprints were all over the apartment, I was exaggerating. Remember, I did find the award Novelli had left for Kim and brought it into her bedroom. Of course I touched things when we were there." Mari was talking faster, breathless.

Sonya looked at her closely. Under Sabrina's pink foundation, Mari's cheeks were fiery red. Her mouth was a thin angry line, her face twisted. She had become another person.

Sonya thought of the guard outside the door. How could she reach him if she needed him?

"Mari, I won't ask you if you killed Kim. I know you did," Sonya said. "But I will ask you this: How did you kill Jefferson Tyler?"

"I don't know what you are talking about. Jefferson Tyler was a cross-dresser, and if he died last night he had it coming to him. Take my word for it," Mari shouted.

Then she sprang. She whipped the battery pack out of her pocket, swung, and hit Sonya across the face. Blood gushed from Sonya's nose and she put her hands up, trying to protect herself.

Mari jumped onto her. Sonya struggled, kicking, punching, and screaming for help. In seconds, Mari had pushed her back in the chair, ripped the cable from the battery pack, and wound the thin, strong wire around her neck.

"That's the end of you," she whispered into Sonya's ear. "I'm in control now."

Sonya fought to get her fingers around the cable and pull it away from her throat, but Mari was too powerful. As Mari tightened her grip, she pushed Sonya onto the floor.

Strength drained from Sonya. Her eyes closed. Her hands fell slack. Her world went silent.

Then, from deep, cold darkness, she heard the shots. Three of them. Suddenly, the band around her throat loosened. She gasped a breath of sweet, cool air and looked into the horrified blue eyes of her guard.

THIRTY-FOUR

Noon, Friday

Sonya put her hand up and ran her fingers tentatively over her injured face. Her nose was almost too sore to touch. But her plastic surgeon had said it would mend without a scar. All she needed was time. Mari had hit her with the battery pack hard enough to make her nose bleed, but not hard enough to break it.

The worst was the pain in her neck muscles. When she fought Mari, she had strained them as she twisted and pulled away from her attacker. It hurt to move her head.

Not that there was much reason to turn her head in the hospital. She had a private room. The television was right over the bed, but Sonya wasn't interested in watching it. There was a window with a view of the gray sky. Occasionally she could discern a snowflake drifting by, but that was all.

Isaac Franklin had sent flowers. They had been waiting for her when they wheeled her back from the operating room— a beautiful posy of yellow roses, mimosa, and daffodils.

Flowers that held the promise of spring, of sun-filled days ahead. The card apologized for his behavior during the shiva and thanked her for asking him to help Grace.

She raised herself carefully and looked into the mirror on the bed table. Most of her face was covered with gauze, but her neck was bare and ghastly. The line where the cable had bit into her skin was red and angry, with a deep purple bruise spreading around it.

Sonya stretched her legs, the one part of her body that didn't ache. She stretched her arms, sore from wrestling with Mari. The phone rang.

It was Isaac.

"Thank you for the beautiful flowers," she said.

"I'm glad you're enjoying them," he said. Then he paused for a moment. "Even though Mari is dead, the police say they will still do a lot of investigating. If they ask you why you didn't call them immediately when Grace telephoned you yesterday," he advised her, "just tell them the truth. Say that Grace was incoherent, incapable of giving straight answers on the phone. You couldn't make out what she was talking about. So you called me and I took over."

It was the truth, or nearly so, Sonya thought. "How is Grace now?" she asked.

"Much better than you might imagine. In a way, I think she's relieved to know what Jeff was up to. She has three great kids and they're a comfort to her, as my three are to me. She always put the children before Jeff. Maybe that was one of their problems."

"And how are your boys doing?"

"They are having a hard time of course, especially Jeremy. He was at the clinic for so long. But Leonard Novelli plans to spend a lot of time with him. For me, the joy is seeing my three boys together. Byron and Henry seem pleased to have their brother home, though of course they miss their mother dreadfully."

Sonya changed the subject. She wanted to know more. She had to understand what had gone on between Mari and Jeff. "Did you have any idea that Jeff was a cross-dresser?"

"No, but Harriett knew. Novelli told me last night that he saw Jeff once at a transvestite bar, and let it slip to Harriett. I wouldn't be surprised if Harriett were blackmailing Jeff. She was determined to get his support in her bid to have her name on the fragrance.

"At the time, I only thought that Jeff disliked Harriett and avoided her whenever he could. He never really spoke to me about any of this. I guess that's understandable. For all his charm, Jeff was a secretive man."

Sonya thought for a moment. "I think Mari not only knew he was a cross-dresser, she played the game with him. I always thought that Mari dressed in a very conservative way for business with her prim little suits and dresses. But that was just one side of her character. Sometimes she would go completely unisex and wear a well-tailored but definitely masculine jacket or coat. It had crossed my mind that she must have two wardrobes."

"She probably did." Isaac laughed. "But let me assure you, the feminine clothes all came from the Franklin Company."

When Sonya eventually put down the phone, her mind was racing. Isaac was an observant man. Perhaps with his help, she could eventually unravel all the details of Mari's personality. It was something she had to do for her own satisfaction.

Donna was right. She had been too close to Mari.

Her next call was from her mother to tell Sonya that she was on her way to New York. She wanted to be there to take Sonya home from the hospital and care for her while she healed.

But she was still at the Minneapolis airport. Yet another storm had delayed her flight—a storm that would sweep across the continent and bombard New York. Sonya shuddered. She was tired of the cold.

"I'm all right," she reassured her mother. "I'm worried about you. I hate the thought of your being out in this weather. Have you done what I told you when you called earlier and upgraded your ticket to first class? Just put it on my credit card. The network will reimburse me."

"Yes," her mother said, and laughed. "But I didn't have to

pay the extra. When I told them who I was, they said the upgrade was on the airline and they took me to the VIP lounge so I could call you. They asked me to tell you how brave they think you were. Everyone in Minnesota is so proud of you."

Sonya found her mother's gleeful tone disturbing. She didn't want to go down in Minnesota history as the woman who was shown being strangled on national television and had a mother who accepted freebies.

She kept her voice low so her irritation didn't show.

"That's great," she said. "Now I won't worry about you." Then she felt guilty. She had no reason to be angry because her mother had bought an economy ticket even though the network had told her to travel first class. Why was she angry that her mother had boasted about getting a free upgrade? She came from frugal stock. She pinched pennies even when the pennies belonged to someone else.

She loved her mother, she told herself. Her mother was the most precious person in her life.

"Mom," she said. "Remember, you're to look for a driver holding a card with your name on it. He'll be waiting at the exit after you pick up your suitcase." She looked up quickly as the door opened. Donna and Matt came in. "Hang on a moment," she said.

"Is that, by any chance, your mother?" queried Donna. Sonya nodded. "Let me speak to her."

Donna put her mink coat and shopping bag on the end of the bed, and reached for the phone. "Mrs. Iverson, believe me, Sonya is fine. We're taking good care of her. All she needs is some rest. I am so pleased you are flying in. It'll do her a world of good to have you with her.

"You know we've arranged to have a car and driver pick you up at the airport. You're to keep it for as long as you need it. The driver can wait for you at the hospital, take you to Sonya's apartment, to the supermarket, to the drugstore, to wherever you need to go. Just take care of yourself. We don't want you sick too."

Sonya realized that Donna and her mother were an almost perfect match. Many things about them were alike.

As Donna spoke, Matt sat down in one of the chairs beside the bed.

"Why didn't you tell me that you suspected Mari was the murderer before you went into the studio to interview her?" he asked. "If she had killed you, it would have meant plenty of mud on Donna's face. You were lucky that the guys in the control room were watching for once and called down the corridor to the guard. You would have been in real trouble if he hadn't been so fast on the trigger. It wasn't very smart of you to keep what you knew to yourself."

Sonya was speechless. Matt was at it again. Turning every point against her.

But Donna wasn't having any of it. She had finished her call and put down the phone. Ignoring Matt, she gave Sonya an encouraging smile. "Your work brought us the highest ratings the show has ever had," she said. "The overnights are sensational. Now tell me, when did you first suspect Mari was the murderer?"

Sonya gave her a smile that turned into a painful grimace. "I had a sense of it as early as Sunday night, when Harriett was murdered. Mari was extremely agitated. Of course, I have known her long enough to know she was a control freak, and she wanted the dinner to be perfect. But Harriett wasn't having any of it. First, she attacked Isaac, then Mari herself. It was a bad scene. I think that's what got to Mari. After the award ceremony, she disappeared. I thought she must have gone backstage to check, but obviously, she followed Harriett.

"Then, after I found the body, when I told Mari that Kim had been in the toilet while Harriett was killed, she seemed to be stunned. It took her a while to understand what I had said. I didn't think much of it at the time, but it kept bothering me."

"Why didn't you come to me with your theory?" Matt's tone was still nasty.

Sonya flushed with anger. She had had enough of him, and was about to say so. But Donna said reassuringly, "Go on, I'm fascinated."

"I didn't have a theory. I just sensed something was deeply wrong with Mari. But after all, her boss's wife had been murdered. I told myself she had every right to be upset. Then on Monday, after Kim's interview, when Mari took Perry to the elevator, Kim asked my advice. She told me that she had heard Harriett say 'no, no, no' before she died. She said she was too afraid to tell anyone because they would think she had done it. I advised her to tell the police. But I got the feeling that she knew who the murderer was, and she was too frightened to talk. Poor, sad Kim."

Sonya looked at Matt. Now that she was into her story, she didn't care what he thought. "The next evening, after we'd had a few drinks, Mari told me that Harriett was a 'no, no, no' kind of woman. Those were the last three words that Harriett uttered before she died. It was just too much of a co-incidence. I realized that later, as I began to mentally put the show together. Harriett's last words must have been playing on Mari's mind."

Matt warmed to the subject. "The police believe that Mari could easily have slipped into Kim's building without the doorman seeing her. They found a faulty lock on one of the service doors."

"Yes," Sonya agreed. "It's a pre–world war building with several side doors and elevators. Mari knew it well. She'd taken reporters and photographers there many times for interviews with Novelli. She was there visiting him that night. She could easily have tested the doors, even left one open."

Donna added thoughtfully, "Kim would have opened her door to Mari. There's no doubt about that. And Mari certainly had the strength to push Kim over the balcony. But what about Jefferson Tyler? How could she have managed that? He was a strong man, a former soldier. He can't have been so easy to tackle."

This time Matt answered.

"The police say he died of several blows to the back of the head. He may have been leaning over. Who knows? But of course, the body was moved. Apparently, his wife went crazy when she found him."

Sonya thought for a moment, then said, "And Mari was certainly familiar with that apartment. When I interviewed Grace, Mari suddenly appeared in the living room. She must have had a key to the front door."

Donna nodded. "That's possible, especially if they played games together."

Sonya continued, "Mari didn't expect the body to be found so quickly. When I spoke to Grace, she muttered something about closing the window. Perhaps Mari wanted to keep the room cold. It's a horrible thought, but maybe she was planning to get away before the body was discovered. After all, the evidence against her was building. And she couldn't keep on killing people.

"It would have been easy to just disappear for the weekend. She could have said she was going skiing to get away from it all. She often did, so everyone would have believed her."

Donna stood and reached for the shopping bag.

"The police will check on it, I'm sure," she said. "The best thing for you now is to stop thinking about it. The nurse told me you had trouble chewing, so I've brought you some soup. I didn't make it myself, so don't get worried. I called the Four Seasons and had them prepare it especially for you."

"The tape? Did you bring it?" Sonya had asked for a tape of her interview with Mari, or of the show, so she could see the result of her work.

Donna shook her head. "It was such a traumatic experience—you need time to recover. And I mean psychologically, as well physically."

"But you have to recover fast," Matt interrupted. "Donna is planning to interview you for the show on Tuesday night."

"I can't do it," gasped Sonya. "I'm not an on-camera person. And I look terrible."

"Yes, you can do it," replied Donna. "It's a natural follow-up after the show. And as Matt says, think of the ratings." She bent over and touched Sonya lightly on the cheek. "As for how you look, don't give it two thoughts. Sabrina is already working on ideas for you."

"Well, if I can't trust Sabrina, I can't trust anyone," replied Sonya, resignation and dismay flooding through her.

Donna motioned to Matt that it was time to leave. She paused for a moment and put her nose to the flowers.

"Beautiful," she said.

"Isaac Franklin sent them and he called this morning," said Sonya.

Donna gathered up her coat and put it over her shoulders, then picked up her bag. "I hope he doesn't send Jeremy back to the clinic again," she said.

Sonya replied, "That was a big issue between him and Harriett. I think Jeremy is home for good."

Donna nodded. "Great. I think that would be the right thing. Isaac is a good man and a good father."

Sonya grinned. "Donna, you're the best judge of character I know."

"You didn't do too badly yourself."

Donna tilted her head and smiled a little smile. The famous Donna Fuller sign-off.

Look for

SHOOTING SCRIPT

by Elsa Klench

Available October 2005
From Tom Doherty Associates

Carnival Pride℠
April 2 - 9, 2006.

7 Day Exotic Mexican Riviera Itinerary

DAY	PORT	ARRIVE	DEPART
Sun	Los Angeles/Long Beach, CA		4:00 P.M.
Mon	"Book Lover's" Day at Sea		
Tue	"Book Lover's" Day at Sea		
Wed	Puerto Vallarta, Mexico	8:00 A.M.	10:00 P.M.
Thu	Mazatlan, Mexico	9:00 A.M.	6:00 P.M.
Fri	Cabo San Lucas, Mexico	7:00 A.M.	4:00 P.M.
Sat	"Book Lover's" Day at Sea		
Sun	Los Angeles/Long Beach, CA	9:00 A.M.	

ports of call subject to weather conditions

TERMS AND CONDITIONS

PAYMENT SCHEDULE:
50% due upon booking
Full and final payment due by February 10, 2006

Acceptable forms of payment are Visa, MasterCard, American Express, Discover and checks. The cardholder must be one of the passengers traveling. A fee of $25 will apply for all returned checks. Check payments must be made payable to **Advantage International, LLC** and sent to: **Advantage International, LLC, 195 North Harbor Drive, Suite 4206, Chicago, IL 60601**

CHANGE/CANCELLATION:
Notice of change/cancellation must be made in writing to Advantage International, LLC.

Change:
Changes in cabin category may be requested and can result in increased rate and penalties. A name change is permitted 60 days or more prior to departure and will incur a penalty of $50 per name change. Deviation from the group schedule and package is a cancellation.

Cancellation:

181 days or more prior to departure	$250 per person
121 - 180 days prior to departure	50% of the package price
120 - 61 days prior to departure	75% of the package price
60 days or less prior to departure	100% of the package price (nonrefundable)

US and Canadian citizens are required to present a valid passport or the original birth certificate and state issued photo ID (drivers license). All other nationalities must contact the consulate of the various ports that are visited for verification of documentation.

We strongly recommend trip cancellation insurance!

For complete details call 1-877-ADV-NTGE or visit www.AuthorsAtSea.com

---

This coupon does not constitute an offer from Tom Doherty Associates, LLC.

For booking form and complete information
go to **www.AuthorsAtSea.com** or call **1-877-ADV-NTGE**

Complete coupon and booking form and mail both to:
Advantage International, LLC,
195 North Harbor Drive, Suite 4206, Chicago, IL 60601